A FACE
IN
THE CROWD

ALSO BY KERRY WILKINSON

KERRY WILKINSON

A FACE IN THE CROWD

bookouture

Published by Bookouture in 2019

An imprint of StoryFire Ltd.

Carmelite House
50 Victoria Embankment
London EC4Y 0DZ

www.bookouture.com

ISBN: 978-1-78681-764-8
eBook ISBN: 978-1-78681-763-1

FIVE YEARS AGO

Ben pats the breast pocket of his suit jacket, then his trouser pocket, his backside and his wrist. Keys, wallet, phone and watch. It's the new head, shoulders, knees and toes.

'Got everything?' I ask, unable to come up with anything better to say.

He checks his trouser pocket once more, removing his phone to make sure it's definitely there. I don't like it when he's nervous; his anxiety feeds mine, a contagion that's spreading along the hallway of our house.

'We're close,' he says, answering a question I hadn't asked. 'If I can just get this bloke to invest…'

He tails off, biting his lip and glancing towards the front door.

'Train tickets,' he says to himself, going back through the routine of checking all his pockets.

Keys, wallet, phone and watch; phone and watch… and eyes and ears and mouth and nose…

Ben eventually finds the train tickets in his inside pocket, breathing a sigh of relief. There's a bead of sweat along his hairline, which he wipes away with his sleeve. He scratches the base of his neck, tugging at the collar of his shirt, where the top button looks as if it's done up a little too tightly. After that, he rubs the scar that's underneath his Adam's apple. He does this a lot when he's worried. The mark is barely there and, if he'd not pointed it out on our very first date, I'm not sure I'd have noticed it unless I really looked. There's a narrow trace of squiggly purple that hoops under the bulge in his throat – an old rugby injury, apparently. He needed reconstructive surgery.

I was shocked when he said he got it playing rugby. He's not particularly tall or broad, and nothing like the rugger-bugger type. He said it happened at school.

'This is it,' he says. 'We might be able to book the venue tomorrow. It'll be the wedding you've always dreamed of.'

I almost tell him that the venue doesn't matter to me. That it feels like, for all the talk of what *I've* always dreamed of, what we've really spent months looking into is the wedding *he's* always dreamed of.

Montgomery Manor is out in the countryside, a massive building that's featured in at least half-a-dozen movies and television shows. We've visited twice, ostensibly to decide the room in which we'd like to be married. There's the Robinson Suite that overlooks the stream at the back, with lots of natural daylight during spring and summer, apparently. If not that, there's the Westley Room, in which Kate Winslet once snogged some actor whose name I can never remember in a film I've not seen. The reason we've committed to neither room is that we can't afford it. Even marrying on a weekday off-season is beyond our budget. I don't mind. I'd get married in a register officer with no hesitation. I'd do it this weekend. I'd do it tomorrow.

Ben breathes out deeply and strides towards the front door. He opens it and then pauses before leaving, taking another deep breath.

'I've been thinking,' he says, half turned. 'Once we've got the house by the park, we could maybe think about getting you those stables…?'

It takes me a second to process what he's said – but it still makes no sense. 'Getting those *what*?' I ask.

'Remember on our second date when you said you liked horses and always wanted your own when you were a girl? If everything comes through today, I might be able to make that happen.'

He stares at me with such clear, unblinking focus that a tingle flickers up my spine, making me shiver. One of the first things I noticed about Ben was those long eyelashes. They make his brown eyes appear even duskier than they are. Some women would kill for eyelashes like those – either that, or pay a small fortune to a doctor somewhere. It is part of what makes him so seductive; so appealing. But the darkness of his eyes is also what makes me feel as if there's something else there. Something about him that I'll never understand.

'I'm not sure if I want stables,' I say, stumbling over the words. The truth is, I'd forgotten telling him about my young dreams of owning a horse. Seven-year-old girls want for all sorts of things. That was eighteen years ago. I've barely thought about it since. I wanted a pink helicopter and an endless supply of Cadbury's Fruit 'N' Nut bars when I was that age, too.

'It was only an idea,' he replies. 'I want to provide for you.'

'I don't mind working. I *like* working.'

He nods, but it doesn't feel as if he's listening. 'You'll be able to do what you want. Work or not work. Study or not study.' There's a momentary pause and then: 'Take a few years off and we can try for kids…'

I fight away a roll of the eyes. We've been through this and I'm not ready for kids. I want to visit Thailand and travel through south-east Asia. I want to finally go to university, or study for a degree from home.

It's not the time to point all that out, however. I don't want to burst Ben's bubble when he's got such an important day ahead of him. I'm hoping that, if today goes well, it'll put an end to the mood swings and the nights by myself when he sleeps on the sofa.

Ben works as a day trader, buying and selling shares from the relative comfort of our living room. I can always tell the type of day he's had by the way he greets me when I get home from work.

Or, indeed, whether he greets me at all. There's darkness and light within him – or, more recently, darkness and dark.

The light makes it worth it, though. The way he smiles; the times we cuddle under a blanket on the sofa to binge-watch some overhyped drama series; even the way he says my name. He's never called me 'Lucy', always 'Luce' – or 'Loose', I suppose. It's hard to describe, but it makes me feel as if I'm at the centre of the world. As if there's only me. That's love, isn't it? When a single word spoken can make a person's throat dry up.

From nowhere, Ben grimaces. He angles forward slightly, as if about to bow.

'What's wrong?' I ask.

He closes his eyes for a moment and then reopens them. 'Last night's sushi, I think.'

'Will you be okay?'

He shrugs, which is something I hate. It's hard to say why, other than that it doesn't suit him. It's like when I try to do something left-handed. There's a lack of coordination; a general sense that the action isn't quite right.

'I've got to go,' he replies. 'I love you.'

'I love you, too.'

A reflex.

Bang.

I love you–I love you, too. I'm pretty sure I do love him. Sometimes I'm certain, other times I wonder if I know what the word means.

'See you later,' he says. He's being kind today, going through the whole routine. He doesn't always say goodbye. I sometimes leave for work and he doesn't look up from his computer. Sometimes, I say I love him and he doesn't reply at all.

'See you later,' I say, parroting him. 'You'll do brilliantly today.'

He steps outside, leaving a hand on the front door.

'Yes,' he says, not sounding convinced.

'Good luck,' I add.

There's a second in which I wonder if I've said the wrong thing. As if I'm doubting his ability by implying he needs good fortune. Luck shouldn't come into it, after all. Luck is what people need if they aren't skilled enough to get the job done.

A flutter tickles my heart, but he doesn't pick up on it.

'Thanks,' Ben replies. He checks his pockets and wrist one final time – *keys, wallet, phone and watch* – then he pulls the door closed.

I stand alone in the hall for a moment, watching through the rippled glass of the front door as his silhouette shrinks its way to the end of our driveway.

'See you later,' I repeat, this time to myself.

ONE

FRIDAY

I'm not sure if there are many things more humiliating than looking at a rolly-eyed bus driver and saying, 'Don't you recognise me?' He has tufty gingery hair and is wearing the weary expression of a man who can't wait to finish his shift. I get on this bus twice a day, five days a week. He drives it three or four times of those ten journeys. We do not know one another, but there's still indignity in that I recognise him, while he's sure he's never once set eyes on me.

'It's two-twenty,' he says with yet another roll of the eyes. I can practically hear his thoughts. *Not another nutter...*

'I'm not trying it on,' I reply, 'I really do have a monthly pass. I use it every day. I was hoping you'd know me...?' I tail off, knowing I've lost the argument.

The person behind me in the queue to get on shuffles and sighs. I'm one of *those* people. The ones who can't simply get on a bus without causing trouble.

My purse gives no clues as to where the pass could be. I always leave it in the front window section, precisely so that it's impossible to lose. It's not there and neither is it in that compartment.

'Two-twenty or you'll have to get off,' he says.

I half turn, ready to get off, but it's at that moment the rain starts to thrash the windscreen like a kid playing whack-a-mole at the fair.

Losing something is surely one of the worst feelings in the world. I've known real loss and pain, but there's something about the way a person's stomach sinks when a valued item has gone astray.

I start to fumble through the coin part of my purse, but this is about more than the two pounds and twenty pence. By the time I've paid rent and all the other bits and pieces, there's so little left that everything else is brutally budgeted. This extra £2.20 means I'll probably have to miss a meal. It's a straight choice: Food – or a six-mile walk home in the pounding rain.

'I'll pay.' It's the man behind me in the queue. No, not a man. A teenager at most. He's probably fifteen or sixteen, clutching a backpack.

I start to say no, but my heart isn't in it because everything about me must be screaming *yes*. Before I can make any sort of fake protest, he's passed a five-pound note to the driver and told him to take it out of that.

I mutter a 'thanks', but it doesn't feel like enough. A wave of relief slams into me as if the bus itself has thundered into a wall. I try to take a step, but my knees wobble.

For his part, the kid shrugs away my thanks with a, 'no problem – it's only two quid'. He offers a thin smile and then edges past, manoeuvring his way as far back into the bus as he can manage.

Only two quid.

Only.

It's funny how far I can make *only* two quid stretch.

I'm lost for a moment, but, as more passengers get on, I find myself following the flow until I'm clinging to a pole. The engine rumbles like a low-level earthquake and then everyone shunts forward as we set off.

It takes me a few seconds to realise that the man next to me has gone full-on chemical warfare. If any government agencies are still hunting for weapons of mass destruction, this guy is hiding in plain sight. He's clinging onto one of those plastic loops that hang from the roof of the bus, thrusting his armpit to within a few centimetres of my face. Showering is free and even I can afford deodorant. How hard is it to not smell like mouldy cheese?

What is *wrong* with some people?

The man is oblivious, holding his phone with his other hand and thumbing his way through Facebook. Someone named Jenny has some seriously ugly children. Someone called Dave has posted a map of the route he ran that morning. Mr Stinky types 'Good going dude' into the comments and presses 'post'. In all the millions of words that have been added to the internet since it was invented, I wonder if there has ever been anything more inane.

I'd move away but it's a Friday, so the number 24 bus is full. I'm never quite sure why so many more people appear on this one single day of the week compared to any others. It's a throbbing, sweating pit of humanity.

I attempt to ignore the smell while also trying not to worry about my missing bus pass. It will be in my bag somewhere. I had it this morning. I still have the receipt at home, too. If need be, I can go to the bus station and get it replaced.

The bus slows and the floor starts to vibrate as the driver pulls into the next stop. There's a collective groan from the people around me. As if the bus isn't full enough. We're British, though, so nobody says anything.

No one gets off, but passengers start to shuffle into one another as, presumably, more people get on. I can't see much past Mr Stinky. His armpit edges ever closer, the chloroform about to smother its target.

I'm in the front third of the bus, with people standing all around me. The unseen door hisses closed again and there's now no room to move. Barely room to breathe. We're packed in like beans in a can.

As the bus pulls away, I wobble slightly and tighten my grip on the vertical metal pole with one hand, while trying to cling onto my bag with the other. It's no wonder the roads are full of cars. Who'd choose to travel like this? To *pay* to travel like this?

It feels as if everyone around me is so much taller than I am. As well as Mr Stinky's armpit, there's a woman in gym gear with one of those drawstring bags over her shoulders. She's holding onto a pole with one hand and thumbing away at her phone with the other. If nothing else, modern technology has turned us into a population of multi-taskers.

The groan of the engine changes as we slow for a set of traffic lights. I take this bus so often that I know the potholes, the traffic lights, the junctions, and the give-way signs, even though I don't own a car of my own.

There's a scuff of feet from behind, but I'm too crammed in to be able to turn. A man in a beanie hat lurches sideways and lightly treads on my foot.

'Sorry,' he mutters, straightening himself as the bus speeds up again.

He's young; early twenties or late-teens. Probably on the way back from college, something like that. He's got a kindly smile but immediately looks back to his phone.

'It's fine,' I reply, though he doesn't acknowledge it.

The bus slows and someone from the back shouts that this is his stop. After that, it's a series of oohs and aahs as a succession of people squeeze through the crowd to get off via the front door. The man in the beanie disappears, along with the woman in gym gear. There's suddenly a little more space and I try to do-si-do myself away from Mr Stinky. There's little respite as he slides around half-a-dozen newcomers who scramble to get the most secure handholds. I'm left clinging to a new metal pole, slightly nearer the front.

The bus surges forward and I'm two stops from sanctuary. There are traffic lights between here and there, which means another wobbling lurch of bodies swaying into one another.

Mr Stinky is still on Facebook, telling someone named 'Big Tom' that his pimped-out twatmobile of a car is 'the dog's'.

We stop at my penultimate bus stop. The boy with the backpack who gave me two pounds wriggles through the horde and gets off. He clutches his phone in his hand and doesn't acknowledge me. I'm not sure why I thought he might, or should. For him, the two pounds was a shrug. It was nothing. He might have rich parents. It simply meant he could get on the bus quicker. For me, it was a gesture that means I get to eat this weekend.

After he's off, more people get on. The bus is now so full that passengers are standing level with the driver. He shouts something about moving to the back, but there's nowhere to go. Someone presses an elbow or an arm into my back, but I don't have enough room to see who it is. In the meantime, a woman who is wearing what can only be described as a faded curtain treads on my toe without apologising and then swings her oversized handbag into some bloke's stomach. He grunts in pain, but she doesn't notice because she's busy huffing something to the woman next to her about 'foreigners filling up all the buses'. She then turns to Mr Stinky and tells him to put his arm down because he 'needs a wash'.

Mr Stinky eyes her incredulously but lowers his arm and puts his phone away, suitably chastened. Turns out there's a hero in all of us – even the racist lunatics.

One more stop to go. Two minutes at the most. After the bus pulls away, I stretch for the bell and the most satisfying of *ding-dongs* echoes along the length of the aisle. Mandela might have had a long walk to freedom, but I'll be damned if he ever spent twenty minutes on the number 24 bus on a Friday.

I'm counting the seconds when the floor rumbles and the bus slows. Moments later, everything swerves to the side and the doors fizz open.

This time, it's me apologising as I clasp my bag to my side and try to clamber around everyone else. I trample on someone's foot, accidentally elbow someone else in the hip and then almost grab a man's crotch as I reach for a metal pole to try to support myself. He snorts with laughter as I apologise and, in fairness, it is the most action I've had in longer than I care to remember.

There are a few more steps, the customary 'thanks' to the driver, more through habit than actual gratefulness, and then – finally! – the crisp, cool, clean air of the real world. My sentence has been expunged and I can walk free with a clear conscience.

The rain has stopped and the pavement glistens bright as I hoist my bag higher and start the walk towards home. Some kids in school uniform are busy kicking a wall because... well, I have no idea. Perhaps this is what young people do nowadays? Better than hard drugs in the bushes, I suppose. I weave around them, eyes down, and then offer a watery smile towards an old woman who is wheeling one of those canvas bag things behind her. I've never seen them for sale anywhere. There must be an old person store for which you only get the address after reaching pension age. She smiles back and carries on heading in one direction, while I go in the other.

I'm halfway across the road when I realise something doesn't feel right. I almost stop right there, in the join of Fisher Road and Allen Street, as I try to figure out what's going on. It's that same sinking feeling when a phone or purse has been lost. Or a bus pass. That panicked realisation of not being in control.

A taxi is impatiently waiting to take the turn, the driver hanging out the window with that flabby-cheeked, dead-eyed gaze of a man who's spent the day listening to radio phone-ins. He gives me that *get-a-move-on-love* look, so I hurry across to the safety of the pavement.

There's a strange moment in which I wonder if I've left my bag on the bus, before realising that it's in my hand. Panic does odd things to the mind. Absolutes are suddenly doubted. My bag is open, however. The zip has been sticking for months and I don't have the money to buy a new one. Brute force sometimes works, but only ever temporarily. I suppose that could be a lesson for life, not just with bags.

It's then that it seems so obvious what's bothering me. My bag is heavier because a padded envelope is tucked inside. It wasn't there before and I find myself sitting on a low wall at the edge of the pavement, holding onto the envelope with a strange sense of awe. The flap is sealed closed and there's no writing on the outside. No address, no markings, no anything. Only a plain, taupe envelope. It's heavy and packed thick with whatever's inside. It must have fallen in there while I was on the bus.

This envelope isn't mine – and yet there are no clues on the outside as to whom it might belong. I have no choice but to open it – if only to find out whose it is.

And so I do.

There's a tingle of excitement, like unwrapping presents on Christmas morning. The anticipation of the unknown. The tab unsticks itself from the envelope and then I pull it away, accidentally tearing off part of the corner. I reach inside, and though I instinctively know what I'm now running my fingers across, there's still a large part of me that can't believe what's in front of me.

It's money.

More cash than I've ever seen in one place before. Hundreds of pounds. No, thousands – all wedged down until the envelope is filled.

There are tight bundles of those new plastic notes. They feel so smooth and clean. So… wrong.

I quickly push the notes back inside and fold the flap down while checking around to make sure nobody has seen. This would be a lot of money anywhere, but, here, on the street, in this little run-down corner of the world…

The envelope is dispatched back into my bag and, this time, I do wrench the zip closed. Brute force is the champion.

I set off towards home, but everything feels muddled and I almost trip over my own feet in my attempt to walk quickly. It's as if I've stumbled into a mirror world. Up is down. Left is now right.

So much money.

So.

Much.

Money.

And, for now, it's all mine.

TWO

It's such a strange thing that strips of printed plastic can be swapped for real, tangible things. For food, for the roof over my head. I can understand something like gold being valuable. It's shiny and heavy and... real. I suppose it's odder that a click of a mouse or the swipe of a screen can lead to numbers changing and then, suddenly, one person has more worth than they did moments before. Life can be full of the weirdest things at which we all simply shrug.

And, for me, right now, there is £3,640 on my coffee table. It's almost all comprised of the new plasticky £20 notes, with only a handful of tens.

No wonder my bag felt heavier.

I found my bus pass, too. It was tucked into the wrong pocket of my purse, barely a couple of millimetres away from where it always is. Sometimes panic can stop a person from seeing what is directly in front of them.

The notes are stacked into piles of £200 to make them easier to tally – and I've done some serious counting since getting home. Over and over I've gone, reaching £3,640 on every occasion, except one. Somehow, I found a phantom £20 that time, which appeared and disappeared from one count to the next.

I pack the notes back into the envelope, seal the tab at the top and then put it back on the table.

I'm definitely going to hand it in to the police.

Definitely.

Billy comes and sniffs at the envelope, but seems nonplussed by it. Dogs deal in food, sleep and affection, which seems like a decent way to live. He turns his head sideways, staring at me with those endless brown eyes that are now encircled with increasing amounts of grey hair. He was once black with white underneath, but now his Staffie face is a pepper pot of dark and grey. It comes to us all, I suppose – the poor sod.

I push myself up from the sofa and cross the apartment. The scratched bareness of the old carpet transitions seamlessly into the ripped linoleum of the kitchen. One of my few solaces from living here is that I haven't made the flat any worse. I scrub the walls and ceiling whenever I find mould. I clear the spider's webs whenever they appear. I get rid of the limescale in the bath and sink. I try to keep the place clean, but it's a constant fight against landlord neglect and age itself.

Billy's tail wags with anticipation – but that's only because he doesn't yet know of the disappointment to come. I fork half a tin of food into his bowl and then put it on the floor next to the sink. He sniffs it and then looks up at me, betrayed.

'Sorry, mate,' I tell him. 'Those tins were four for a fiver. Unless you fancy getting a job, it's all there is.'

He sniffs the food once more and then takes a reticent mouthful.

As he eats slowly, I open the mail. It's the end of the month, so my usual credit card bill has arrived. I have no idea how I got approved for it – but it is, essentially, the only reason I can afford to live. The minimum payment is £15, but I owe a little over £200 in total. It's not much, not in the bigger picture of inflated house prices and brand-new cars, but it *feels* like so much more than it is. There was a time when I wouldn't have thought twice about spending £200 on an evening away, or a new dress for some posh function.

Not any longer.

It doesn't feel as if I'll ever clear it. I never thought I'd end up as one of those people who always owes money – but here I am.

Billy is getting into the swing of eating a little more now, not quite so put out by the treachery of cheap food.

I find myself staring at the envelope of money on the table: £3,640 that I'm definitely going to hand in.

Before I know it, the envelope is in my hand and I'm not entirely sure when I crossed the room. The apartment's *only* room. I lift the envelope flap slowly, peering at the packed rows of twenty-pound notes.

I'm lost in thoughts of the good I could do with the windfall. The way I could turn my life around… which is when a noise thumps through the apartment.

I shriek and possibly even jump a little. Literally jump. There's somebody at the door. I cram the envelope into the drawer underneath the television and then shout 'hang on' as I double-check the money is definitely still inside the envelope. There's an addictive intoxication to it. A lure.

Billy is still in the kitchenette, half watching the door in case this newcomer is interested in his food.

The identity of the person at the door is no surprise. It's not as if I have a gargantuan circle of friends who pop in unannounced at regular intervals. I don't live in a sitcom.

Karen is leaning on my door frame, half turned to the door opposite.

'You seen 'im yet, then?' she asks.

'Who?' I reply.

Karen nods across the hall. 'Our new neighbour.'

She looks between me and the closed door expectantly, as if whoever it is might appear through the sheer force of her will. Nobody does, of course.

'I don't know why you think it's a him,' I say.

'I saw Lauren on her way out today and wheedled it out of her. She's still fuming that Jade up and left without paying the rent.' Karen turns from the closed door back to me. 'Did you know Jade left all her stuff? There wasn't much, but Lauren reckons she had to pay someone to come and take it all. Guess that's what happens with students.'

Karen pushes herself up from leaning into a standing position. She's still eyeing the door across the hallway as if there's a prize behind it. If I was in there, I'd probably be hiding from Karen, too. She's lovely – and my best friend, if I'm honest. That's partly because a single woman in a crappy flat with a crappier job and no money isn't really in demand among the social circles of society. It's also because we really do get on. She does enjoy the gossip a lot more than I do, however, and the identity of our new neighbour is something that's been a constant source of speculation and conversation since we found out Jade had left a few months ago.

I always liked Jade. She seemed assertive enough and, more importantly in a place like this, never made any noise. The fact that she upped and left without telling Lauren, our building manager, seems a bit unlike her – but then I guess we never had a real conversation. It's funny how much you think you know about a person through snatched snippets of interaction.

'He's probably hiding,' I say.

Karen turns back to me. 'Who?'

'Our new neighbour. He's heard you're prowling around the hallway and is keeping his head down.'

I grin and Karen acknowledges the truth with a smirk. 'I'm not prowling,' she says. 'I baked a welcome-to-your-new-home cake – and then no one's seen him in two weeks.' She pauses, biting her bottom lip. 'I reckon it's a rich businessman using it as a place to meet his mistress. Y'know… cheap flat… no one's gonna suspect he'd bring anyone here.'

She's right about one thing. Hamilton House has been around for more than six decades and is gradually becoming more and more run-down. The people who live in the flats do so not through choice but because there's hardly anywhere cheaper in the local area. It's the sort of place where people can spend decades and it's a competition to see whether the building is condemned before the tenants die of gas poisoning or respiratory lung problems brought on by the damp. We literally live in an eyesore.

There's no way a rich businessman is bringing anyone here, secret mistress or not, but I can't be bothered to talk about it any longer.

'You're probably right,' I say.

'Did you hear 'im playing Elton John the other day?' Karen asks.

I blink at her, silenced for a second before I find my voice. 'Really?'

It's only a single word, but I still manage to falter in saying it.

Karen looks to me, picking up on the crack in my voice. She frowns: 'You okay?'

'Yes, I um…'

If she noticed my momentary stumble, then Karen moves on quickly. 'I'm going to invite him to my birthday party,' she says, before taking two steps across the hall and rapping her knuckles on the door.

We wait in silence as nothing happens. Karen tries knocking a second time but gets the same response, so she shrugs, crouches, and slips an envelope under the door. She turns back to me.

'You're coming, aren't you?'

I shrink back into my apartment. 'I don't know. It's on bonfire night and Billy gets scared by the fireworks.'

As I glance back into the flat, Billy's ears prick up at the sound of his name. He's finished his food and is sitting next to the cupboard underneath the kitchen sink. Sometimes, it feels like he's the bouncing, excitable dog he once was; other times, it's like he can barely muster the energy to move.

'Didn't I tell you?' Karen replies. 'The Rec Centre says dogs are okay. I asked especially. The party's in the room at the back, so you probably won't hear the fireworks in there. There'll be music to drown it out anyway.'

Damn.

Parties are not my thing and haven't been for a long, long time. It's all true about Billy and bonfire night, but, as much as I like Karen, I was also hoping to use him as an excuse to get out of going to her party. I think, deep down, that's how everybody feels about this sort of thing. The minute a wedding invite arrives, or there's a mention of a birthday or anniversary party, those summoned start thinking of the best way to get out of it. Sickness is an obvious one, but we pray for an altered work rota or to be hit by a taxi. Sure, it might mean a shattered limb – but it will provide the sweet, sweet respite from an evening's pretence of enjoying ourselves.

With Karen's party, the Rec Centre is only a street away, so it's not as if I can even claim to have no way of getting there.

'Oh,' I say. 'I'll be there then.'

Karen checks something on her phone and then takes a step towards her own flat at the end of the hallway.

'You working tomorrow?' she asks. 'I was wondering if we might do another Parkrun. I could knock at eight…?'

It's all a stream of words, touching on three different subjects in what is barely a sentence. It takes me a moment to de-spaghettify it all.

'I am working,' I say. 'But I can do Parkrun before.'

She breaks into a smile. There's nothing like struggling through a 5K run with company.

'I've gotta get back,' Karen says. 'If I turn my back for two minutes, Quinn and Ty end up playing UFC with each other. They're banned from watching it – but I think someone at school has it on their phone.' She stops for breath and then adds: 'Are you still okay to take the kids trick or treating on Sunday?'

'You've sold them as such angels, how could I say no?'

The truth is, I'm not looking forward to it – but Karen and I do our best to help out one another. It's not as if we have families on whom to rely. Not so long ago, I'd have been happy to go trick or treating. This time of year – Hallowe'en and Bonfire Night – used to be my favourite days of the year, even above Christmas. I'd love the sulphur in the air; the ever-increasing whizzes and bangs that would light up the sky leading up to the fifth of November itself. Now, I have too many bad memories of the week.

Karen smirks. 'They're not bad kids, really.'

'I know.' A pause. 'Have you got some fella on the go…?'

I'm fishing, because Karen has been cagey about precisely what she's doing on Sunday night. She does agency work but only during the day so that she's home for Tyler and Quinn. This is the third Sunday in a row that I'll have kept an eye on her boys. Not that I mind.

Karen glances away to the other end of the hall, suddenly unable to meet my eye. 'Something like that,' she squirms.

She doesn't want to talk about it, so I leave it.

'I'll see you in the morning,' she adds, before scurrying down the corridor to her flat. Boys' screaming voices echo out momentarily as she opens the door and then there's quiet.

I take a moment to eye the door across the hall. There's a peephole in the centre and, for some reason, it feels as if there's someone on the other side. I hug my arms across myself, feeling the stranger's eyes scanning me. Billy takes that as a cue to poke his head into the hallway. He shifts his head in both directions and then turns to look up at me and he licks his chops.

'Fat lot of good you are,' I tell him as I usher him back inside.

I've almost closed the door when a solitary creak ekes ominously from across the hallway. From inside Jade's old apartment. I stop to watch, but seconds pass without any other noise; without any hint of movement or acknowledgement. It's an old building, after all.

It's when I eventually click my door shut that I wonder if I heard anything at all.

THREE

The money is stacked on my table again, all £3,640 of it. I leave it there, as if it's an invited guest. It feels comforting to have it in front of me and I find myself slightly reordering the piles so that the cleaner, newer notes are all together. It's only when Billy comes to lie at my feet that I notice I've spent almost twenty minutes simply looking at – and touching – the money.

In the end, I force myself to get my laptop from the drawer underneath the television. It was a Christmas deal on Amazon nearly two years ago, although cheap for the same reason most things are cheap: it's barely useable. I flip the lid and turn it on and then put it down. Booting up takes a minimum of five minutes – and that's if it loads at all. Using the computer is something like raising a toddler. Sometimes it does what it's told and everything's happiness and light; other times it's uncooperative, even against threats of extreme violence.

Perhaps I shouldn't be allowed to raise a toddler.

I wait for the laptop to go through its usual routine of deciding whether it's going to actually do something today – bit like those workmen digging up the road – and then it finally reaches the main screen.

There is work for me to do and I load the Open University website, but, before I actually get on with anything, I find myself googling 'missing money' and the name of our town. I'm not sure what I'm expecting, but there's nothing of note. I try 'stolen money', but that only brings up a few news stories about minor robberies going back over the past few years. There's nothing recent, so I try searching for the exact amount.

Nothing.

The £3,640 could be part of a larger figure, of course. Some sort of robbery, or drug money? I don't know. I've probably seen too many crime dramas. *Drug money*? I might be naïve but I don't think my sleepy little corner of the world is up there with the South American cartels when it comes to laundering cash.

I pack the money into the envelope once more, but it's like trying to cram toothpaste back into a tube. Each time I remove all the notes, the envelope seems to shrink slightly. Eventually I reseal the envelope and put it into the drawer, but it's almost as if the money is calling to me. Whenever I look to my laptop hoping to do some university work, I find my attention drifting to the drawer.

It's not long before I move the envelope to the cupboard underneath the kitchen sink. Because I still can't focus, I then hide it underneath the mattress that's part of the bed which folds down from the wall next to the sofa. My flat is so small that there isn't anywhere better to conceal it, not without ripping up floorboards.

That doesn't stop me from thinking about it. It's hard to know where the money came from. I noticed it after getting off the bus – but the number 24 doesn't seem the type of place that someone would be carrying around so much cash. That said, I'm not sure I frequent any places in which people would be carrying these sorts of amounts. The envelope wasn't in my bag when I was looking for my bus pass, so it appeared either on my walk from the bus stop, or on the bus itself.

I'm lost in a daydream when my phone starts to ring. It's an old, battered Android that I've dropped more times than I care to remember. If it wasn't for the £1.99 case I bought from the market, my phone would have been a goner months ago. I pay £10 a month, which is one of my more extravagant outgoings. There is no landline phone in the flat and it's hard to lead a life in these times without a mobile: I am texted my shift times and I have to call our building manager, Lauren, if there are any problems at the flat. Even my banking, for what it's worth, is done through an app.

The phone's screen is scratched and scuffed but the word 'unknown' beams bright. I wouldn't usually answer – it'll almost certainly be a life-sapping marketing call – but there's a part of me that somehow believes it might be the money-owner calling.

'Hello?'

There's silence from whoever's at the other end, not even one of those tell-tale clicks that happen when it's a telemarketer. I check the phone, but it's back to the home screen. Whoever called me rang off the moment I answered. The previous caller's option reveals only 'unknown'. I stare at it for a second to two, wondering if there's anything I can do to trace the call and then deciding I'm not that bothered.

By now, Billy is back on his feet and hanging around by the front door. When he was younger, he'd actually paw when he wanted to be let out – but he's far savvier now. He knows that it only takes a look for me to understand what he wants. He likes to roam the corridors of the building, pacing around for a few minutes to go up and down the stairs. I take him out in the mornings and evenings so he can go to the toilet, but it's like he learned to walk himself in between times.

When I open the door, there is a corgi also wandering around. He is named Judge and he turns to look up at me, as if I've caught him up to no good. Judge's owner, Nick, lives two doors down and we sometimes take the dogs for joint walks. The two dogs sniff at one another and then head in opposite directions along the hallway. I guess it isn't only me who has become a reclusive loner.

I leave the door slightly open, ready for Billy's return, and then perch on the edge of the kitchen counter as my phone buzzes once more.

It's a message this time – and there are no questions about who it's from. I was on the street a couple of months back when one of those chugger-types enthusiastically bounded towards me. I try to stare at the floor in such situations but somehow ended up with a promo card that offered three free months' membership of a dating website. I wasn't going to do anything with it, but then, for a reason of which I'm still not completely sure, I ended up signing up. It was probably the word 'free' that did it. There's very little I turn down when it's not going to cost me anything.

An actual dating website seems old-fashioned given the amount of left- and right-swiping that goes on nowadays. I guess that's how quickly times move.

Either way, I have a message from one of my matches, a bloke named Harry.

So… are we ever going to meet?

I've been putting him off, with a part of me hoping he'd go away. It's not that his pictures aren't appealing, nor that he hasn't entertained me with his messages, more that Ben's legacy still seems so close. There are mornings when I wake up and still think Ben is lying next to me; times when my phone beeps and I'm certain it's him.

It's been five years – *five years* – and I'm still not sure I'll ever quite forget everything that happened.

I think about not replying, about letting Harry's messages drift until he gets bored and stops contacting me.

Surely five years is long enough?

Tomorrow evening?

Harry pings a reply back almost instantly:

Perfect! Where would you like to go?

I start a reply and then stop myself. There's etiquette to think about. Do people split a bill on a first date? I've never been the sort of person who's comfortable with allowing a bloke to pay for everything just because he happens to have different genitalia. This is the other issue with dating, even if I hate that word, it's expensive – or it can be.

As I'm trying to figure out how best to suggest the cheapest place I know without making it sound like I'm skint, another message arrives.

How about The Garden Café?

I've never been but Google says it's within walking distance of where I live. It's funny how, when travel costs are hard to meet, every place is judged by whether it's walkable. I hold my breath and check the menu. There are expensive items – plus a dizzying array of wine – but I can stick to tap water. Free is always good. More importantly, the soup and salad is cheap, there's an all-day breakfast that's a fiver and plenty of fancy-sounding dishes that won't cripple my finances for the rest of the month. I might have to go without food for the rest of the day, but I could likely handle it.

I find myself glancing towards the bed that's folded up into the wall. Towards the envelope of money.

Sounds good.

We send a couple more messages back and forth, finalising the time, and it all seems very normal. Very simple. It's like I'm a real human being. Like the shadow of Ben isn't hanging over me any longer; as if everything *will* be all right in the end. That's what people kept saying five years ago and I'm still waiting.

Our messages dry up as Billy nudges his way back into the apartment. I close the door behind him and then take my space on the sofa, him at my feet, curled up and ready to sleep. I should be doing some of my university work – my Childhood and Youth Studies course isn't going to complete itself – but it's almost impossible to concentrate.

I'm home alone, just me and Billy.

And the money.

It's still calling, wanting to be counted. To be touched. So much money.

I turn on the television to distract myself, flicking through the Freeview channels until I find something that isn't full of gurning, grating idiots shouting at one another. It takes a long time. With the background noise sorted, I do some more searching on the laptop, looking for news stories or social media posts about missing or stolen money in the local area. There's still nothing.

I'm definitely going to hand it in to the police. It's a bit late in the day now, so probably tomorrow.

Somebody must have noticed it missing by now. It's too much money to ignore. I wonder if it's dodgy. I know the new plastic notes are supposed to be impossible to counterfeit, but, if that's the case, then… what? It has to be real, so someone will want it back.

My stomach gurgles, reminding me that I've not eaten since the Weetabix I had this morning. Billy grumbles as I remove my foot from under his chin and head to the fridge. It takes me a second or two to realise that there's even less inside than I remember. There's a bottle of chilled tap water, a couple of carrots, a tub of almost-finished margarine, two eggs and an apple. There's also a large bag of porridge oats underneath the sink that was on offer six weeks ago and will last for months, plus the remaining Weetabix in the box. It's not real Weetabix, of course. It's the own-brand Weety-Bits. Aside from Billy's food, that's all there is to eat in the flat.

It's a little after seven p.m. but I make myself a bowl of porridge on the hob, measuring out the oats and water because I don't want to make too much and end up wasting it. By the time I get back to the sofa, Billy is in full-on snoring mode. It's gently melodic, as if he's keeping time for an orchestra. I'm careful not to step on him as I curl my feet under myself on the sofa and check the web one more time to see if anybody has reported the missing or stolen money.

Not yet, but I'm sure they will.

If I'm honest, this is my life now. There was a time when it might have been the odd dinner party, or nights out at the cinema. Where I'd pay £6 or more for a glass of wine and not even think about it. Where I'd get a taxi home, tipsy and giggling. Now, it is bowls of porridge, a snoring dog, nonsense on the television and me attempting to do my university course. I tell myself it's all a means to an end. I'll graduate one day and then I can look for a job that pays more. When that comes through, I can find somewhere bigger and better to live. Time is all it takes. Well, time *and* money. I want it to be *my* money, though. Money *I've* earned. Something I've worked for.

I'm definitely handing this money in. I've got Parkrun in the morning, then work, then I'll go to the police station after that.

My phone rings once more and one of Billy's ears pricks up, even though he doesn't open his eyes. The screen reads unknown and I let it ring off. Whoever it is will leave a message if it's important. I find myself staring towards the bed that's hidden in the wall once more. The money is calling me again, but it'll be gone tomorrow and everything will get back to normal.

Definitely.

FOUR

SATURDAY

Out of everyone I know, there is one of us who really enjoys the five-kilometre Parkrun – and it is definitely not me. I tolerate it and Karen more or less does the same, citing the greater good. Billy, however, seems to know when it's Saturday. He strains on his lead the entire way to the park. He might be getting slowly, heartbreakingly, more lethargic – but this day is always his favourite of the week.

Karen and I hang around close to the line as the rest of the Parkrunners mingle and wait for the start. The crumbling path serves as the route, looping its way around the green of the park, up and over a ridge and then back down the other side. We circle the pavilion, continue along the riverbank for a bit and then follow the trail back around to the start. Two laps of that is 5K – and then we can all, mercifully, go home.

There's a bit of everything here; a bit of everyone. Some skinny lads are in vests and short-shorts that are borderline pornographic. They look professional, with their watches, chest straps and general focused stare whenever they get somewhere near the start line. There are women, too, of course, with their toned, tight abs and bobbing ponytails. Others are in jogging bottoms, loose T-shirts and scruffy trainers. Someone behind me is wearing jeans, as if he didn't have to time to get changed from whatever he was up to last night.

A whistle signals the start and then, predictably, those at the front with all the gear go bombing off. For me, I'm certain the tortoise had the right idea against the hare: slow and steady is the way to go. Although, if that *were* true, I'd be beating those that have gone off fast – and that definitely doesn't happen.

Karen likes the company of running with someone, even if she's too out of breath to actually talk after we start. I'm a little faster than her, but there's not much in it, so I happily plod along as Billy bobs at my side. It took me a few weeks to realise that, if I start near the back, I can jog past more people than overtake me – which gives a stab of satisfaction.

It is also at events such as this that I realise Billy is way more popular than I will ever be. The fellow slow runners usually have a wave for him, even as they fail to acknowledge my existence. Not that I mind. Not really.

It doesn't take long for the field to thin as everyone settles into their respective paces. There's a comforting rhythm to the steady beat of my trainers hitting the tarmac, but my stomach is grumbling, possibly because, in the previous 24 hours, I've had only two bowls of porridge. I'm almost certain it's not the best way to prepare for a run.

The air is cool and bites at my throat and lungs. This was much easier in the summer months. I've never been much of an athlete. Running, swimming or cycling were the confines of someone else. It was when I turned thirty earlier in the year that I figured I should probably make an effort to get fit. I'm not completely sure why – I think it's something that happens when a person reaches a certain age. We spend a decade getting fat and enjoying ourselves, then another decade trying to right all the wrongs we've foisted upon our poor bodies.

It was never quite like that with me, not after what happened with Ben. I stopped eating entirely, working my way through an eating disorder and back out the other side. I think this is part of me taking control of my life.

Karen is six years older than me and had been talking about running and going to the odd fitness class. It was when I found out that Parkrun was free that I agreed.

And here we are.

I up my pace as I reach the first slope. The cold air is beginning to stab into my lungs as breath spirals up into the air. Billy doesn't seem to mind as he remains at my side. I stay with Karen every week, but today, for once, I allow myself to go at my own speed. I pass half-a-dozen runners on the incline and, even though I'm not particularly competitive, it's hard not to feel satisfied. Billy starts to pull at his lead, enjoying the pace – and so I kick again until the cold air suddenly feels hot within me. No matter. I can do this.

It's only as I'm crossing the finish line for the first time that I realise I've only been overtaken *once* by the leaders. It's so unexpected that I almost stop to make sure something catastrophic hasn't happened to those at the very front. I twist to look over my shoulder and, sure enough, one of the skinny lads in a vest is a few metres behind, ready to charge over the line himself.

I've completed one lap in the time it's taken him to do two – but it's better than what usually happens, when I'm overtaken twice. It might be silly but it feels like an achievement. It's a confirmation that I'm in a better place than I was a week ago.

I should be tiring, but, as I get to the slope for the second time, I feel surprisingly fresh. As I clasp Billy's lead tighter, I press on, knowing I should beat my best time. Everything is going fantastically until, from nowhere, my shoe comes off. I take two steps without it until I fully realise what's happened. My socks are little protection against the scratchy scattering of small stones underfoot as I hop to a stop. Billy strains on the lead before turning to look back over his shoulder, giving me an angsty, *Why-have-you-stopped?* look.

As soon as I retrieve my shoe, it becomes apparent why it came off. It's not because the laces were too loose, or that one snapped, it's because – somehow – the entire leather has split from the tongue at the top, through to the sole. I find myself staring at the wreckage, wondering quite how it could have happened. Runners start to overtake as Billy completes the humiliation by sitting on the grass. Even he's given up on me.

Something sinks within me. The trainers were a charity-shop find. A miracle of circumstance in that the cashier was putting out a new set of donations and I got hold of them before anyone else could. I paid £15 for something that should have been £140. I know that because I looked them up afterwards. It sounds pathetic – I know – but finding the bargain feels like one of my greatest achievements of recent years. I don't really get to have nice things, not any more. If I need a new item of clothing – actually *need* – I'll go through sale racks and hope to find something that isn't either enormously huge or microscopically small. The £15 for these trainers were a stretch but I wear them for everything – work, getting around, and, of course, running.

Karen slows as she passes, huffing 'You okay?' in my direction. I hold up my broken shoe for her to see – but she's already past, perhaps on for a personal best herself. I don't blame her.

The grass is dewy and the water soaks through my sock as I set off to walk back towards the start line. I can hear myself wheezing – but it's not from the exertion of running. Panic attacks used to come regularly, but it's been a while since I've been overwhelmed by one. That's not who I am any longer. I can control it.

I stop and crouch, smoothing the hair on Billy's back as he stares up at me with confusion. Breathe in through the nose, out through the mouth. Concentrate.

It's hard to describe the desolation. They're only shoes and yet they represent so much more. I don't know how I'm going to be able to replace them. The fact it's all so stupid, that it's *shoes* – of all things – that are getting me emotional, only makes it worse.

I am almost back at the start line, one shoe on, one off, when I feel my gaze being pulled towards one of the benches over by the trees at the entrance to the park. A steady stream of runners are jogging past, but it's not them I notice. It's not any of them who are staring back at me. I spot the red anorak first and, before I know it, I'm drifting across to the woman whose eyes have not wavered from me.

'Melanie,' is the word I go with as I stand over her. Say what you see and all that. I don't know what else to come out with.

Her face is craggier than I remember, the wrinkles deeper, her hair a wiry scrubbing pad of grey and rusty brown. Some things never change, however. There was always spite and fury in her eyes – and, if anything, it burns brighter in the years since we last saw one another. Billy must feel it, too. He sits behind my legs, not daring to look at her.

Melanie continues to stare but says nothing. Eventually, she twists away to gaze out towards the water on the far side of the park. Red-faced runners continue to bob past, huffing and puffing their way to the finish line.

'I didn't know you got to this end of town,' I add. The silence between us is agonisingly awkward.

Melanie tugs her red anorak away from her collar and gasps a loud gust of breath.

'Are you, um…?' I'm not sure what I'm asking; not even particularly certain why I'm continuing to talk to her. It's been four years since we last saw one another. She was a venomous inferno of anger then. I've moved on and I suppose I'm wondering if she has.

In a flash, she spins back to me, eyes blazing. 'Oh, you'd like that, wouldn't you?'

She spits the words with such spite that I take half a step backwards, almost treading on poor Billy.

'Like what?' I manage.

In a blink, Melanie is on her feet. She glares daggers and then turns with a swish and stomps off towards the park exit. I watch her go and it's only as she disappears out of sight that I feel able to move again.

I suppose I thought she might have moved away from here and found herself some peace elsewhere. A little place near the seaside, or a flat in a city centre where everything and anything is on the doorstep. It's no surprise she's still around, of course. It's not like I moved; not like I found peace elsewhere. We live in the same big town, but it's easy to get lost among so many people. To be invisible. Her in her space, me in mine.

It's only as I release a large rasp that I realise I've been holding my breath. I shiver with relief and, suddenly, it feels as if I'm still the shaky, traumatised woman I was in years gone by.

The thing is, it's not that I don't see her point of view. There's a part of me that understands exactly why she is how she is. Melanie doesn't like me, which is completely reasonable given that she believes I killed both her sons.

FIVE

When it comes to fashion statements, shoes that are literally being held together by sticky tape certainly sends a message. Admittedly, the message is: 'This person cannot afford to buy new shoes', but it's a clear statement nonetheless.

My only other option of shoes to wear to work is a low pair of heels that are leftovers from my school days more than a decade ago. There's no way I'll be able to stand in those all day – so it's my taped-up trainers or bare feet.

I have to go to work but cannot resist opening the envelope of money to check it's still there. It is, of course, precisely in the way I repacked it all with the neat, uncrimped notes at the top. The small voice telling me to take what I need for new shoes is starting to become louder. There's still nothing online about missing or stolen money. If nobody's missing it, then what would be wrong with taking a bit for myself…?

I reluctantly put the envelope of money into the drawer underneath the television and then say goodbye to Billy. He's used to being by himself while I'm at work – but it's still hard to escape the guilt for leaving him alone. In between showering and changing, I've had another missed call from 'unknown'. There is no number to call back, no clue as to who is trying to get in contact.

After closing my door, I pause for a second, drawn to the flat opposite. Good or bad, Hamilton House is the type of block in which everyone recognises everyone else. There is a certain amount of all being in it together, as they say. We know it's a bit of a crappy place to live – but it's still ours. There are three floors of six flats and that creates a community. If someone *has* moved in opposite, there is a strangeness in that nobody has seemingly seen the person.

I head downstairs and there are posters for Karen's birthday party at the bottom with 'all welcome' written on each in felt tip. Karen's written her flat number on there, inviting anyone who wants more details to knock on her door.

Outside, and the chill is still clinging to the air. I pull my coat tighter and take a few steps towards the bus stop before halting. Before I know what I'm doing, I'm back inside and rushing up the stairs. I wrench my door open and almost fall inside with the speed of it all.

Billy is lying on the sofa and his ears perk up with confusing expectation. I whisper a 'sorry' in his direction and then grab the envelope of money from the drawer. It's comforting and feels like something I need to have close. I tuck it into my bag and then wrench the zipper shut. After another apology to Billy, I close the door and then I'm off again. This time I don't change my mind.

It's only when I pass the low wall on Allen Street that I remember the feeling of first seeing the money in the envelope. The thrill of it all. It was nearly a day ago and yet I can still feel the buzz. There's an urge to open my bag and check it over, but I force it away and continue on until I arrive at the stop just as the bus is pulling in.

The difference between Saturday morning and Friday evening on the number 24 bus is ridiculous. Today, there are barely half-a-dozen people spread out among the seats. I show the driver my pass – my biggest monthly outgoing aside from rent – and then get a double space to myself. One of the other passengers is seemingly passed out across two seats, his beanie hat pulled low over his eyes as he rests his head in the crook of his elbow. Everyone else is on their respective phones and I copy their lead. There are still no hits for missing or stolen money. I would hand it in but, if I was to take it to the police, who's to say it wouldn't end up being divvied out among them? If anyone should get it, surely it should be me?

I glance towards the front of the bus, eyeing the spot near the pole where I was standing last night. There's nobody there now, but there can't really be any doubt that this is where the envelope appeared in my bag. Could it really have been by accident? Surely the alternative is weirder – that someone *gave* me this money? But who? And, if it was deliberate, why not simply hand it to me?

So many questions.

I open the zip of my bag and finger the top of the envelope, craving to touch what's inside. I know it's strange – I know, I know – but I can't help myself. I picture those poor, hungry people that appear on television appeals every time it's *Comic Relief, Children In Need*, or whatever. If someone gives them food, it gets eaten. There's no need for politeness or reticence. The amount of money in the envelope is close to three months of wages for me – why shouldn't I treat it in the same way that hungry people treat food? I've not *stolen* it.

For some, it's pocket change. I read once that if Bill Gates was to drop a $20 note, it wouldn't be worth the time it would take him to pick it up. He earns more from carrying on with his day. For someone like that, this money is nothing. For me, it can change my life.

I'm so lost in the dilemma that I almost miss my stop. It's only when the lad with the beanie hat jumps up in alarm that I notice where we are. The driver has started to move, but I call a 'hang on' and he stops once more for me to get off. From here, I only need to cross the road to get to work.

Crosstown Supermarket is something of a throwback to times that are almost gone. Somehow, the owners have held out against the giant superstores and are still running a singular, medium-sized, independent shop. Nobody – most of all the people who work there – can quite believe it's not been bought out yet.

When I get into the staff changing room at the back of the store, Daff – who does *not* like being called Daphne – is arguing with someone on her phone. She nods at me in acknowledgement as I get my uniform out of my locker and then she continues to ask whoever's on the phone quite why they've charged her interest on a credit card payment she says she's already made. I listen in without making it obvious and inspect my taped-together trainers, which have held together remarkably well.

Daff finishes her call with a flourish of, 'Yeah, well, you can whistle for it, darling', and then tosses her phone into her bag.

I ask if everything's all right and she snorts what is probably the filthiest laugh I've ever heard.

'Can't let 'em grind you down,' she says, before taking an envelope out of her locker. There's a moment in which I'm confused, as if everyone I know has been delivered an envelope of cash, but it's not that at all. She waggles it towards me.

'You got a pound for the lottery?' she asks.

It's hard not to sigh at this. I've never been interested in gambling – even a pound twice a week for the lottery. The problem is that everybody else who works here – literally every single person – *does* chip in two pounds a week for the syndicate. Rationality tells me we'll never win and yet I know I couldn't face seeing all these people around me sharing out the millions as I rue hanging onto my two pounds. I don't know how anyone could ever deal with that. I know I couldn't – and so I go along with it all. It's lose-lose, of course – because if I was to count the number of weeks I've been chucking in two quid and add it all up, I'd only depress myself at the money lost. We once won ten pounds, but that went back into 'the pot' and was, of course, lost in the following draw.

I pass Daff a pound coin and she drops it into her envelope, before writing my name on the front.

'Cheer up,' she says with an enthusiastic grin.

I return hers with a forced smile of my own, wondering what precisely people think might happen when they tell others to 'cheer up'. Oh, great, all the things I was dealing with are solved because someone told me to be a bit happier.

Daff starts wittering about some night out she's planning this evening. 'Everyone's coming,' she promises, presumably referring to the people with whom we work. It's little incentive for me. These are the people with whom I've been thrown together. It isn't as if we chose to work with actual friends, not that I have many of them either. Even though I never left the town in which I went to school, I have no real friends left over from those times. I gave that up when I moved in with Ben all those years ago.

Either way, I have numerous issues with going out that involve, but are not limited to:

I have no money

I like being in bed early

I have no going-out clothes

No group can ever make a decision as to a venue

I'm too old for morning-after hangovers

I make small talk with Daff and give a non-committal 'maybe' when she asks if I fancy coming out with 'the girls' later. If I was honest, I'd tell her, 'Not a chance'.

As the clock ticks around to the start of our shift, Daff puts her bag in her locker – as-per company policy – but I know I can't do the same. Not with the envelope of money inside. I need to feel it close. I stuff mine under my arm and head to the tills, before burying it in the space underneath the conveyor belt.

A person can learn a lot about others when working on a supermarket checkout. It's a bit like sharing a bus, I suppose: there's a bit of everything – of every*one*. Everybody needs to eat and so everyone uses a supermarket sooner or later. Most go about their business as quickly as they can – a swift in and out and they're done until the next time. There's always a minority, of course. Those who drop something like milk on the floor, watch it splat and spread, and then walk off as if nothing has happened. It happens almost every day. Then there are people who scatter trolleys here, there and everywhere in the car park because a short walk from their car to the front of the store is seemingly too much.

Some ignore the '10 items or fewer' and wheel through full trolleys but then act incredulously when told they need to check out in a different place. A surprising amount try to use coupons meant for one product to try to get money off another – and then there is the thing that makes it clear to absolutely everyone that the person involved is a horrendous human being. It's not as if I want a lengthy conversation with the people who pass by my till. A nod and a 'hello' is usually enough. Sometimes people ask about my day (how do *you* think it's going, seeing as I'm working at a checkout?) – or I'll ask about theirs. It's all fine. What is really hard to stomach, though, are those people who spend the entire process talking into their phone, ignoring me as if I'm some sort of robot at their beck and call. I want to slap their phones away, to stare into their eyes and remind them that I'm an actual, *real* human being. To let them know that I have feelings and that it's really not that much to ask that they acknowledge me in the merest way imaginable. A good start is actually looking at me, or muttering 'hi' – even if they don't mean it.

I don't do any of that, of course. I scan their shopping, take the money, and let it simmer.

Time always seems like it passes quicker on Saturdays, mainly because there are more people trying to get their shopping done. At times, it is a stream of one person after another. Through it all, I think of the seven pounds and fifty pence I'm making every hour. With my lunch break, it is £52.50 a day and it's hard not to calculate how many days of work there are sitting in my bag at my feet. How I could remove three twenty-pound notes right now and be better off than I am spending seven-and-a-half hours in this job.

I'm lost in those thoughts as a young woman arrives at the till cradling a baby in one arm and pushing a trolley with the other. Her dark hair is dirty and there are some murky-looking stains on her top. She has to be twenty at the most and struggles to make eye contact as she places her items on the conveyor belt. Her child has no such worries, gazing at me with deep blue eyes that haunt and charm in equal measure. The mother is so gaunt, so small.

There is a packet of formula, a box of rusks, a bottle of lotion and a bag of nappies. Everything is the cheap, own-brand items that we sell. Other than that, there are four packets of ten-pence noodles and a large bag of porridge oats.

We share a look that lasts barely a second, but, in that moment, it's as if we are sisters. Out of everything, we've bonded over porridge oats.

She pulls out a tattered shopping bag and waits at the end of the conveyor belt, still balancing her child with one arm.

'I'll pack,' I tell her and she nods. There is acne around her mouth and unfilled piercings in her ears. I wonder when she last ate.

I pass the rusks over the scanner, waiting for the beep and the price: £2. The girl stares at the amount and then her eyes give her away as she glances back to the trolley. It's impossible to miss now: there are two further packets of nappies sitting on the rail underneath the main trolley. I look at them and then at her. She holds my eyes and we're still sisters.

I scan the lotion, the noodles and the porridge oats; then hold my hand over the barcode of the formula as I pass it directly into the shopping bag. There's no beep.

The total is a little under £15 and we both know it's not right.

Another customer slots in behind the girl, talking on his phone, and neither of us pay him any attention. She's shaking as she counts the notes and coins out of her tatty purse into my hand. The amount is correct to the final penny – and I suspect much of her budgeting is done like this. Pennies count and pounds certainly do.

I lean in, so the man on the phone can't hear, even if he was listening. 'Use the small door by the magazines,' I say, 'You can squeeze around the scanner no problem.'

Her eyes widen a little, but she nods to say she's heard. I don't know about her, but my own heart is racing.

She shuffles away, switching the nappies from the trolley to her bag and then heading in the direction of the smaller door without risking a backwards look. I watch her go before turning to the man who is still on his phone.

Sometimes life isn't black and white and, as I nudge the bag at my feet, I figure not everyone can be given envelopes full of money.

SIX

It's only as I'm getting off the bus close to home that I get a message from Harry asking if I'm still on for tonight. With spotting Melanie and spending a day at work, it had fallen from my mind. I can't stop thinking about the girl at the checkout, wondering if she'll eat today; or how the baby is getting on.

I wait until I get home and have given Billy a quick walk before replying to Harry. I'd rather have an evening in with my dog – but that describes almost every other night of my recent existence. Instead, I send back 'of course!', spending almost ten minutes agonising over whether to include the exclamation point. I go for it in the end, figuring it can be part of the new me. Old me would go without; new me is way more fun.

That done, I try to figure out how I'm going to make myself somewhat presentable given my lack of options. I don't have many choices, especially considering one of my two pairs of shoes are taped together. I go with my ancient school shoes and my job interview clothes of a dark skirt and white blouse. Not that I've had an interview in years. In an attempt to lessen the office worker appearance, I dig a floaty blue scarf thing from the bottom of my drawer and tie it around my neck. It's still a bit low-rent airline attendant but it will have to do. Beggars and choosers and all that. It's almost a relief that I have so little. In the old teenagery days, I'd have spent hours figuring out what to wear and changing my mind dozens of times. Sometimes, it was like that when I was with Ben. Now, it's as if that worry has been taken from me. If these clothes, if my appearance, isn't good enough, there's not a lot I can do about it. I should be nervous and yet this realisation gives me a strange calmness.

I get to The Garden Café fifteen minutes before the time Harry and I agreed. After asking the waiter for some tap water – being very specific about the word 'tap' – I spend time looking through the menu again. There are a few differences to what was online and, because of the prices, I rule out almost eighty per cent of everything listed. It's automatic now, not only with food, I check the prices first and the actual item afterwards.

'Lucy?'

I turn at the sound of my name and then stand to meet Harry. I'm not sure what I expected. We've swapped photos, but there's still something of a shock that he looks like his pictures. He doesn't have three additional chins that he's been hiding with flattering lighting, or a bald spot that is far more than simply a patch. I don't necessarily mind any of those things, it's more the deception of using old pictures or selective lighting. It's been years since I was on anything close to a date and the world has moved on. I've read stories of sexting, ghosting and all sorts of other 'ings' that weren't around a decade ago.

Harry and I shake hands and it feels fine and normal. We're not into the hug territory yet; even the bums-out, lean-in kind of hug.

He's refreshingly ordinary. Shortish dark hair, jeans and a jacket – which is forgivable in this instance, especially given my own clothes. He's average height, weight, and whatever else.

There is something about the way he looks at me, though. It's hard to place at first, but then I realise he reminds me of Billy when I wake him up unexpectedly. There's a sideways tilt, a glimmer of recognition.

'Do I know you?' I ask. 'You seem like you know me…?' I tail off, not quite sure how to phrase it. We've only met seconds ago and, already, I'm blowing things.

There's a pause. I first think it's because he's considering it, but then it seems clear that he has no idea how to reply. Of all the things I could have said to him, this would have been somewhere at the bottom of the list. Level with, 'So, Genghis Khan. He was a bit of a rascal, wasn't he?'

'I don't think so,' Harry replies, hesitantly. 'Perhaps I have one of those faces?' He cracks a smile and strikes a comedy catalogue pose, pointing and gazing off into the distance. From nowhere, I'm giggling and everything is fine.

Harry motions to pull my chair out to allow me back in, but I tell him not to be so daft and then we're sitting opposite one another. He has one hand on the menu but doesn't open it and there's a moment in which we simply look at one another. Size each other up, I suppose.

It's broken by the waiter arriving with the timing of a red light when someone's in a hurry. He rattles on about the specials and then recommends half-a-dozen wines. Harry eyes my water and then orders a pint of some lager whose name he rolls his tongue around.

When the waiter has gone, he leans in. 'You're not one of these wine people, are you?'

'What counts as a wine person?'

He pokes out his bottom lip. 'Someone who talks about different types of grapes and can spend an hour banging on about weather patterns in certain Mediterranean regions.'

Harry has an infectious smile which spreads as I reply: 'I am definitely *not* a wine person.'

He nods approvingly. 'That makes two of us.' He nods at the menu that's open on the table in front of me. 'What sounds good?'

There's a moment of panic that's hard to push away. I don't particularly think of things as being 'good', more 'cheap'. I can't stop eyeing the tomato and basil soup, because it comes with bread and a salad – and costs less than a fiver.

'I've not really looked yet,' I lie.

He nods acceptingly but doesn't open his menu, instead nodding at my drink. 'Are you sure you're okay with water? I was only joking about the wine. If that's what you're into, we could share a bottle…?'

It's a question I've been asked before when ordering water, as if not getting trolleyed on a dozen pints of Danish lager is the weird option.

'I've got uni work to do tomorrow,' I reply – which is true, but not the reason for my choice.

He taps the side of his head. 'Of course. I forgot you're a student. It's Childhood and Youth Studies, isn't it?'

There's no way he's remembered that off the top of his head and I wonder if I should have done some revision on him based upon the information we've swapped and his profile. Is this another one of those 'ings' that have appeared in dating since I was with Ben? 'Revising', or something like that.

'That's right,' I say.

He nods along. 'I guess this means you like kids…?'

Harry says it with a smile, but I have another moment of panic. How are we on to talking about kids within minutes of meeting for the first time?

'Um…'

He laughs and waves it away. 'Sorry, I didn't mean it like that. The reason I first contacted you is because you said you were a dog person – so what I really want to ask about is your dog…'

Finally, we're onto something I can talk about confidently and warmly.

'Billy,' I say. 'He's a Staffie. I got him from a shelter about four years ago. He's almost ten now.'

Before I know it, my phone's out and I'm proudly showing off photos as if I've got a newborn. Perhaps he's humouring me, but Harry seems interested. He laughs at the silly pictures and goes 'aww' when I would.

'Have you got a dog?' I ask.

'I wish I did. My building doesn't allow tenants to have pets. Someone could probably get away with a fish or a guinea pig, but that'd be about it. No cats or dogs.'

'Why?'

'I think someone went on holiday and left his dog at home for a week. One of his friends was supposed to be going around to feed him and let him out – that sort of thing – but there was some mix-up. I don't know all the details. It was before I moved in. Either way, the building council banned pets after that.'

I try to think of the last time I had a holiday away but can't come up with anything more recently than the time six years ago when Ben and I went to Cornwall for a week.

'The poor dog…' I say.

Before we can get much further, the waiter is back with Harry's lager. I wonder if workers in places like this can spot the couples on first date. Perhaps they have some sort of radar for it and sit in the back trying to guess which pairs will reach a second date. If things were reversed, I would definitely do that.

The waiter asks if we're ready to order food and I'm on the brink of saying 'soup' when, for a reason of which I'm not entirely certain, the word 'ravioli' pops out. I almost correct myself, but he's already moved onto Harry. I glance down to the menu and feel a rising panic at the '£14' that's listed. Harry orders a risotto (£13.50) and then everything is cleared away. I'm left wondering how I can possibly justify spending so much on a single meal. It's more than I might usually spend on food in a few days.

I bat away a yawn that's crept up on me from nowhere and Harry makes the obligatory 'Am I that boring?' remark.

'I've been at work all day,' I reply. 'And I went running this morning.'

'I'm afraid I spent the afternoon at the football. My team lost.' He pauses to sip his drink and then adds: 'You're in a supermarket, aren't you? Do you work every weekend?'

I had forgotten letting that scrap of information out. 'Not always,' I say. 'I'm sort of assistant manager, so sometimes I have to cover.'

It's a lie but the words are out before I can call them back. The assistant manager's job was up for grabs eighteen months ago – but the applicants all needed degrees. I figured that, if I was going to spend time and money getting those sorts of qualifications, I'd rather find something I thought I'd enjoy. I'm in the circle of not being qualified for better jobs and not having experience to go for jobs within industries that interest me. I'm hoping my part-time course can change that.

'I work in internet security,' Harry says. 'It's all a bit boring, I suppose.' He holds up his phone. 'I'm on call in case one of our clients have a major problem. I alternate with a few others from the team, but one of us always has to be ready to drop everything.'

I fumble something close to a question about what that means, while simultaneously trying to appear as if I know what I'm talking about. It feels like he's trying to downplay what he does while I'm trying to make what I do sound more important than it is.

He tells me that he looks for security holes in company's websites and then effortlessly turns the conversation back around on me: 'If you're doing an Open University course now, does that mean you've been working since you were a teenager…?'

It's a reasonable question, I suppose – especially if this is us getting to know one another. I'm thirty, so why wouldn't he ask about what I've spent the rest of my life doing? I could go on about the past four and a bit years where I've been going nowhere in a supermarket, but it doesn't feel like an achievement. Then there are the years before that…

'I nearly went to university when I was eighteen,' I say, starting to stumble. 'I had a boyfriend at the time and we chose to move in together instead.'

Harry nods along. It's all normal – except, before I know it, the rest is coming out.

'His name was Ben,' I say quickly. 'He died five years ago on Tuesday.'

It's not enough to splurge about what happened to Ben on a first date, I have to be precise with the timing.

'Twenty-four others died, too – including Ben's brother, Alex. There was a train crash.'

Harry gulps and I have little doubt he's regretting being here.

'Ben was off to a work thing,' I add, apparently unable to shut up. 'I didn't know he was going with his brother. You can google it – the crash was a big thing. You might remember it. We were going to get married, buy a house, all that…'

I tail off, suddenly breathless.

It's a flood of information Harry doesn't need to know. Not yet, anyway. It's hard to know why, but I couldn't stop myself. The voice in my head was screaming for hush but out it came. I reach for my glass, but the water is gone. Harry slides across his lager and I don't hesitate, swigging a couple of mouthfuls and then passing back the glass with a whimpered apology. I don't even drink beer. I've not had alcohol of any sort in months. Years. It costs too much.

'It's all right,' he says, with a closed-lip, though kindly, smile. 'If something like that happened to me, I'd want to talk about it, too. It must be one of the biggest things that has ever happened to you…?'

It's such a reasonable response to my dump of information that I have to blink away tears. I mask it – or try to – by flapping an arm to catch the waiter's attention and pointing to my empty glass.

'Do you miss him?' Harry asks. 'It's fine if you do. I'd miss someone if they'd died like that.'

This time I have to glance away. I focus on a poster that's advertising Christmas meals and scan the details over and over until I'm certain I can talk without losing the plot. As first dates go, I've turned this into a disaster – but there's no going back now.

'It's not that simple,' I manage, surprising myself by not cracking. 'There were debts…'

He waits, saying nothing. Moments ago, there was a low chunter of other people chatting to each other, but now it feels as if everyone is silent, wanting to know what happened.

'He took out loans online,' I say. 'I still don't really know how he did it, but he used my name and ID. It was tens of thousands. After Ben died, I started getting letters about payments being overdue. He must have intercepted anything like that before. I'd call the banks and say I didn't know anything about them – but they had my signature and things like that. They didn't believe it wasn't me who'd applied for the money.'

I stop for a breath. It's a long time since I've said any of this out loud. Karen was the last person I told – and that was three years back. I have no idea what's come over me to go through it now.

'We had savings,' I add. 'It was all in joint accounts for the wedding and a house – but that had gone, too. He must have spent it on business trips, but it's not really clear where all the money went. It wasn't in our account when he died. He spent his money and mine.'

The waiter proves he really does have the worst timing by sauntering over and placing a newly filled glass in front of me. Perhaps it's me, my state of mind, but I think he makes a point of saying '*tap* water' when he does so, as if to point out how cheap I am. Either way, he disappears after that.

Harry is silent for a moment. He's drumming his fingers on his cheek and, though I know he's staring at me, I can't meet his eyes.

'How did he get away with it?' Harry asks.

'I guess he didn't. Not in the end. Karma and all that. He said he was a day trader, buying and selling shares usually from home. Other times he said he had conferences to go to, people and investors to meet. That sort of thing.'

Harry nods, but I'm not sure he understands. I'm not sure *I* understand. It sounds so pathetic out loud. How did I fall for it all? Maybe he *was* a trader and lost all our money in some stupid stock market gamble? Perhaps he blew it all on holidays and who knows what else?

The truth that I can't say is that I don't know what to think of him. I feel nothing and everything. I despise him but I don't. Despite everything I found out after he died, there's a part of me that still doesn't feel like it's all real because I didn't see any of it when we were together. Seeing is believing and all that. I loved him once, but there's hate there, too – because this is the life he's left me with. Spending the pittance I earn on paying off his debts and getting close to a panic attack because I ordered a meal that costs fourteen pounds.

Harry takes a deep breath and glances towards the door. I wonder if outside, away from me, is where he'd rather be. I wouldn't blame him.

'Well…' he says. 'I didn't expect that.'

SEVEN

I apologise but Harry waves it off.

'It's a big thing in your life,' he says, which is quite the under-statement. 'It'd be ridiculous to expect you not to speak about it.'

He's right – but there's a time and a place, and I fear this is neither.

There's an impasse between us, a moment to let the dust settle. I look to the waiter on the other side of the restaurant, hoping our food can arrive to stop me saying something else stupid, but there's no such luck. The gentle clatter of the other diners has risen again – or perhaps it was always there and the quiet was only my imagination.

'What about you?' I ask, somewhat hoping there's something in his past that will take the attention from me.

He snorts slightly. 'I've had a few girlfriends but nothing major.' He stops and waits for me to catch his eye. 'No train crashes,' he adds. It could sound mean but it doesn't. There's a shyness to the slight upturn in his lips. He's testing the boundaries of what I might find acceptable. I don't need to force myself to smile back because it comes naturally. I didn't think I'd ever laugh about everything my life has become, but here we are.

I'm taken back out of the conversation by the beeping of my phone as I scramble into my bag to shut it up. It's buried under-neath the envelope of money, but, by the time I get to it, all that's on the screen is another missed call from 'unknown'.

'My friend's dog-sitting,' I say, holding up my phone. It's not *quite* a lie. Karen is keeping an eye on Billy – but it has nothing to do with the phone in my hand.

Harry asks if everything is okay and I tell him it is.

After that, the food finally arrives. We eat and we chat. I find myself trying to listen to him, while compulsively adding up what each mouthful of food costs. Aside from that, it's all very pleasant. Very... *normal*. It feels as if I've got rid of the madness and, now it's in the open, I can attempt to be a human being capable of having conversations about the weather and whatever else it is people talk about.

I sometimes think most of the struggle in being an adult is maintaining that fraudulent face of normality. If others knew half the mad things that jump into a person's thoughts, everyone would be single and have no friends.

I take my time with the food – it's the most I've eaten in one go for weeks. Harry finishes first, but that's fine because he's telling me about the American states he's visited through the course of his work. It's the kind of thing I used to dream about, perhaps even plan. I wonder if I ever told Ben about it. There was always something about the top-down road trip of Hollywood movies that seemed so romantically appealing, even if real life would make that impossible because of the heat and wind. Then life gets in the way and, before anyone knows what's going on, existence is a one-bedroom flat and forty-hours-a-week on a checkout till.

The waiter returns and removes our plates, before asking about dessert. My mouth waters and I so want to say yes – but it's an extravagance too far. Harry has no such reservations, opting for some cherry-chocolate thing and specifically asking for two spoons.

We sit for a few moments, neither quite sure what to say.

It's Harry who breaks first. He angles his head towards the street. 'Would you like to do this again?' he asks.

If I'm honest, it's not felt like a date; more a meal out with a colleague. That's my fault, of course. I've never been a big believer in the fairy-tale world of love at first sight and butterflies in the stomach. I'm not sure if I think soulmates are a real thing, either. I never had that with Ben, nor with anyone else. I didn't feel it when I first saw Harry, or when we shook hands. It might be me. I know that.

'Sure,' I reply, almost through politeness. It should be him that's running for the hills, who's texting mates to say, 'I ended up with a right basket case tonight'. It feels wrong that he's asking about a second date and I'm the one who doesn't know.

He claps his hands together softly and breaks into a grin. 'Fantastic. How about this week? There's a big bonfire out at—'

'I can't,' I say. 'It's Billy. He's scared of the bangs and people will be setting fireworks off all week. I can't leave him alone.'

Harry scratches a little behind his ear. 'I'd invite you over to my apartment – you *and* Billy – it's just off Livingstone Street, but there's the no pets rule.'

There's a moment in which I could be honest, say I'm not sure I'm ready for all this. And yet, if I don't believe in love at first sight and all that, then it follows that it would take a few meetings to get to know someone.

'I suppose you could come to mine,' I say, instantly panicking that he'll see my one-room bedsit and figure out that I really am a lost cause.

'I don't want to intrude,' he says.

'It's fine. We can figure out a day later in the week.'

'Great! I'll bring dessert…' He pauses. 'And wine!'

The waiter chooses this moment to return with Harry's cherry-chocolate thing and the two requested spoons. Harry forces me to try a bit and it's hard not to feel a stupid sense of longing that this is the kind of life I've not been able to lead. It's not much to ask for, is it? The odd meal out without hyperventilating over how much it might cost.

By the time we finish eating, the restaurant has almost cleared. Hours have passed and I've barely noticed. I ask Harry to tell me more about the states he's visited and it's nice to listen to someone else talk. He claims he drove through a place called Bald Knob in West Virginia – although it sounds suspiciously made up.

The spell is broken when the waiter arrives with a bill.

Perhaps Harry's one of those gentleman-types who wants to pay for everything, or maybe he senses the intake of breath I take.

'I'm paying,' he says firmly, reaching for the leather card.

'I should pay my half,' I reply.

He picks the paper out from the little booklet and waves the waiter back. 'I insist.'

I should let it lie. Not everything has to be a tug of X chromosome versus Y. Of feminism against patriarchy. Sometimes, one person can buy another a meal and that's the end of it. I can't stop myself, however. I know I've only spent fourteen pounds on the pasta, but before Harry can get his credit card out of his wallet, I've plucked a twenty-pound note from the envelope in my bag and dropped it on the table.

'That's my share,' I say.

He frowns at the money and then at me. 'You're not going to let me pay, are you?' he says.

'No.'

EIGHT

It's gone eleven as I make my way down the stone steps of Hamilton House in my socks. I've always done my laundry late, mainly because it lowers the chances of running into anyone else. There's also a strange, melodic peace about the rumble of the machines that makes me feel tired enough to sleep.

I'm not even on the ground floor when the thumping beat of someone's terrible music infects my ears. Why is it always the people with appalling taste who feel the need to crank up the volume?

It's coming from the door at the opposite end of the corridor from the laundry room, so I sigh in my very British way and ignore it.

The laundry room itself is more of a large cupboard, with two washers, a single dryer and twine that's been looped around the light fittings to create something close to a washing line. There's not really room for more than one person, which is why there's a small yelp of alarm as I push my way inside.

'Oh,' a woman's voice says, 'it's you.'

Vicky is a single mother who lives on the ground floor. She has short blonde hair in a pixie style that I'd never be brave enough to try to pull off, as well as a ring through her septum. She's so tiny that it's hard to believe she gave birth relatively recently. We've occasionally played cards together or shared well-thumbed paperbacks.

She glances across to where a crib is blocking the dryer. 'Sorry,' she adds. 'I didn't think anyone would want to do their washing this late.' She yawns and it's immediately infectious as I find myself doing the same. We smile through watery eyes to one another.

'Are you okay?' I ask.

Vicky rubs her eyes and fights another yawn. 'Mark's having a party next door to me and Yasmine can't sleep. I brought her in here. I think she likes the hum of the water going through the pipes.'

I peep towards the crib, where Yasmine is bundled under a series of blankets, her eyes closed, chest slowly rising and falling. It's hard not to envy the peace and beautiful unawareness.

'Do you think she'd mind if I put the washer on?' I ask.

Vicky laughs and it's so wholesome, so full of charm, that it's hard not to join in.

'You can ask her if you want,' she replies. 'But *I* don't mind. The clocks go back tonight anyway, so we all get an extra hour's sleep.'

I take my dirty clothes out of the bag and cram them into the washer, before pushing two fifty-pence pieces into the slot to set it going. The resealed envelope of money is left at the bottom of the bag and I fold the material around it. I don't like letting it out of my sight.

I'd almost missed what she said but reply with an unsure: 'The clocks go back?'

'Mum messaged me on Facebook earlier. I didn't know. I never know if they're going forward, back, or whatever.'

I think that's probably true of everyone. The only thing of which we can be sure is that they're definitely going back or forward an hour. I nod up to Karen's party poster that's stuck to the back of the door. 'Are you going?' I ask.

The smile has left Vicky's face. She's resting her elbows on her knees and doesn't look up. 'I have no money,' she says, bigger things on her mind. 'They've stopped my benefits again.'

'Why?'

She holds both palms up. 'I had to turn down a job because the hours were all over the place. It would've cost too much to put

Yasmine into care. I'd have ended up losing money overall, plus seeing less of her. I couldn't afford to take it – but when I turned it down, they stopped the benefits. I was screwed either way.' Vicky rubs her eyes and sighs once more. 'Rent's due on Monday,' she adds. 'Do you think Lauren will give me a couple of weeks?'

I want to be supportive but I've been living here long enough to know that Lauren is only acting on behalf of the building's owner. Rent extensions do not come often.

'I'm not sure,' I say. 'How short are you?'

'A hundred. I've got the rest. I'm hoping I'll be able to scramble something together.' She nods at the crib. 'Her dad's behind on maintenance and my Mum's always saying she'll help.' Vicky huffs out a long breath but doesn't need to say it. There's defeat in going back to parents, or asking for money – if only in perception.

We're interrupted as the music from down the hallway is nudged up a notch and starts to battle with the washer for dominance. Yasmine rolls over in her crib and there's a moment in which it feels as if she's going to open her eyes. I can sense Vicky holding her breath until her child settles once more.

'I'll have a word,' I say, indicating the corridor.

It takes three separate knocks until Mark opens his door.

It's not that Mark and I have never got on, more that we've barely exchanged anything other than a glance to acknowledge we recognise one another. Sometimes people know when they have nothing in common. When he first moved in, he was carrying a life-sized cardboard cut-out of some semi-naked model under his arm and I knew then we were very different people. He's tall and broad, the type of person who is intimidating simply because of size. Mark is clinging onto a can of Stella in one hand as he nods towards me. I'm still cradling the envelope that's wrapped in my dirty washing bag.

'A'ight?' he says.

'Could you turn the music down a bit?'

He stares at me as if I've thrown some advanced algebra in his direction. The stench of weed floats out from his apartment and I struggle not to cough.

'What?' he says.

'The music… it's a bit loud.'

Mark turns between me and the inside of his flat. He shifts his weight from one foot to the other. 'How about you mind your own business, yeah?'

I step away and then turn back and sniff the air dramatically. 'That's fine. I'll call 999 instead. I think there might be something on fire in here.'

His eyes narrow and there's a moment in which I think the subtlety has gone over his head. It takes a couple of seconds, but it's almost as if a light bulb goes off behind his stare. His top lip curls and he thrusts a pudgy finger in my direction. 'You should watch yourself,' he says with a snarl.

'I will,' I say politely. 'You should turn the music down.'

He stands his ground for a second and then steps backwards, slamming the door behind him. Moments later, the volume dims.

Just another day at Hamilton House.

NINE

SUNDAY

I slept with the envelope under my pillow last night. It's mad, I know. Ridiculous, really. I put it in the drawer underneath the television at first but found myself lying awake thinking about the cash. Poor old Billy wasn't happy at being accidentally kicked awake as he slept on my feet – but it was only when the envelope was safely within touching distance that I finally started to drift off.

The first thing I did after waking up was fumble under my pillow to make sure it was still there. After that, I lay the cash out on the table again, counting the full £3,620. I can replace the £20 I spent. I'll use my credit card to withdraw the money so that I can return the full amount.

I find myself sitting in the window, watching the street below. The bins have been kicked over, but that's about the most controversial thing that happens around these parts. There's not a soul outside, not a car passing. This serenity is part of my Sunday routine and yet I feel the constant tug back to the money on the table. I make a cup of tea to distract myself and then check last night's lottery numbers. Our work syndicate didn't win, so that's another pound gone. Another pound wasted.

A text is waiting for me from Harry:

Last night was great. How about we do it again on Tuesday? Do you still want me to come to yours? We can go out if you want?

I read it a couple of times but leave it for the time being.

Google still offers no information about missing or stolen money in the area, so I go to the local police website, but there's nothing there. I search Twitter, Facebook and anything else I can think of, but there are no clues. I keep thinking someone will come asking for the money. Cash doesn't just appear. It doesn't grow on trees and drop into envelopes. It has to belong to somebody.

Billy is sniffing around the sink, so I give him his food and watch him eat. It's only as I'm doing that I realise I'm not hungry myself. I'm so used to the gurgles and groans, to having to fight the cravings, that it's an alien feeling to actually be... satisfied.

When he's finished, Billy licks his chops clean and then crosses to the door. He is many things, but subtle is not one of them. I pack the money back into the envelope, resolving to leave it there this time. I can't keep removing it to count. It's becoming an obsession.

I put on my trainers, but they instantly feel looser than yesterday. It's hardly a surprise – there's a reason shoes aren't held together with sticky tape. If I'm lucky, I'll get another day out of them before I have to figure out something new.

We do a lap of the estate and Billy's in a particularly inquisitive mood, dragging me off into every alley we pass to have a sniff. My phone rings twice – both times 'unknown'. I miss the first call but answer the second, only to discover the same as before – that there's no one there. I stop and peer up at the buildings around, wondering if the phantom caller is watching. It's starting to feel ominous, more than an auto-dialler at a call centre that won't give up.

Billy eventually leads us back to Hamilton House and sits expectantly on the doorstep as I fumble for my key. When we get into the flat, he finds his spot next to the sofa and sits waiting for me to join him. Sunday is the day I get most of my university work done and, aside from walking Billy, it wouldn't be uncommon for me to spend the entire day here.

It's hard, but I have to force myself not to touch the envelope of money that's in the drawer. I missed handing it in yesterday and the police station will be closed today – presumably because no crime ever happens on a Sunday – so I'll have to do it tomorrow. I tell myself I'll definitely do that.

Billy finally puts his head down when I sit on the sofa with the laptop. He nuzzles into my foot until he's comfortable and then closes his eyes.

The computer goes through its usual routine of considering booting without actually doing it and I use the time to tap out a reply to Harry's text:

Tuesday is fine. I'm busy in the day, so 7pm?

His reply takes barely thirty seconds:

Fab! Let me know your address and I'll see you then.

There is a part of me that's wary of letting him know where I live. It's probably one of those things on every guide about dating – public places, good lighting: that sort of thing. But it's hard not to think that, of the two of us, I'm the nutty one. I dropped bombshell after bombshell on him and he still wants to see me again. After a minute or two, I reply with my address and leave it at that.

The laptop is still booting as I rub Billy's ear with my big toe. He lets out one of those huge, appreciative huffs that never gets old. After what feels like an age, the laptop finally stops whirring and allows me to load the web browser. The Open University site is set as my homepage, but, the moment it loads, the screen flickers and goes dark.

The first time this happened, I panicked, partly because I thought I'd lost my work – but also because I knew I'd struggle to find the money for someone to fix it. I'm calmer now as I hold down the power button and count to ten. If only this worked with people. Everything gets a bit mixed up, a bit out of sync, and all it takes to fix is a ten-second press of a button.

I let go of the button, wait and then tap it to start the laptop booting all over again.

Nothing happens.

It's now that I feel my chest tighten. I'm holding my breath as I press the button once more. The laptop crashes more often than an F1 driver on a wet track – but it always starts again. Always.

Not this time. There is only a blank screen.

I spend more than a minute staring at it, hoping for a miracle. When that doesn't arrive, I close the lid, unplug it, plug it back in and try again.

Still nothing.

The rushing begins immediately. It starts with the walls zooming towards me and then it's like I'm being swallowed by something much larger than myself. Billy pushes himself up and clambers onto the sofa, resting his head on my lap and staring up at me.

'I don't think you can fix this one,' I tell him, closing my eyes and trying to blink it away. My throat is dry and rasping. I have work to do, deadlines to meet. This course is my out. I've hinged everything on it being the way to change my life, to make things better. Without my laptop, I can't study. Without my studies, this is all I'll ever be.

I take a breath, gulping away the sob that feels close, but when I open my eyes, the walls have me crushed. I push myself up, but the ceiling starts to fall as I stumble across the room and clasp onto the kitchen counter. I'm in a box, confined and trapped, so disorientated that the first drawer I try to open is the one that's not a drawer at all. It's a handle that's attached for either decoration or to confuse someone on the brink of a panic attack. It's too hard to open my eyes all the way, so I fumble along the counter until

I reach the proper drawer. There are medicines and painkillers inside and I riffle through them, eyes now screwed closed, until I find the inhaler. I haven't needed it in a long while, but I suck on the bottom and then pump the trigger twice in quick succession.

It only takes a couple of seconds until the clouds begin to clear. When I open my eyes, the walls are back where they're supposed to be and the ceiling hasn't fallen at all. Billy is at my feet and I slide down until I'm sitting and smoothing the fur on his back. He twists to lick my hand and there's such a purity that I realise I'm crying on top of him.

I'm not sure how long passes before I move next. The inhaler is still in my hand but the memory of needing it is fresh. I thought I was past this; thought I was moving on.

Eventually, I push myself up and cross to the sofa. The laptop is on the floor, upside down. I must have dropped it – not that it was working anyway. When I press and hold the power button, nothing happens.

'Please work,' I whisper. '*Please.*'

I press it again, but there is still only a blank screen.

It's inevitable, I suppose. From the moment I sat on that wall and opened the envelope that had, literally, fallen into my life, I think I knew it would always come to this.

TEN

Hunting through charity shops and bargain bins has happened largely through circumstance, but I'd never been much of a shopper before what happened to Ben. It's nothing to do with money and everything to do with a lack of patience. Trying on so many different items feels like such a faff compared to the end result. Shopping feels like a social thing, too – a team game – and that hasn't been me for a long time. I can't really remember when I stopped having friends, but it probably happened at around the time I moved in with Ben.

The number 24 bus takes me straight to work, but, if I remain on, it continues out to the Twin Oaks Shopping Centre. Hanging around there on a weekend was a fixture when I was a teenager who had friends. That feels like a distant memory.

When I last spent any significant time here, there was a massive HMV and a Virgin Megastore. Teenagers craved the CDs and DVDs that were packed onto rack after rack along the full length of the store. My friends and I would waste hours browsing for things we had no intention of buying. Now, everything like that is in the palm of our hands. It feels like life has moved on and it's somehow skipped me.

As I wander along the wide, bright halls of the mall, it's all mobile phone stores and pound shops. There are so many people, too, aimlessly going about their lives. I spend so much of my day around others – customers at work, or, of course, on the bus – and yet there's nothing real about those interactions. They're people I see and forget; people who'll see me and forget. I feel surrounded but alone.

Many of the stores are decorated with orange and black streamers, with various standees of werewolves, Frankenstein's Monster and, for some reason, sexy doctors and nurses. Not only that, the country seems to have undergone some sort of pumpkinisation at this time of the year. It's American, of course. Everything is. Not like this in my day, and all that.

I continue meandering, getting lost until I stumble across a huge sports store. Another new thing since I was young is being pounced upon by a sales assistant the moment anyone steps into a shop. Most of my work history revolves around being in retail. When I was sixteen, I got a job on the checkout in a stationery shop that's no longer there. The norm then was a general indifference to any customer who walked through the door. Speak when spoken to and all that. Now, I am barely into the sports shop when two separate people in red polo shirts descend to ask if I need any help. I tell them I'm fine, which I suspect is the sanest of answers, and then follow the signs to the footwear section. Someone wants to talk to me about gait and pronation, but I wave him away and pick out half-a-dozen different sets of running shoes that look comfortable.

There's a wonderful release in being able to look at things I like, rather than have to check the price first. This is what it used to be like when I was with Ben. I wasn't particularly extravagant then but I'd look for things I liked, rather than things I could afford. Now, I try on all the shoes and walk around in them, simply because I can. Perhaps shopping isn't so bad? I take my time and eventually settle on a pair of Asics that claim they will make me run faster. It sounds unlikely, but I'm at the point where I don't care.

Seeing the price would usually make me anxious. It's three days' wages. Twenty-four full hours of sitting on a checkout scanning people's shopping – all for a single pair of shoes. As the cashier asks for the money, I reach into my bag, into the envelope, and remove eight twenty-pound notes that I hand over.

It's so simple.

The cashier is a young guy, who I doubt is even twenty. He's all fuzzy chin fluff and spiky hair. He could be me all those years ago; could be me now, I guess. He barely looks twice at the cash, scooping up the notes and counting them into the till. I get less than £10 in change – and that's that.

The shoes are mine.

I ask him to cut off the tags and enquire as to whether he can keep the box. He says that's fine and so I find myself walking out of the shop in brand-new shoes. My taped-together monstrosities are immediately dumped in the bin outside – and I'm done.

I expect there to be guilt, but there isn't. Perhaps I deserve this money?

My next stop is an electronics store and, this time, I do let the sales assistant talk at me. I feel like the star of the show; the centre of attention. He's older, probably in his forties, padding out a suit that doesn't look like it has fit him in years. He reeks of desperation, or cheap aftershave. Perhaps both. There is hunger in his eyes and it's hard not to wonder if that's how I look to others. Whether desperation of living pay cheque to pay cheque is something a person wears on their face.

He leads me to the laptop aisle and I stop at the first one. It's the cheapest they sell – the very one that's sitting unresponsive on my table at home. It costs even less than I paid when Amazon had it on special offer. I look up and the salesperson can't hide the disappointment. There won't be much commission on this. This will be from a stock of which they've been unable to rid themselves. The lowest of the low. This is me.

But not today.

'What do you have that's better than this?' I ask.

The man's lips slip into a smile and then he catches himself, leading me along the aisle into the next.

'What type of thing are you looking for?' he asks.

'Something for my university course. Small – but fast. It has to boot up quickly.'

He nods along and then points to a pair of laptops at his side. He talks about the new Windows, plus RAM and CPU speed, but I'm not sure if I care about the specifics. He continues to talk, but I've already switched off. For all I know, he's telling me about how they can sing, dance, do the dishes or hug a person on those cold winter nights. None of it matters. I can barely contain myself because I know I can afford either.

'… how does that sound?' he concludes.

I blink back into the shop. 'Do you take cash?' I ask.

He stares at me, wide-eyed, not needing to say 'nobody ever pays this much cash', because it's obvious. 'I guess…' he replies.

The man talks to me a little more about the two machines and I end up choosing the cheapest one – but only because it's the same size as the piece of junk I have at home. It feels a little more manageable; a little more me.

When I've chosen, he practically frogmarches me to the front and then radios someone in the back to bring a brand-new laptop from the stockroom. He bangs on about extended warranties, but I tell him I'm fine. My mouth is watering as I reach into the envelope and dig out a fistful of twenty-pound notes. I count them onto the counter until there is a little over £500. It's ten days of work for me. Half a working month all sitting in a neat pile.

For some reason, the voice in my head that was so insistent I spend the money is now telling me that this is someone else's. The hypocrite. It's so brash that I almost shush it out loud, only stopping myself when the till starts to chunter out a receipt. When it's finished, the salesman hands me the box and the computer is mine. I walk to the exit and pause by the security gates, half expecting them to sound an alarm. I take one step towards them, then a second to get past, but there's no sound.

It's mine, all mine.

The box isn't heavy, but it is awkward. I lug it around the shopping centre as if clinging onto a newborn child. Young and old look at me as I pass. It's probably the oversized box, but it feels as if I'm special. It's been a while since groups of people turned to look at me – if it ever happened at all.

After a few minutes, I have to stop on a bench to rest my arms. It's then that I notice I have yet another missed call from an unknown number. One after another, after another. This mystery caller is literally the only person who has phoned me for three days. I tell myself it's nothing, but it's hard to ignore the fact that the calls only started after the money had been left in my bag. If the unknown caller knows something about the envelope, then why not say so? They have my number. I've tried to talk to the person twice – and he or she could have left messages on any other occasion. Instead, it's silence. It feels… ominous – and yet I'm on such a high from spending the money that I blink it away.

I'm on my way towards the front of the shopping centre and the bus stop beyond when I notice the pet store. I stop, take a step towards it and then another away. But it's hard to resist.

I spend ten minutes squishing various toys, before noticing the sign about a 'dog cake'. I picture Billy's scruffy, grizzled face beaming at the idea of a cake that's entirely for him, and so I spend another £20.

I waddle my way towards the exit, somehow balancing everything, when I find myself passing the food court. Even with everything I'm carrying, I march with a purpose over to the McDonald's window. There are screens now, where orders are tapped into the system and paid for without having to talk to anybody. I pick a Big Mac, fries and strawberry milkshake, then feed the machine a ten-pound note. It is only a few minutes until I'm sitting in my new trainers, with my new laptop at my side and a doggy cake on the table, all while dipping fries into a milkshake.

Life, as they say, is wonderful.

ELEVEN

I'm not entirely sure how anyone thought it was a good idea that, one night a year, kids should be given their own body weight in sugar. The streets around our estate are like the aftermath of a bombing raid. Children are screaming and running in all directions – and a good proportion are dressed up to look as if they've dragged themselves bloodied and battered from a crumbling building.

Tyler is dressed as a tree… sort of. He has taped twigs to a green top and is going around telling everyone that 'I Am Groot'. Quinn, meanwhile, is wearing a football kit. I'm not sure what that has to do with Halloween. As for Billy, the two boys made him an orange jumpsuit and have strapped a toilet-roll gun to his back, so that he can be Rocket Raccoon. I've somehow ended up supervising two members of *Guardians of the Galaxy*, plus a four-foot footballer.

Compared to some of the other children, Karen's pair are incredibly polite and well-behaved. It helps that, once again, Billy is the star of the show. So many kids and adults come over to say how terrific his costume is and then rub his head or his back. He never seems to tire of the attention, even rolling onto his back for a belly rub at one point and slightly squashing his toilet roll gun.

As we traipse from door to door, I keep an eye on the lamp posts we pass. To the untrained eye, it's a weird new hobby; to the *trained* eye, I'm reading the various posters people have put up. There are crudely made ones advertising gigs and quiz nights at some of the local pubs. Somebody is hosting a sit-in on the green to protest the new one-way system, which, if you ask me, sounds like grounds for sectioning. There's one that screams: 'Wanted: Flatmate', which is probably a good way to get stabbed while sleeping.

Nothing about missing money, or a lost envelope.

The voice in my head can't make up its mind. It's now saying I should enjoy the money; that it's mine and I deserve it.

Even if I wanted to repay what I spent, it's gone past the point of feasibility. With the dinner, the laptop, the trainers, Billy's cake, the McDonald's and a couple of other odds and ends, I've spent more than £700 in less than twenty-four hours. I've kept the receipts as proof of my theft – if it *is* theft. The numbers burn inside me.

I'm so lost in thinking about myself that I almost miss the 'NO trick or treaters' sign that's pasted to a gate. Quinn is halfway down the path before I call him back. We carry on along the street and there's no question that some of the adults have used this night of trick or treating as an excuse to go over the top with their own costumes. There are a couple dressed as Rey and Kylo Ren who are having a lightsabre fight in the middle of the street, all while their kids – I assume it's *their* kids – watch on, bored.

It's as we're about to head along the next driveway that Tyler stops. He picks at one of the errant twigs angling out of his shoulder and nods behind me.

'I think that wolf is following us,' he says.

At first I don't notice who he means – but then I spot the figure striding along the pavement on the other side of the street. The person is tall, wearing a wolf mask that covers the entire head, plus a full body suit of hair, with a basketball jersey and shorts over the top. Whoever it is has no children with them. Because of the height, I assume it's a 'he' – and the wolf turns to look at us before stopping momentarily and then continuing on.

'Why do you think he's following?' I ask.

'Dunno. He's just always there.'

I turn from Tyler back to the other side of the street, but the wolf has already disappeared around a corner.

'There could be more than one wolf,' I say.

'I guess…'

Tyler suddenly loses interest in the way kids do. Quinn is waiting at the next house, impatiently bouncing on his heels and Tyler skips away to join him. We head along the path as a foursome and the owner has the front door open before we've got there. He asks Tyler if he's a tree, tells Quinn he hates Manchester City and then asks if Billy is 'a giant rat'. Poor old Billy doesn't seem to mind, probably because he'd gone through a quarter of his doggy cake before we came out.

The homeowner scratches his head as Tyler explains about the *Guardians of the Galaxy* – but he does dump handfuls of mini chocolate bars into the boys' carrier bags and follows it up with an ear-rub for Billy.

We carry on along the street, ignoring the houses with the lights off, and continuing until the boys' bags are full of sweets and chocolate. It's as we're about to head home that I notice the wolf again. This time, he is standing in the shadows of an alcove next to some bins at the back of a housing block. The lighting is dim, but the orange glow from the apartments beyond casts his hairy shadow across the pavement. The wolf isn't watching us; he's turned in the opposite direction, thumbing a mobile phone. The head of the costume is hinged upwards, resting on top of his head as the bluey glow from the screen illuminates his stubbled face. His jaw is sharp, his cheekbones angled, though it's too dark to see much else.

There's the fleeting glimpse of passing a celebrity in the street and realising a few seconds too late who it is. And in that moment, only a moment, I feel a tug of recognition. The shape twists away slightly, peering closer at the screen. I take a step towards him but then…

'Auntie Luce…' Quinn tugs on my sleeve and I turn to see him, knees clamped together. 'I need a wee,' he adds. I turn between him and the wolf, but the moment is lost. The slant of the light has changed and the man in the costume now seems like the stranger he is.

It was Ben, of course. It's always Ben. I've seen him everywhere in the five years since the train crash. He'd be a customer walking out of the supermarket, or someone on the opposite side of the street. It was always half glimpses, or sideways stares, never anything firm. I looked it up on the internet and the pseudoscientists and blogger therapists all say it's normal after a trauma. Ben's in my mind again after I dumped my life story on poor Harry. His debt became my debt – and that became my life.

'Are you okay?'

I turn back to Quinn, but both boys are now staring up at me with puzzled expressions.

'Of course,' I say, 'let's get back home.'

I risk another quick glimpse towards the wolf – but he's no longer in the alcove and the only other people at that end of the street are the *Star Wars* parents with their weary kids.

Billy is flagging – he's not used to all this late-night walking – and I have to carry him up the stairs of Hamilton House until we're on our floor. I take the boys past my apartment to Karen's and then use the spare key to let them in. Quinn shoots straight off to the bathroom as Tyler starts trying to pick the rest of the twigs from his costume. Billy wanders around, confused at why we're in the wrong flat. I'm about to flick on the kettle when the front door creaks and pops open, to reveal an out-of-breath Karen.

'You're back,' I say, apparently unable to do anything other than state the obvious.

Karen unbuttons her coat and bats Tyler away from taking up the entire sofa before flopping onto it herself. She thanks me for looking after the boys and then Tyler pours his entire haul of sweets onto the floor to show her the type of night he's had. Quinn returns and does the same and then they start trading back and forth. It's a bit like the stock exchange, but with less childishness.

Probably unsurprisingly, Karen leaves them to it and joins me in the kitchen.

'How was your evening?' I ask.

She looks towards the boys and says 'Fine,' seemingly unwilling to say much more about it. 'How was yours?' she adds.

'Not bad. Tyler had to keep telling people he was Groot and not a random tree – but good other than that.'

We watch them for a moment and then I remember the other thing I spent money on. I dig into to my bag and take out the pair of £50 gift cards.

'I got these for the boys,' I tell Karen as I pass them to her. 'I didn't want to give them over tonight without checking with you.'

Karen twists the cards around and squints to read the words on the back. The children will be able to upload the credit to their phones and use it to buy games, apps, music, or whatever.

'It's so much money,' Karen whispers.

I hold my hands up to say it's fine and she bats away a yawn, before apologising. Her eyelids are sagging and she looks ready for bed.

'You shouldn't have,' she adds. 'It's too much.'

She doesn't need to say it because I can practically hear her thoughts. This is money I'd usually need for rent, food and to get around. One hundred pounds is more than I can afford. Strangely, when I saw the cards near the till at the shopping centre, it hadn't crossed my mind that I'd have to justify buying them.

'I won a bit of money on a scratch card,' I say, surprising myself at the ease of the lie.

Karen's eyes widen. 'You lucky cow!' She leans in and lowers her voice: 'How much?'

I shrug non-committedly. She can read into it what she wants, but my lies are already piling up.

'Bloody hell,' she mutters. 'Well, if anyone deserves it, it's you. I hope you spend the rest on yourself.'

I smile wanly, not sure what to say.

'How are the party plans going?' I ask, hoping she doesn't notice the obvious segue.

Karen's features brighten. 'Good. The boys are off to their dad's for a bonfire, plus everything else is all booked. Just got to hope people turn up.'

'I'm sure they will.'

She yawns again, which I take as my hint to go. I leave my tea largely unfinished on the counter and she leads me to the door. Billy trudges behind, also ready for bed, as I say goodnight to the boys. They're more concerned with hedging whether two mini Bounty bars are worth a single Snickers, with Quinn insisting that 'nobody likes Bounties'.

It feels dark as I head into the corridor, something I seemingly missed when I was rushing inside with a toilet-bound Quinn. Karen notices it too and we take a moment to realise the light in the corner is out.

'I don't think it was like that yesterday,' Karen says as she leans on her door frame. 'I'll text Lauren.'

We share a look because we know how efficient our building manager is. Late rent: Lauren will be on it within minutes. Anything needing fixing will take a full assessment and tendering process that means it'll be lucky to get done within a month.

Karen pulls the door until it's almost closed behind her. 'Thanks for having the boys,' she says, before taking a big breath. She bites her lip and it's obvious there's something there.

'Do you want to talk about it?' I ask.

She opens her mouth and there's a moment in which I think the reason for her Sunday disappearances is going to come out. Instead, she yawns once more, covering her mouth with her hand.

'Sorry,' she says, though I'm not sure if the apology is for the yawn. 'I hope you enjoy the money.'

I crane my neck, taken aback, before realising she means the fantasy scratch card win. 'Thank you,' I reply.

She gives a little wave and then disappears back into the apartment.

It's only a few steps to my flat, but Billy is ahead of me, waiting outside the door and peering back over his shoulder to see where I am.

'I'm right here,' I tell him as I creak across the floorboards.

Billy turns back and then pushes his way into the apartment. I almost do the same before I realise what's wrong.

I never unlocked the door.

I stop and turn to look around the empty hallway. The corner near Karen's is shrouded with darkness, but the rest of the space is filled with the dim orangey glow from the cheap bulbs. I push into my own apartment and stop to take in the room.

Billy is twisting himself in circles as he pads down the blanket in his bed. He does this every night, even though he ends up sleeping on my bed.

I hurry to the other side of the room and pull the bed down from the wall. I'm barely thinking and the hinge catches on the wall, wrenching backwards so violently that I feel a snap in my shoulder. All that does is make me heave harder until the foldaway bed pops out from the wall and crashes into the floor with a *whump*. The stabbing pain in my chest is such that I pat a hand to my top, fully expecting there to be blood. There's not, but I'm gasping for breath as I slip my hands underneath the mattress.

The money has gone.

TWELVE

I almost took the envelope of money out with me when picking up the boys – but thought it would be safer here. How could I have been so *stupid*?

I stand, turning in a circle, before noticing that the front door is still open. I dash across the room and slam it closed and then stand to take in the room. Aside from the sheets that have tumbled from the bed, everything else is in place. It's easy to say that because I have so little. I check the drawer underneath the television, but my brand-new laptop is still there. The old, unresponsive, one is there, too. I couldn't bring myself to throw it out.

Billy is sitting in his bed, staring up at me with confusion. I still need to help him out of the trick or treat costume, but he's ready for bed and the toilet roll gun is long gone.

There's a flicker of something in the corner of my eye, but, when I turn, there's nothing there except the bare wall, which is sliding slowly towards me.

I stand as still as I can, closing my eyes and willing calm. It's hard – somebody has broken into the apartment and taken the money – but I push those thoughts away and instead think of a wide, open field. Acres of lush, bright green stretching in all directions and endless blue above.

Breathe.

When I open my eyes, the walls are where they should be. I shuffle into the kitchen and open the drawer, allowing myself two deep puffs on the inhaler.

'Be calm,' I tell myself.

And I am.

I'm not sure how or why, but I suddenly realise I was looking for the envelope on the wrong side of the bed. My thoughts are clear now and I round the kitchen counter, step across to the askew mattress and reach underneath.

The envelope of money is exactly where I left it.

I pull open the flap at the top and dig inside, removing the neat bundles of cash and placing them on the table by the sofa. As Billy watches on and scratches at his costume, I count the money. Then I count it a second time. And a third.

It's all there.

Nobody has been in the apartment and nothing is missing.

When I first moved in, Lauren told me the door would sometimes stick. I went out five or six times thinking I'd locked the door, when I'd not pulled it all the way into the frame. I've not done it in at least two years – and it does stick more depending on whether it is a hot, cold or mild day. Perhaps I made the same mistake I did those years ago?

I open the door – which doesn't catch – and head into the hallway. There's nobody there and no hint of noise from either above or below, but I can't escape the feeling of being watched. It's unlike any other sensation; more of an intrinsic knowing than anything else. I take a step across the hallway to Jade's old apartment and then, as if I've stepped on a hidden switch, music starts. It's not loud, and if my door was closed, I wouldn't be able to hear it, but it still stops me on the spot.

Karen said she heard Elton John playing from inside the apartment and I wasn't sure if I believed her. It's not that I thought she was lying, more that she was mistaken and perhaps the music was coming from elsewhere, or that it was a different singer. It's not, though. Elton is singing about packing bags and being as high as a kite. I feel frozen, listening to the words and piano until he reaches the chorus.

Different times.

It's only when my door creaks that I'm released. Billy is there, still scratching at his costume. I crouch and ruffle his ears, then release the straps underneath and help him to wriggle free. He immediately turns and trots back into the flat. He'll be asleep within thirty seconds.

The song continues to play and I take a couple of steps until I'm eye to eyehole with the opposite door. I can't see anything, obviously, and yet I still have that sense of being watched.

It's at this moment there's a clunk from behind and Karen emerges into the hallway with a basket of laundry under her arm. We do a double-take at one another and there's a second in which the thought flutters through me that she might have been watching through the peephole in her own door.

'What are you doing?' she asks.

I step away from the door and stumble over my words, eventually managing: 'Elton John.'

Karen moves along the corridor until we're level. The music has stopped. 'I didn't catch what you said,' she says.

'I, um…'

She puts down the wash basket on the floor and turns to look at the closed door opposite, from which there is nothing beyond but silence.

'My door was unlocked,' I say. She spins to look past me and I hastily add: 'Nothing was taken. I think I must've left it like that. It sticks sometimes.'

We look to each other and there's a moment of understanding. I can see it in the deepness of her eyes and I'm certain she can see it in me, too. I'm keeping something back, but so is she. Sometimes that's what friendship is – knowing that, for a while at least, secrets have to stay as such.

Karen picks up her washing once more and takes half a step away. 'I'll see you tomorrow, right?'

'Yes,' I reply.

Then we go our separate ways.

THIRTEEN

MONDAY

Billy seems a little uninterested on his walk the next morning. He's usually straining at his lead, trying to drag me off into various gullies and alleys, but all he does now is amble along at my side.

I check the lamp posts once more, but there are no signs up asking about missing envelopes. As I'm getting back to Hamilton House, the door opens and Nick emerges with Judge, his corgi. The two dogs immediately begin their ritual of sniffing one another as greeting. Nick and I stand together like proud parents of children about to walk down the aisle. Nick is a little older than me and one of those types who seem painlessly, effortlessly stylish and skinny. I realise it's likely down to a significant time in front of a mirror and working out, but I only ever see the final result. With most of the people who live here, it's easy to see why; with Nick, I'm less sure. It *feels* as if he could move away if he wanted.

He nods towards one of Karen's party posters. 'You going?' he asks.

'Yes. What about you?'

He nods towards the dogs. 'I've got to stay in with Judge. He doesn't like the fireworks at this time of year.'

I tell him that dogs are apparently welcome and can tell from the glazed 'oh' that he was also hoping to get out of having to socialise. Perhaps this is why he doesn't move – it's easy to keep to oneself while living here. No big turnover of tenants and nothing in the way of nosey neighbours overlooking back gardens.

'Has Mark been onto you about Billy?' Nick asks.

'Huh?'

Nick nods towards the front door. 'He was having a go about me letting Judge onto the stairwell.'

'He doesn't even live on our floor.'

'I know! He aimed a kick at Judge the other day when we were coming back in.'

'What?!'

We stare open-mouthed at one another. Mark has said the odd thing in passing about dogs being in the hallway – but nothing directly. The spat we had the other night is the most we've ever spoken to one another.

'He didn't realise I was there,' Nick adds. 'He only saw Judge and then, when he noticed me, claimed it wasn't a kick.'

I crouch and give Judge a rub on the back. He seems nonplussed and continues sniffing around Billy.

'I didn't know if he might've done something similar with Billy,' Nick says.

I stand again and can feel my pulse racing at the very idea someone might lash out at my dog.

'I don't think he's ever done that,' I reply.

Nick nods and we stand and sigh together because it seems like the only thing we can do. There are no specific rules about dogs being allowed in the halls unsupervised, but, I suppose, nothing that expressly allows it.

We say cheerio to one another and then I head into the building. I'm in half a mind to knock on Mark's door to tell him to mind his own business – but stop myself, figuring it's not going to make anything better. Instead, I stop outside Vicky's flat and slip an envelope under her door. I stop for a moment, wondering if I should knock in case the envelope has disappeared underneath a mat. In the end, Billy makes up my mind as he pulls at his lead and tries to drag me up the stairs.

This time, my door is definitely locked – but, as I let myself inside, I still can't get past the feeling of being watched.

Friday evenings might be a crammed-in hell of a journey on the number 24 bus, but, for whatever reason, Monday mornings are the opposite. There are still people getting on – but everyone has a seat and there's a steady calmness to the ride.

It's as I'm sitting a few seats from the back that I notice the CCTV camera inside a domed curve of dimmed glass on the ceiling. I've taken this bus hundreds of times and it would have been there, unnoticed, for every one of those rides. It's strange the things that can hide in plain sight. Perhaps it's this new-found observation, but I suddenly seem very aware of myself.

I turn and eye the people around me in a not-eyeing-them kind of way. I pretend to look through the window, then act as if I'm staring at my phone.

There is a pair of women in the seats opposite dressed for the gym; some kids in uniform who are seemingly late for school; two blokes in suits across from one another, oblivious to how much of a mirror image they are. An old guy with a red face is swigging from a two-litre bottle of cider at the very back, while, one row in front of him, a woman is tucking into an iced bun while nodding her head along to whatever's playing through her headphones.

There's nothing abnormal, but it's hard not to wonder if someone here is missing £3,640. I find myself looking at the men in the suits because there's a natural assumption that suits = money. It's nonsense of course. The manager of the local mobile phone shop wears a suit, while some millionaire web design wizard wears skateboard shorts and Converse. Books, covers, assumptions and all that.

But whoever it is will see my bright new trainers and *know* where I got the money to buy them. When I'm on the bus, I usually try to make myself as small and unnoticeable as possible. Sometimes I will read a book I've had from the library, or skim around a few websites on my phone. Johnny Depp could be standing behind me and I'd not notice. Today, I keep my eyes up, watching everyone new who gets on.

It's not long before we pull in close to the park and the house that Ben always promised he'd buy for me. I'm not sure why it was always phrased in that way – but he had a thing about buying things *for* me. We didn't do things such as make joint purchases, and he would sometimes get angry if I bought something for myself. It seemed so normal then.

It's next to the park where Karen and I do Parkrun each week. There's a large hedge that separates one from the other and I run past it each time. The house is so different from the pop-up red-brick housing estates that now seem to populate every town and city. It's set back from the road, with three storeys and probably an attic and basement. I always liked it because it was different and, when I said this to Ben in passing one time, it was as if it flicked a switch within him. It suddenly became his mission to buy it – and not just that, to buy it *for me*. Then he mentioned stables on the day he went to catch the train. I was never quite sure what to say, because telling him the wedding, house and stables didn't matter to me would only send him into a spiral of despair. He'd think I was saying that because we couldn't afford such things – which was true – but then take it as a personal insult because he felt he didn't make enough money. It was as if his entire self-worth was linked to the money he made.

A lady in a wheelchair pushes onto the bus and manoeuvres herself into the handicapped space next to the luggage rack that is almost never used. I wonder if she's £3,640 short, but then find myself focusing on the sticker that's in the window behind her. It's one of those 'please let us know how we're doing' notices, with a phone number underneath. Companies must post these hoping they'll either get no feedback or positive remarks – but it's only ever going to attract the green ink brigade.

I tap the number into my phone in any case and then continue to eye newcomers until the bus arrives opposite Crosstown Supermarket. I make the call after crossing the road. It's all, 'press one for this, press two for that', which is, presumably, to make someone lose hope in humanity before they ever get to talk to an actual person. I'm sitting on the low wall outside the staff entrance when I finally hear a real voice. It's then that I realise I'm not sure what to ask about and find myself waffling about CCTV on buses and whether the footage is stored.

I'm suddenly part of the green-ink brigade. I can imagine the person on the other end of the line drawing a circle with his finger around his ear. The universal symbol for 'loony'.

'I'm sorry, ma'am,' he replies. 'I'm not sure what you're asking.'

'There are CCTV cameras on your buses,' I reply. 'I was wondering if you keep the footage, or if you delete it.'

There's a pause, which somehow seems very loud. 'Sorry, what did you say your name was?' he says.

'I was on the number 24 bus on Friday and I was wondering if I could have a look at the camera footage.'

It's only as I say the words that I realise how mad it all sounds.

There's another pause, longer this time. The handler is probably wondering if this is some sort of wind-up.

'I take the same bus every day,' I add, nonsensically.

He replies with a bit of a cough and then: 'Was there some sort of incident, ma'am…?'

It takes me a second to realise he's asking if there was a crime.

'There was this man,' I say. 'We said hello, but I didn't ask for his number. I was hoping to run into him on the bus today, but he wasn't there. I was hoping that you might be able to help me ID him…?'

I'm one of those people who are excellent after a crisis. When it comes to thinking on the spot, to sounding plausible when needed, I'm a joke.

There is another, far lengthier, pause. It's agonising and I know I must sound like some sort of desperate stalker. This is what it's come to. First there was online dating, then Tinder, now stalking people on public transport. There's nothing lower.

'I don't think I can help,' the poor man says.

'I can pay.'

It comes from nowhere. It's suddenly my default answer to everything – buying myself out of trouble.

There's more silence, then a shuffling and then the voice replies much lower this time. 'I guess I might be able to do something,' he says. 'It might take a day or two.'

He asks about which bus I was on, what time, roughly where I was located and whether I was sitting or standing. I answer all his questions, almost through politeness. After that, he takes my phone number and says he'll call back if he comes up with anything.

By the time the line goes dead, my chest is hammering once more. It's partly through embarrassment but also because I wonder if the images that might come will show whoever dropped the envelope in my bag. I suppose this is how the world really works. Money gets people what they want.

When I get into the staff changing rooms, Daff is already there. She talks about how she was bladdered on Saturday night, which is reason enough for avoiding work nights out. We don't talk about money, but I do wonder how people afford it all. Even if I wanted to be an alkie, I couldn't afford it.

I'm about to head towards the checkout when the manager, Jonathan, waves me across. He's always in a suit and shuffles around the supermarket, permanently looking as if he's lost something. Despite that, he's also the type who's stacked the odd shelf in his time. I've seen him do aisle clean-ups while still in his jacket. He's always been fair to me, allowing me to skip shifts at short notice when Billy has been ill.

'Can I have a word?' he asks. His features are stony, which isn't entirely rare.

I follow him into his office, which is a windowless room at the very back of the store, next to the toilets. I doubt anyone dreamed of this sort of thing as a boy – not that working on a checkout is the stuff of which dreams are made, either.

He sits behind his desk and cathedrals his fingers into one another to form a triangle. The room is cold and it's hard not to shiver as I sit.

'Is there anything you'd like to tell me?' he says.

My stomach knots. The money from the envelope is his and now he wants it back. How can I explain everything I've spent?

'Like what?' I reply, somehow keeping my voice level.

He twists his monitor around and taps the space bar. A video starts to play and it now seems so stupid, so obvious, that I can't believe I did it in the first place.

The dirty-haired girl from the other day steps around the security barrier at the small door by the magazines and leaves the store. She cradles her baby in one arm and the stolen shopping in the other. There's a second in which she gazes back to the camera and then time is frozen.

'Like this,' Jonathan says.

FOURTEEN

It's stick or twist time, I guess.

'I don't know what you're asking,' I say. I'm like a kid with chocolate around her mouth, telling her mum that she hasn't raided the Easter Eggs hidden under the bed.

'Three bags of nappies,' Jonathan begins, 'four packets of noodles, a bag of oats, a bottle of lotion, formula and rusks. That's what she carried out of the store, and yet her receipt shows something quite different from that. Would you care to explain?'

There is no explanation, of course. There will be footage of me passing items over the scanner while covering the barcode, more still of the girl wheeling the nappies past me on her trolley and then moving them, unpaid, into her shopping bag.

'It's not the first time, is it?' Jonathan adds.

He's watching me, trying to make eye contact, but I can't match him. I stare at the floor and my throat has swelled to such a degree that it feels like I'm trying to gulp down a whole melon. There's no point in arguing because he knows. Of course he knows. I try to speak, but all that emerges is a croak.

'You can continue to lie,' he says, 'and I'll call the police right now.'

He reaches for the phone on his desk, but I get there first, grabbing for the receiver and accidentally knocking it off the desk. There's a clatter of plastic and wire as it tumbles and Jonathan reaches to pick it up.

'Sorry,' I say. 'Please don't call them.'

Jonathan spends a few seconds detangling the cord and then replaces the phone on the holder. 'Give me a good reason why I shouldn't.'

I glance around the room, searching for anything that might help, while still trying to avoid his eyes. There are certificates on the walls showing Jonathan's qualifications, plus more from when we won third place at the Grocer of the Year awards. It was a big upset considering all the larger companies involved and everyone got one hundred pounds as thanks. Mine went on paying off the interest on my debts.

'She had a baby,' I say, nodding at the girl on the monitor. 'And she was so thin herself. I knew she couldn't afford it, and…' I tail off. What is there to say?

'How many times have you done something like this?'

I was wrong. Now is the time to stick or twist.

'Not often,' I say quietly, still staring at the floor. 'Now and then. The odd item. Never for me.'

It's the truth. I've never once stolen food or anything else from this place *for me*. It's also true that the girl with the baby wasn't the first person for whom I've passed items over the scanner, or ignored the odds and ends on the bottom of a trolley. I can see the despair in people's faces sometimes.

'That's not really the point,' Jonathan says.

'No…'

He motions for the phone but not in any serious way. 'Tell me why.'

I look up at him, finally meeting his gaze. 'Because I know what it's like to budget,' I say. 'Things go wrong. I've missed meals because I'd rather my dog eats. He sometimes needs things at the vet, too. In the choice of him or me, I always choose him.' I take a breath and wave a hand towards the rest of the supermarket. 'I see it in other people, too. When they have to put back items, or when coupons don't work. I know they've got kids and that they're going to miss meals themselves.'

Jonathan turns away first. He focuses on the third-place Grocer of the Year certificate. It's strange the things of which we are proudest. What counts as a success for one person is a chronic failure for another. Companies report billions in profit, but it's a disaster because they made slightly more the quarter before.

'It's still stealing,' Jonathan says, more quietly.

'I know. I'll pay you back, I'll—'

'How will you do that?' He turns to me and his eyes are like ice. 'I know what you make.'

I shrink into my seat, unable to speak.

There's a long, awkward silence and I can only think that I seem to bring out the worst in people. I wonder if people go to prison for this, or if it's just community service? Would there be a fine? And, if so, how does it make sense to fine a person who steals minor items from a supermarket? Surely that person is stealing because they're short of money?

Jonathan sighs again and then turns back to me. 'I'm not a monster,' he says softly. 'I know that people complain about me in the back. I'm the boss and it's all fine.' He bites his lip and puffs out a small breath once more. 'But this is still a crime. I should call the police. If I don't, I can't make any sort of insurance claim.'

He pauses and glances to the photo of him and his wife. It's as if time has stopped. I'm holding my breath and it feels like my life is in his hands. Turn left and the police show up; turn right and…

Jonathan shakes his head. It's barely a movement, but it's enough. 'I'm not going to do any of that,' he says – and I can finally exhale. 'I'm going to have to fire you. I know you've been here two years and I don't really want to train someone new, but I don't have much of a choice.'

He sounds so reluctant, so sorry, that I almost reach forward to comfort him. I start nodding along, agreeing my firing is fine.

'Of course,' I say. Somehow, I didn't see this coming, although it's predictable. Who expects to steal and then not be fired?

'I need your key,' he says, reaching across the desk.

It's as if I'm watching myself as I take the keys from my bag and unloop the one that opens the door to the staffroom. My thumb gets caught in the metal hoop and I give a little gasp before tugging it clear. Jonathan waits with his palm extended and I drop the key into it. It's only then that I notice I'm shaking.

'Is there anything in your locker?' he asks.

'Only clothes.'

'I'd like you to go to the staffroom, change and leave your uniform in the locker,' he says. 'I'll let you in and wait outside.'

It's like some sort of death march as I loop around the edge of the store to get back to the changing area. I can sense Jonathan behind me, matching my pace, not letting me get too far ahead in case I do something mad like make a run for it. When we arrive, he unlocks the door and then I re-enter the area I left a short while before. Life was different then. I had a job. I wasn't a confessed thief.

The room is empty and I take off my uniform, then hang it up. I stand in front of the full-length mirror and look at myself. Look at what I've become. I can see my ribs and the boniness of my hips. There are bags under my eyes and a few threads of grey around my ears. I'm only thirty.

I'm a zombie as I put my own clothes back on. It's not the best job and I've never been sure if I actually liked it. It was hardly a career choice and yet, for two years, this has been my life. Sometimes, it's felt like this is all I've had. It's been regular money, regular hours. People who, if not friends, know my name. What will Daff and the rest think now?

There's a moment in which it feels as if my legs can't support me any longer and then I am sitting on the bench staring at myself. That's my life changed in an instant. It's hard to take in the enormity of it all and I reach for my bag, fingering the envelope within, wanting the comfort it gives.

When I manage to leave the changing room, I find Jonathan standing outside. He's staring past me and motions towards the staff exit at the back. I take the hint and move past him towards it.

'What will you tell the others?' I ask.

He scratches his head and our roles have reversed. It's now him who cannot look at me. 'Just leave,' he says.

I hover for a second – but only that – and then I'm gone. The door clangs closed behind me, echoing out into the breeze of the car park. It feels as if everything has changed.

I've been fired for being a thief.

There isn't a better way to dress it up than that. What will I do now?

I set off in an aimless meander across the tarmac, which is when I spot the red anorak. I think it's a flapping carrier bag at first; so bright against the grey that it's impossible to miss.

There's a figure sitting on a bench next to a taxi rank. Even from a distance, I know who it is. I knew when I saw her in the park two days ago. I drift across the car park towards her and then change my mind – because she is unquestionably watching me.

Ben's mother, Melanie, glares across the car park and the chill that surges through me is nothing to do with the weather. I'd not seen her in years and now it's twice in three days. Could she have set me up with Jonathan? How could she have known I'd go for the girl's silent sob story? It's not as if she *asked* for me to let her walk out with free goods. And yet, at one of my lowest moments, here Melanie is.

I stop, unsure what to do with myself, and then skirt away from the bench. I tuck my head into my jacket, clasp my bag tighter and stride to the bus stop.

FIFTEEN

I'm on the number 24 bus when Unknown rings my phone again. I answer but there's nobody there. I hadn't expected there to be. I stare at the blank screen, numb from everything that's happened in the past hour.

I google phone hang-ups, but all the internet has to say is that call centres are probably responsible. Something about auto-dialling and then not having enough staff to take the calls. I put my phone on silent and drop it into my bag.

Billy is confused when I get home. He's on the farthest side of the flat, apparently amusing himself with one of his cuddly toys. I like the idea of him playing while I'm away; that he's not desperately lonely by himself. When I get home, he usually flings himself at me and is full of licks and affection. Now, he stands and stares, as if to say he was quite happy by himself, thank you very much.

He tilts his head to the side and I give him a rub, before laying down a little more of his doggy cake. He doesn't complain at that.

As he eats, I get on the new laptop and start looking for jobs. I'm no snob, but it's hard when everywhere wants experience, even for some of the lowliest positions. I could go for a job at a different supermarket – but how could I explain what I've been doing for two years? I don't think Jonathan will be giving me much of a reference.

The KFC on the retail park wants junior cashiers, or kitchen staff – but the salary is less than I earn now. There's also something about being surrounded by people almost half my age that I know will drive me to despair.

I search around to see if anyone is looking for bar staff, even though I'm not sure if it's a job I could manage. There's nothing online, but it's not that kind of work anyway. I'd be better off going door to door and asking. I half think about doing it, but then realise the hours would mean leaving Billy by himself in the evening. We have a routine.

Had a routine.

I watch as he sniffs the plate he's already cleared and then saunters off to the cabinet below the one in which his cake is stored. He looks between me and the closed door mournfully and then sits. His tail flicks across the lino floor as he continues to stare.

'Later,' I tell him and it's as if he understands.

He potters across the floor and then takes a spot on the other side of the room from me. His lids are half-closed, but he's watching with treachery in his eyes. I've kept his cake from him; I've denied him his time alone – therefore I am, temporarily, the enemy.

I go back to job-hunting and look up a couple of agencies. They only seem to have factory work on offer, which specifically states 'shift work'. It'll mean early mornings, late nights, or overnights. That's more disruption to the life I've built. If I'm on lates, how will I cope with fitting my university course into the morning? How will Billy cope?

It's hard to understand why I did what I did at the supermarket. I felt sorry for the girl – but does that mean I should have allowed her to steal? I risked so much and now I've got my comeuppance. At the time, I was grateful Jonathan didn't call the police but now it is sinking in how much I've lost.

My thoughts are invaded by the ringing of my phone and another call from Unknown. I should ignore it – it probably *is* a call centre – but I can't stop myself.

'Leave me alone!' I shout into the phone. 'Stop calling me.'

There's a pause and then a cough from the other end. 'Is that Lucy Denman?' a woman's voice asks. She's tentative, which isn't surprising considering I've just shouted at her.

'Yes…' I reply. 'Sorry about that, I—'

'This is Gloria,' she says. 'You probably won't remember me, but my husband, Kevin, was on the train.'

I'm so surprised that the best I can manage is a weak, 'Oh…'

'Are you coming to the memorial tomorrow?' she asks, not missing a beat.

There are a few seconds in which I have no idea how to respond. I met a lot of people in the months after Ben died. There were faceless officials, lawyers, journalists – and then the other women and men who'd also lost loved ones on the train. I was one of them at first. Then I became the fraud because they would talk of love and loss and I couldn't see past the lies.

I try to place Gloria, but there's nothing. If I know her, then it'll be by looks, not by name. She will be online, of course. We all are. Look for my name and Ben automatically appears alongside me. We're forever entwined.

'I'll be there,' I say. I'd tried to forget the memorial service, I always do, but it creeps up on me.

'Great,' Gloria replies. 'I was hoping you'd say that.' She's speaking quickly, as if this is precisely what she thought I'd say. There's a moment in which it sounds like she's typing something on a keyboard and then: 'Can we talk about money?'

I glance across towards my bag and the envelope within. 'Money?' I stumble.

'Perhaps it's best if we talk tomorrow?' she says.

'But—'

'I'll find you and we'll talk after the service itself.'

'Can you—?'

Gloria isn't listening. She cuts across me with 'Safe journey. We'll talk soon' – and then, like that, she's gone.

I'm staring at the blank screen and, when I press to look at previous callers, all I see is 'unknown'.

She wants to talk about money, except the only money I have is that which is sitting in the envelope that's still in my bag. Perhaps it's me, but perhaps it's her, because, for whatever reason, it sounded as if she already knew that.

SIXTEEN

I get back to what I've spent so many hours doing – googling to see if anyone has reported missing or stolen money in the area. It's reached the point where I'm hoping there is something. Perhaps a robbery in which the perpetrator had to dump the money? It would be an answer – and yet there's nothing.

Billy has gone to sleep and I'm not used to being at home during the day. I'd usually be an hour and bit into a stint behind a checkout and, even though the end of my shift can never come quickly enough, I now want to be at work. I sign up for overtime on my days off; I give up holidays because the money is more important. I spend so much of my time wishing I didn't have to do such a job and, now I've been fired, I want it back.

I continue searching for jobs and find a posting that someone has linked to on Facebook where a sandwich shop is looking for a person to do early morning to lunchtime shifts during the week. It's minimum wage, less than I was making, but the hours mean I'll be home for Billy by mid-afternoon. I look the place up and realise it's closer than the supermarket. It would be simple enough to keep my bus pass and use the same route. On nice mornings in the summer, I could walk. If anything, although the pay is worse, the hours are a little better. There are no weekends and I'd be home earlier.

I send the woman a message and then allow myself a little self-indulgence by making a cup of tea. It's only as I'm picking out a teabag that I realise I'm not going to have my five per cent staff discount at Crosstown. It doesn't sound like much – it's *not* much – and yet it has totalled a lot of money over the years. Everything comes back to money in the end.

By the time I get back to the sofa, I already have a reply from the sandwich shop owner.

> Hi Lucy.
> Thanks for your interest. Can I ask what experience you have in the food industry and also what your current job is?
> Thanks.

I read the short message three times over. The answers are simple enough. I have no experience and I am currently unemployed after stealing from my previous job.

I think about lying, replying to say something like I'm 'between jobs' because I'm also studying – but there are already too many holes in my life history for someone who is thirty.

Instead, I return to the websites for the pair of job agencies. I fill in forms to say that I am, essentially, looking for anything. It reeks of desperation, but it's not the first time I've debased myself today. I have rent to pay and debts that were never mine to clear.

When that's done, I remove the remaining cash from the envelope and stack it on the table in piles of £200. I'm going mad, I know. This is surely not the way normal people behave. I count it all five times in a row and there's a little under £3,000. It's a huge amount, but it won't last long if I have to start paying rent and bills from it.

So much for handing it in.

Billy is pawing at the door, so I let him out to go wandering the halls and then return to the sofa. With all the free time I suddenly have, I can catch back up on my university work.

I don't, of course. I sit in front of the laptop, occupying myself with nothing of note. I can't even make myself log onto the site.

Even Billy's return doesn't raise me. It's worse that he seems to sense it, too. He clambers onto the sofa and rests his head on my knee, wanting to be of comfort. I count the money over and over until I get so frustrated with myself, that I pack it all back into the envelope. The afternoon is largely wasted by thinking about the things I could buy with it.

It's almost a relief when there's a chatter from the corridor to signal that Karen and the boys are home. I shoot off the sofa, startling poor Billy, and then catch Karen just as she was about to close her door. We do the faux 'fancy seeing you here' thing and then she invites me in.

'I was thinking about trying that new takeaway pizza place,' I say. 'Do you think the boys would like a treat? On me.'

Karen wavers in the doorway. 'I'd already taken their tea out of the freezer,' she says. 'I can't ask you to do that.'

'I want to,' I insist. A pause and then: 'I think the pizza place does ice cream, too.'

Tyler is close enough to hear. He spins on his heels and looks up to his mum – and that's enough to sway it. Bully for me: I've guilt-tripped a mother into feeding her kids junk because I'm desperate for company.

The four of us and Billy head out of Hamilton House and along the street. The boys speed ahead, setting themselves short races from lamp post to lamp post that Tyler always seems to win. Karen and I talk about the same kind of nothing we often do: weather, the state of parking at the front of our building, how the nights are drawing in, and so on. It's meaningless, but the comfort of having somebody by my side outweighs all of that.

You Wanna Pizza Me? is one of those shops that are constantly opening and closing in different guises. It was a coffee shop a year ago and then sat empty as the graffiti mounted on the shutters outside. It's on a small rank of shops, along with a betting place, a newsagent and a launderette.

The kids are still ahead but wait outside, checking to see that this is definitely where they're allowed to eat tonight. When Karen nods, they whoop with joy and jump up the step to get inside. I tie Billy outside and head after them.

When they ask what they can order, I tell them whatever they want, and they start to plan a pair of created feasts.

We watch as they relay their order and Karen leans closer to me: 'Thank you,' she whispers.

It's a struggle but I manage, 'Don't worry about it.'

'You deserve this,' she adds.

It takes me a second to remember the lie about a scratch card.

'This bit of money could turn things around for you,' she adds. 'I know it's been hard after everything with Ben, but this is going to change it all.'

She nudges her shoulder into mine and there's such care in her tone that it's hard to bite away the tears. I'm using money that isn't mine to pay for everything. I've lied about where it came from – and all this on the day I was sacked for theft. If only she knew the truth.

I pay for the order but can barely eat more than a few bites of my own food and end up carrying the box home. It turns out the pizza place doesn't do ice cream – but a bribe is a bribe, so we take the kids into the newsagent, where they raid the freezer at the back. I pay for the Magnums, too – no ten-pence Mini Milks here – and Karen is so overwhelmed that she's almost in tears. It will have been a fair while since Tyler and Quinn have been able to have such an indulgent treat. They'll remember today because small gestures mean a lot when a person has so little.

We amble back to Hamilton House and each step along the pavement gives me a growing dread that I'm going to be alone. I'm not usually like this; the opposite is true. It's Billy and me versus the world and I'm fine with that. But now, after today, I need people around me.

I trail after Karen until we get to her door, as if there's no question of me returning to my own flat. She doesn't seem to mind, unlocking it and waiting for Billy, Tyler and Quinn to head inside before we follow. She kicks off her shoes and mentions the kettle, so I say I'll do it. The layout of our apartments is identical – except that Karen has two bedrooms tagged onto the main area. I have a bed hidden in a wall, but she has the equivalent of the penthouse suite.

Karen relaxes on the sofa as Tyler and Quinn head off to their room. After flicking the kettle on, I hunt through the cupboard above for the box of teabags, but the results are catastrophic.

I hold up the single teabag for Karen to see. 'Tragedy has struck,' I say.

She looks up from her phone and laughs. 'There's more somewhere around there.' She presses down on her arms but doesn't actually move. It's the half-hearted motion people do when they're already sitting and don't want to get up. I don't blame her.

'I'll find them,' I say.

A new box is not in the cupboard with the others, so I open a few doors and start looking. My kitchen is largely barren – a testament of only buying the things I need – but Karen's is full of food for the boys. There are cereals and packets of biscuits; plus a cupboard seemingly devoted to sandwich fillings. No sign of teabags.

I start opening and closing drawers and am moving so quickly that I almost miss it. I've already moved on and have to backtrack to make sure my eyes weren't lying. Sitting in the drawer next to the fridge is a taupe envelope. I glance to Karen, who is busy tapping away on her phone, so I turn my back, blocking her view as I remove the envelope from the drawer. I flip it over, but there is no writing on the front or back. It's padded but squishy, with the tab loosely held in place by a thin strip of tape.

It's all horribly familiar…

I risk a glance over my shoulder to Karen, but she is still not paying attention. The tape comes away under my nail and then I raise the flap to peer inside.

I'd been expecting it from the moment I saw the envelope – but it's still a shock. Still inexplicable. There's money inside – scruffy ten-pound notes bundled in haphazardly and shoved to the bottom. I hold the notes for a moment, running my fingers over the smooth plastic.

There are hundreds of pounds packed into the envelope, perhaps more than a thousand. I have an almost unescapable urge to tip it onto the side and count it all.

Then there's a knock at the door.

I'm not sure if I've ever moved so quickly, but, within a flicker of a second, I've crammed the money back into the envelope and dropped it into the drawer. By the time Karen has made a token gesture of getting up, I've called 'I'll get it' across to her.

I want to ask where the money came from; if she somehow had it drop into her life in the way I did… but there's no time for that because it's one surprise after another.

Standing in the doorway are a pair of police officers.

SEVENTEEN

The officers are both in uniform. The taller of the two is cradling his hat in his arm and stoops to look down at me. Jonathan must have changed his mind and they're here to talk to me about what happened at the supermarket. If not that, they know about the money that was dropped into my bag. They want it back and I'm going to have to somehow explain why I've spent so much and why I never handed it in.

'Miss Atkinson?' he asks.

I turn towards the inside of the flat, where Karen is on her feet. 'That's me,' she says.

'Karen Atkinson?' he presses.

'Right.'

She moves across to me and opens the front door wider, but the four of us remain on the cusp; the officers a little outside, us a little in. The second of the two officers gives a weak smile but stays mute, standing rigidly with her arms at her side.

'I'm Constable Beaman and this is Constable Grant,' he says, indicating the woman at his side. 'Do you know a Jade Johansson?' he adds.

Karen looks to me and then nods. She points towards the door opposite mine. 'She lived there,' Karen replies, before touching my arm. 'This is Lucy. She lives opposite.'

Beaman checks something on a notepad and flips a page before focusing back on me. 'Miss Denman?' he asks, with a nod.

'Yes.'

'Can we come in?'

Karen steps backwards to allow them in and then lowers her voice. 'I've got two sons,' she says. 'They're in the back room. Is that okay…?'

The officers exchange a glance and, in that moment, I know what's coming. There's a grim finality about it all.

'Perhaps we're better here,' the officer says.

We step out and Karen pulls the door almost closed behind us. The hallway isn't overly wide and the four of us huddle awkwardly as a breeze billows up from below. Someone's left a door open.

Beaman turns between the two of us: 'I'm sorry to inform you that we found the body of Jade Johansson forty-eight hours ago,' he says.

Karen gasps and grips my arm. She's so unsteady that she almost topples back into the door. There's a moment, a fraction of a second, in which it feels like it's too dramatic. Like someone in panto faking a heart attack.

'She's dead?' Karen says.

'I'm afraid so.'

When Karen turns to me, I'm ashamed at ever doubting her. Her eyes are wide with shock. I wonder what it says about me in that I thought her compassionate reaction was over the top, while my solemn acceptance was normal. I've been finding out a lot about myself in recent days and I'm not sure if much of it is good.

Beaman focuses on me. 'We're going to need time to sit with each of you at some point. That's not necessarily today because this is all very recent.'

Karen and I nod along, but I can't stop myself from looking past the police towards the door opposite mine. I can picture Jade on her way to classes with a tatty badge-covered bag over her back. She always seemed to be cold and would be layered up, regardless of the time of year. In the winter, she had a coat that was like a converted sleeping bag. She would sometimes buy doggy biscuits as a treat for Billy.

'What happened?' Karen asks.

The officers exchange another glance. 'It's early days,' Grant replies. It's the first thing she's said. 'But we've confirmed it's definitely her.'

'Where did you find her?'

Constable Grant shakes her head. 'We're not ready to confirm that for the moment, I'm afraid.'

She flips open the page of her notebook and then Karen interrupts by saying, 'Perhaps we can go to Lucy's?'

The officers glance to my door and then turn to me.

'It'd be a bit more private,' Karen adds. 'The boys will be okay for a couple of minutes.'

There isn't actually a moment in which I agree to this, but there's an inevitability to it. I can hardly tell the police that they're not welcome.

As Karen nips back inside to tell Tyler and Quinn she has to head out, Billy follows me to the apartment, while having a good sniff of the officers to make sure they're up to his high standards. They both crouch to show him some attention as I unlock my door and head inside. I leave them in the hall, telling them I need a moment to clean up and then I hastily make sure the envelope of money is still in the drawer underneath the television. I think about moving it, perhaps hiding it under my mattress again, but it will take too long. I have to tell myself that they don't know I have it and this is not why they're here. Then I remember the money that Karen had. It's all a confusing mess.

It's not long before Karen, myself and both officers are crammed onto the sofa and single chair. Much of the furniture was left by the previous tenant, which was a good thing, considering I'm not sure how I would have been able to afford my own. Billy is pacing, unhappy at having such a full apartment and strangers in his space. Constable Grant offers him her hand, but he ignores it and trots over to the corner instead.

'I do have that effect on men,' Grant jokes, though nobody laughs.

Beaman is flipping through his notepad. 'I know somebody spoke to you when Ms Johansson first disappeared,' he says, 'but I'd like to ask if you know of any reason that someone might have harmed her.'

Karen and I look to one another blankly and I can't help but wonder if this is how police do things. On television, it's all metal walls, bolted-down tables and two-way mirrors. After Ben died, someone knocked on the door of the house, even though I'd already heard about the crash on the news. The officer asked a few basic questions, but that was more or less it. I've not had much contact with the police in my life.

'I can't think of anyone,' Karen says.

I shake my head. 'I don't remember ever seeing her with anyone,' I say. 'I'd catch her on the way out or back quite often. She'd be off to class, or the gym, something like that – but always by herself.'

'Were you friends?'

'Not as such,' I say. 'We would always say hello, but that's about it. We didn't spend any time together.'

Karen confirms the same, but we seem only to be ratifying what the officers expected.

Beaman finishes whatever he's writing and then looks up. 'Are there ever any problems in the building?'

'Like what?' I ask.

'Trouble with any other tenants? People coming and going? I'm not sure.'

'It's a bit noisy sometimes,' Karen says. 'Music through the floors, that sort of thing. That's about it, though. Normal things.'

'What's it like to live here?' he presses.

'It's cheap,' Karen replies. 'Nobody's going out of their way to live here otherwise.'

The officers nod along and I have little to add.

'Did Ms Johansson ever talk to either of you about money?' he asks. 'Or any other kind of problem she might have found herself in?'

Karen and I each shake our heads, but I catch myself glancing off towards the drawer underneath the television at the very mention of money. It's a protective reflex.

He turns to me. 'How long have you lived here, Miss Denman?'

'Four years.' I fire back the answer immediately, the number burned into me. It somehow feels like a long time and no time. If I close my eyes, it was yesterday that I was wandering into the flat with barely a bag to my name. I scrubbed the sealant around the window because it had gone a browny-black with age and neglect. There was a bang from the street overnight and I jumped up, panicking, even though it was only a bin being knocked over.

So much of my life wasted in this little space.

If there's an edge to my tone, then Beaman doesn't mention it. He turns to Karen: 'And you?'

'Almost two years,' she replies.

The officers check a couple of other things, largely to do with timings and when we last saw Jade. When we're done, they leave a business card each, thank us for our time, say goodbye to Billy – who is still avoiding them – and then continue along the corridor to knock on Nick's door.

After seeing them out, I turn to see Karen still on my sofa. She's blank and staring aimlessly towards me. 'Makes you think, doesn't it?' she says airily.

I'm not sure what to say, so offer a consolatory shrug instead.

'That poor girl,' she adds. 'I thought she'd done a runner on her rent. That's what Lauren was saying. I didn't think it'd be anything like this…' She glances towards her own flat and sighs. 'I'll have to keep the boys inside. No letting them out by themselves after this.'

'How do you mean?'

Karen cranes her neck slightly and stares at me as if I'm stupid. 'It's obvious, isn't it?' she says.

'What is?'

'They said they'd found a body and wouldn't give any other details. It can only mean one thing.' She pauses for breath and then adds: 'Someone round here killed her.'

EIGHTEEN

TUESDAY

I seem to spend much of my life fretting over the amount of space I have on public transport. I've caught myself dreaming about the number 24 bus in the past, where I've got on and found it empty. Then I've realised there's no driver and that I'm naked. If I were to seek out a therapist, I'm sure it would be a signal for some sort of mental anxiety – that's what dreams always seem to be. I wake up panicked and confused, before cursing myself for being so stupid. It's only a bus.

On the train this morning, I have a double seat to myself. There's someone talking far too loudly on his phone across the aisle, but there's always one. He's telling someone that he's not going to be effing walked all over by that effing slag and her effing husband. The woman in the seat in front of him catches my eye and we share a silent moment of knowing. I remember Ben having shouting fits like this when he'd had a bad day at work.

I worried about this journey for so long. The price of train tickets seems to be harder to figure out than quantum mechanics. Apparently, they are cheapest exactly twelve weeks before a travel date, so I poached them online for the lowest price as soon as they went live. It seems so silly now, with all those thousands of pounds in that envelope.

The train chunters into a tunnel, thrusting the carriage into darkness as the rattling of the rails thunders up a gear. The sound eclipses the bellowing of the man, who has probably lost phone signal anyway. I close my eyes and listen to the bounding thump of the wheels rushing across the rails. This isn't the first time I've been on a train since what happened to Ben. I wondered if it would be hard, if I'd break down and demand to be let off at the nearest station, but it wasn't like that at all.

I felt nothing. I wasn't scared, or emotional. I didn't associate being on a train with what killed him.

There's a rush of air and then I open my eyes into the blinding light as the train rumbles out of the tunnel. The man across the aisle is staring angrily at his phone but doesn't try to make the call again.

I push back into my seat and turn to look out the window. The blur of green flashes past, with only the hint of a distant village on the horizon. The sky is a wash of greys.

With everything the police told us about Jade, I'd almost forgotten about the money stashed away in Karen's drawer. There was a mix of ten- and twenty-pound notes. It could be her own savings… but would she really have it in cash? In a drawer?

It doesn't feel right. If she'd won it in some lottery or bingo, she'd have surely said something when I told her about my own invented scratch-card win? She must have a reason to keep it to herself – and I'm hardly one to talk, given I've been hiding my own haul for days. We're two people with very little to our name. She's never quite got into what happened between her and her former partner, other than that he left her for someone else. I get the sense they were both left with debts.

My phone starts to buzz and I fish around the envelope of money in my bag to dig it out. I'm expecting to see 'Unknown', but there's a local phone number flashing. I answer and there's an enthusiastic-sounding woman on the other end. I'm always a little suspicious of people who show a great deal of gusto for their work. She's from one of the job agencies with which I signed up and talks me through a questionnaire that goes over much of the same ground I covered when I filled in their online form. It's almost a relief when the line starts to crackle as the signal gets close to cutting out. She says she'll be in contact if they find anything that suits and finishes with a cheery 'Ciao' and then she's gone.

Ciao?

I wonder if this is who the man opposite was having a conversation with because, if so, I can somewhat understand his tone.

The rest of the journey passes uneventfully and by the time we slide into Reading, the carriage is almost empty. I head out of the station and past the row of taxis until I spot a familiar face leaning on a wall at the edge of the car park. She's typing on her phone but looks up as I get near.

''Ello stranger,' I say.

Annie beams and then promptly bursts into tears. She almost throws herself at me, tucking her head onto my shoulder. Her entire body shakes as she sobs tears onto my neck. There's little else I can do other than pat her on the back gently.

I think I can make out a series of 'I'm sorry' grunts through the snuffles, but it's not easy to tell. When she pulls away after a minute or so, her face is a smeary mess of drizzled mascara and her reddened hair is so tangled that it looks like she's been walking in a hurricane.

'How are you?' she manages.

The fact that she's a tear-stained wreck and I'm a slightly bemused onlooker is not lost on either of us as, from nowhere, we each start to laugh.

'I've had warmer welcomes,' I say.

She coughs another laugh and then fishes a tissue from her pocket and blows her nose long and loud.

'Sorry,' she repeats. I tell her it's fine and then she uses her phone's camera to help clear herself up. 'I told myself I wouldn't cry,' she says.

'How long did you last after that?'

'That was when I pulled into the car park, so roughly seven minutes.'

It's hard not to laugh at that and, all of a sudden, the mood has lifted.

Annie's husband and son were on the same train as Ben and Ben's brother, Alex. They were on their way to a football match and her son was the only child to die. They had gone early, to try to make a day of it. If they'd gone closer to kick-off, they'd be here now. It's hard to comprehend the enormity of how the world turns on such small decisions.

We get into Annie's car and she sets off away from the station, out of the town, heading west towards the M4.

'Thanks for coming,' she says.

'Of course I was going to come,' I reply, even though it's not entirely true. The only reason I still attend these memorial events is for people like Annie. It's five years since the crash and, in the immediate aftermath, before my life fell apart completely, it was hard not to be drawn to other people who had also lost someone. It's easy to say, 'I know what you're going through', but there was a group of us who genuinely knew.

In the time that's passed, we've all come to the annual ceremonies, plus there's a secret Facebook group. Some of us are closer than others and we send intermittent messages back and forth to see how people are.

'How have you been?' Annie asks.

'Great,' I lie.

I think it's a lie lots of people tell. What are we supposed to say? That life is terrible and that each decision made seems to make it that little bit worse?

She tells me about a new relationship she's in, insisting it's early days but that there's definitely a spark. I tell her I'm pleased – and I am – but the reason I'm on the fringes of this group is because there's a part of me deep down that's jealous of people like Annie. She has a conclusion to what happened. There was life insurance and joint accounts.

None of that is worth the two people she lost, of course – but her life can still go on. Like it or not, money matters. It's why those with it have longer life expectancies than those without.

It's good to hear Annie's voice and I let her talk. As well as the new boyfriend, she's up for a promotion at work and her life seems to be coming together. When she asks about me, I fudge things in the way I do. Work's going great, my boss loves me, I'm acting up as assistant manager, it looks like it might be a permanent thing, my university course is cracking along… and so on. Lie after lie. When does it become too much to continue thinking of myself as an honest person?

Annie gets off the motorway and follows a series of winding country lanes with ease. 'I can't remember if I told you,' she says, 'but I have to leave more or less after the service. I'm supposed to be interviewing at work and I'd rather stay on top of it. There's a buffet somewhere after, but, if you want to leave with me, I can drop you back at the station.'

'I'm not much of a hanger-arounder,' I assure her.

The roads narrow as the hedges soar and it's not long before we're surrounded by green. All Saints Church is the same venue as the past four years. A beautiful steeple soars high above the surrounding countryside, topping a blooming patch of emerald that will always be quintessentially British.

Cars are parked nose-to-tail along both sides of the road and Annie pulls in at the back of the line. She checks herself over in the mirror and straightens her hair before we set off along the crumbling tarmac.

By the time we reach the gates, there are so many people in black that it could be either a funeral or a goth convention. Many are close to tears, but I feel a distance from their emotion. There are faces I recognise and we offer the standard mini waves and grim smiles. I stick close to Annie because she's probably the only person from this group I've ever been close to. We've always been able to laugh at one another and some of the absurd situations in which we find ourselves.

When everyone else starts to traipse into the church, we get into line and follow. It's not easy to admit, but, with all things like this, there is a pecking order with grief. When everything happened, there were those who stepped forward to become the face of the bereaved. Perhaps it was coincidence, though I doubt it: the media decided the faces of our loss had to be the most attractive among us. Presumably because of this, Elaine gets a spot on the front row. She's a pristine lawyer who lost her husband – also a lawyer – in the crash. She wears a suit like a lamb wears its wool, as if it's a part of her.

She's sitting next to James, a silver fox who was once a local television personality in the south-east. His grown-up daughter was on the train and it was he who set up the Facebook group and organises this memorial each year. He emails relentlessly upbeat messages every three months, as if we've signed up to a mailing list from which we cannot escape. It's like he thinks he's our counsellor, peppering each note with lines like, 'Hope our spirits are still high' and 'You've all been in my prayers'. He starts each mail with something along the lines of, 'Hey, guys. It's me again'. There's no unsubscribe button at the bottom and I'm not brave enough to reply and say I wish he'd leave me off. I should probably just block him.

The truth is that it's only the crash that connects us as a group. We're a collection of individuals who were unlucky enough to be thrown together as one. Apart from Annie, I feel no affinity for anyone.

Melancholic organ music sets the tone as Annie and I slot into a row two-thirds of the way back. It's a stunning building, with stained-glass windows lining both sides, wooden benches in perfect parallel symmetry and echoing stone floors. It's as we're taking our seats that I spot Melanie sitting on the opposite side of the church. She's wearing a net veil and a black dress, while staring unmovingly towards the front of the church. If she can sense me, then she doesn't shift. I've seen her three times in a week now.

As the music stops and the rector begins to speak, Annie takes my hand. She links her fingers into mine and squeezes gently. I don't say anything, but I feel like a fraud. I'm not in mourning.

Before long, we're on our feet and miming along to a hymn. The bloke in front is belting out the chorus with the full fire and thunder.

The service continues in the way that services do. Almost nobody believes in God until there's a birth or death – and then we want to trust that things have meaning.

After a while, the rector stands aside and James heads to the front. I've not seen him in twelve months, but it's as if each year of ageing makes him more attractive. Without a word, he demands the attention of everyone present and, from there, he starts to read the list of all the victims. He goes one at a time; slowly and poignantly. Most people would stumble over a name or two – but not James. I suppose it's his training from when he was a newsreader.

Sobs spring up from the watching crowd at regular intervals, but he never pauses the cadence, not even when he mentions his own daughter's name. When he gets to the name of Annie's son, I rest a hand on her knee. She sits a little straighter, holding her breath as her body tenses, but there's no hint of a sob this year. As soon as her husband's name has been read, she slumps a little and lets out a long, low gasp. The torment is over and I wonder for how many more years we'll do this. There was the original memorial service a couple of weeks after the crash – and then one on the actual anniversary for each of the years leading up to now. Five years is a landmark – but will we come back for six? For seven? Or will there now be a gap until ten years have passed? Where does grieving end and wallowing begin? It's not quite Princess Di, but will we still be congregating here in twenty years? Twenty-five? Thirty? Is this my life from now on?

I'm so lost in those thoughts that the name 'Alex Peterson' takes me by surprise. Annie touches my knee as reciprocation, but I glance sideways to Melanie in the opposite row. She is sitting stoically, her back straight against the unforgiving wooden bench.

'Benjamin Peterson.'

Annie squeezes my knee a little tighter. It's reassuring and yet unnecessary. I feel empty and out of place. I loved Ben once – but, if he loved me, then how could he leave me in such a state? How could he tell so many lies?

Melanie's chest rises and she reaches to pinch the bridge of her nose. She brushes something away from under her veil and then continues to sit rigidly.

'Luce…'

Annie is whispering my name and I turn to her.

'You're staring,' she adds softly.

It's only then that I realise James has almost completed the list of names. He reads out the final one and then stands solemnly for a moment before bowing his head and returning to his seat. Somehow a minute, perhaps two, has passed without me noticing.

There's no time to reflect because we're on our feet once more for another hymn. The man in front again launches himself into the chorus, but, this time, I don't even pretend to mouth the words. I shouldn't be here.

The rector talks a little more; Elaine does a reading; there's another hymn – because everyone likes a good ol' sing-song at a memorial – and then that's that for another year. The organ hums as we filter out into the chilled November sun. The grass of the cemetery beyond is covered with a layer of dew that I'd missed before and a breeze has started to skim across the fields beyond, fluttering the evergreens that line the edge of the graveyard.

There's always an awkward moment after anything like this in which nobody quite knows what to do. People stand and smile awkwardly at one another, or exchange the most mundane of small talk.

Lovely service, wasn't it?
At least the weather held out.
How was the journey down?

Someone I barely recognise and of whom I'm not sure I've ever known the name tells me I look lovely, so I say the same to her. Nobody ever strides up to another person at a funeral or memorial and tells them they could've made more of an effort.

It's as we're meandering that a woman appears at my side as if she'd materialised there. She's in a tight black dress with a ridiculously oversized hat. If it wasn't a dim grey, she could've been off to ladies' day at the races.

'It's Lucy, isn't it?' she says, extending her hand. We shake, but I'm suddenly aware of my chewed fingernails against her manicured talons. She has glossy dark hair to match her dress and, though there is a glimmer of recognition, I definitely don't know her name. 'Gloria,' she says as a prompt – and it's only now that I remember her phone call. She wanted to talk about money and I'm suddenly clutching my bag tighter, feeling protective over the envelope within.

Annie is still at my side and glances between us curiously. I get the sense she knows Gloria better than I do.

'Can we have a word?' Gloria adds. 'There's a pub down the road and they're putting on a buffet. Perhaps there?'

It feels so British, like this is our national catchphrase. Forget 'tally-ho, old chap', it's 'they're putting on a buffet'.

I glance between Gloria and Annie, jammed in the obvious tension between them.

'Sure,' I reply, 'but I don't have a way back to the station. Annie drove me here and—'

'Oh, I can give you a lift,' Gloria says dismissively.

I don't particularly want to bail on Annie, but Gloria mentioned money and I know I need to hear what she has to say. When I turn to Annie, she's already set.

'It's fine,' she says. 'We can catch up another time. I'll text you later or tomorrow.'

There's yet another moment in which it feels like I'm missing something. Gloria and Annie eye each other for a withering second and then Annie waves goodbye. We do the air-kiss thing that nobody does in real life and then she strides away.

'So…' Gloria says conspiratorially, 'shall we talk money?'

NINETEEN

It is seemingly a well-known fact that nothing pays tribute to victims more than getting lashed in their honour.

The Thirsty Fox is one of those stone-brick postcard pubs that I suspect only exists in Britain. It's next to a stream and a neat humpback bridge but otherwise surrounded by vast swathes of green. Chuck in a red phone-box next to a black cab and American tourists would be throwing their money at it.

A fire is crackling at the back of the function room and the walls are decked out with landscape prints of various countryside scenes. Almost everyone from the church is here mingling with one another, but I'm off to the side, in a booth by myself, feeling invisible. I'm ready to move on from all this but many aren't. Who am I to judge?

Considering how little I eat and how much I worry about money, a free buffet should be right up my alley – but I can do little other than pick at the bite-size sausage rolls and triangular cheese and pickle sandwiches.

I've been at the pub for twenty minutes, but, almost as soon as Gloria pulled into the car park, her phone rang. She told me she'd catch me up – and that was the last I saw of her. There's a part of me that wonders if I've been dumped and I'm now going to have to actually talk to people before finding my way back to the train station.

I've got half a sausage roll in my mouth when Gloria suddenly appears once more, clutching a phone in each hand.

'Do you want to sit outside?' she asks, in a tone that makes it very clear it's what *she* wants to do. 'It's not that cold.'

She's my lift back to the station and I feel a certain obligation, so I trail her out and we find a spot on the picnic tables in the beer garden.

'You wanted to talk about money…?' I say, hoping she'll get on with it.

Gloria looks up and tugs an errant strand of hair away from her eyes. 'Did you get anything when your husband died?' she asks.

I've never been a fan of talking around a subject – but Gloria's bluntness still feels like a physical smack.

'Ben wasn't my husband,' I reply.

A momentary frown etches across Gloria's face and then, as quickly as it arrived, it's gone. 'Oh, of course.'

I'm confused for a second, thinking she's going to add something – but then I realise she's still waiting for an answer. The directness is unnerving.

'I didn't get anything,' I say. She nods along but doesn't reply. 'Why are you asking?' I add.

'No reason,' she says.

I stare at her, but she's now busy flicking at one of her shiny black fingernails.

'There must be a reason,' I say. 'You brought me here and wanted to talk about money. Now you say there's no reason…'

Gloria looks up and I feel like I'm back at school. The cool kids are playing the we-know-something-you-don't-know game.

'I'm not sure if I should say…'

I press back into the wooden chair and stare at her. It's then that Melanie appears on the other side of the fence surrounding the beer garden. She's holding a phone to her ear with one hand and smoking a cigarette with the other. She angles slightly and there's a moment in which we see one another. Her eyes narrow as she continues to talk to whoever's on the other end of the line and then she turns her back to me. It's right that she's here, of course – she lost two sons – but it feels as if she's everywhere I turn.

I blink back to Gloria, trying to push away the thoughts of Melanie. 'Why me?' I ask.

'Sorry?' Gloria replies.

'Why are you asking *me* if I got any money after Ben died?'

'I've been asking the others, too. You were a little more difficult to get hold of. I didn't have your number or email address.'

It occurs to me that she got my number from somewhere, seeing as she called me. There's a short silence, which I break: 'I still don't understand why you're asking.'

Gloria weighs me up but doesn't say anything.

As I feel for my bag, a thought suddenly occurs.

'Did somebody give you money?' I ask.

She reaches for her own bag – a knock-off designer monstrosity, inside which could fit most of what I own. I picture an envelope stuffed with cash in there. She bites her lip, glances sideways and then says: 'I've got to go.'

In a flash, she's on her feet, hurrying towards the car park. It's only as she disappears from sight that I remember she's supposed to be taking me back to the train station. I trail after her but only arrive in time to see her car exiting the gate at the far end. A few stray stones fizz backwards under the wheels and then she's gone. I watch for a few seconds, unsure what's transpired. She wanted to talk to me and then, from nowhere, she was running off.

When I turn around, Melanie is at the corner of the pub, still talking into her phone. I pretend I've not seen her and head inside. I feel like a wedding crasher as I mooch around the small groups of people who are deep in conversation. The atmosphere is different than at the church now the alcohol is taking hold. There are laughs and smiles and the morbidness has lifted.

I walk around, doing the closed-mouth smile and nod thing, hoping somebody might welcome me into their circle and that I can bum a lift. Perhaps surprisingly, it is Elaine who catches my eye. She's still immaculate in her all-black suit and standing tall at the back of the room, where the large double doors overlook the moors beyond.

'How have you been?' she asks.

'Oh, y'know…' I reply, which is standard for this sort of thing. Nobody argues with this type of banality, even though it means nothing.

Elaine looks over her shoulder and then quickly back to me. I'm not sure she listened to my reply. 'Can you see the bloke over by the bushes?' she asks.

I stare beyond her, out past the fence of the beer garden towards the green on the far side, close to the stream.

'Do you know him?' she adds.

There's a bit of a distance, but the shape is distinctive enough. There's a large man in wellington boots and an olive-green fleece, standing with his hands in his pockets. He has some sort of dodgy comb-over but mutton chops that curve around into a beard.

'I've never seen him before,' I reply.

Elaine makes a *hrm* sound. 'No one knows him,' she says. 'But he was hanging around at the church and now he's here.' She turns and the two of us stand side by side watching as the man stares back towards the pub.

'I didn't see him at the service,' I say.

'He was over by the cars as we were coming out,' she replies.

'He could be some sort of photographer…?'

'Where's his camera?'

She has me there. If he is from the media, there are people here who'd be happy to talk.

Perhaps sensing he's being watched, the man takes a tentative step towards the bridge. He clambers up over the fence, turns to look at the pub once more and then continues over the arch. After a few seconds, he is swallowed by the shadows of the trees.

'I get the sense,' Elaine says, 'that we've not seen the last of whoever that was.'

TWENTY

It's not long before the endless, meaningless small talk becomes too much. I ask the barman to order me a taxi and then pay in cash for the driver to take me to the train station. It's money from the envelope, of course.

By the time I'm almost home and hurrying along the street towards Hamilton House, it's almost four p.m. The sky is already starting to look gloomy. Nick is on his way out of the front door but stops when he sees me.

'Did you hear about Jade?' he asks, breathlessly. He doesn't wait for a reply, before continuing: 'It's shocking, isn't it? I cried most of last night.'

'I don't know what to make of it,' I reply – which is largely true.

'It makes you think, doesn't it?' he adds, which is word for word what Karen said.

I agree that it makes people think and then he starts to pass me before stopping once more. 'How's Billy?' he asks.

'He was fine when I took him for a walk this morning.'

Nick winces slightly. 'Judge has been a bit down for the past day or so. He's sleeping a lot and only eating little bits. He's stopped begging for food, which shows how poorly he is. I wondered if he might have picked up something from Billy, or vice versa?'

I shake my head. 'I don't think so. I'll keep an eye on Billy and let you know if I see anything.'

He nods along and mutters the word 'vet'. I pat him on the arm and say I'm sure it'll all be fine – then he disappears off to wherever he was going.

When I get into the apartment, I head straight for Billy, who is lying in his own bed. He raises his head and looks at me with tired eyes. His new squeaky toy is drizzled with doggy saliva, next to his nose. At least one of us has been having fun today…

I pet his head and he rolls onto his side.

'You all right, mate?' I ask him.

He laps my hand gently and, though everything is fine on the surface, I get the sense that something isn't quite okay. Billy rarely sleeps in his own bed and prefers, essentially, literally anything else. It could be that Nick has put the idea of illness in my mind and that I'm reading too much into his general sleepiness.

I continue to smooth his fur until he closes his eyes and then I empty the envelope of cash onto the table. I count it three times over until I'm certain of the amount. I sit and stare at the piles, trying to work out what's happened because, somehow, I've blown through very close to £1,000 of someone else's money in four days. There is the obvious stuff in front of me – the laptop, the shoes, and then… what? I gave Vicky some money for rent. Little things here and there.

Is this what it's like to be rich? Money spends itself simply because it's there?

When I barely had anything, I'd budget to every last penny and knew what everything cost. Now, in no time at all, it's as if I've forgotten all that.

I have *got* to stop spending. I have no job and, wherever this money came from, it has got to last me until I figure out something else.

My buzzing phone is a welcome distraction: a text from Harry.

Hey! Just checking we're still on for later? Looking forward to it! X

It takes me a few seconds to remember what he's on about. With the memorial, the news of Jade, the money in Karen's drawer and my own firing, things have passed me by. I scroll up and see our previous messages. I invited him over for seven. He's bringing dessert and, possibly, wine – despite our joking about 'wine people' at The Garden Café. That means I'm supposed to provide a meal, even though there's barely anything in the flat. I type out a reply, asking if we can do another time and hover a thumb over 'send'.

There's an M&S Food down the road that does pre-packed cooking bundles. Everything is ready for the oven and, voila, even the worst of cooks can pull off an apparently gourmet meal in an hour or so. I've never bought a single thing from that shop, largely because everything is more expensive than at Crosstown. Shopping there is a class thing, not a necessity. That's what I tell myself, but I'm taunted by the stacks of cash still on the table.

I'm immediately going against the pledge I made myself barely minutes before. The bundle of food will be more expensive than individual items – and there would be cheaper places to stock up. It's unnecessary spending, more waste. More money gone. One more step to oblivion.

I delete my first attempt at a reply and send a different response instead.

Deffo! See you then!

It's not who I am. 'Deffo'? What's wrong with me? His reply doesn't take long:

Fab! Am bringing chocolate volcano cakes!

I'm not sure if we're going to get along, after all. Not only is he mad for exclamation marks but he's drawn me into it. I tap out a wimpy 'OK' – no punctuation – and then turn to Billy. He's still in his bed, watching me through half-closed eyelids.

'Are you going to clean up or do I have to do it?' I ask him.

He yawns and then puts his head down.

'Fine,' I reply. 'I'll do it.'

There is a knock on my door at precisely seven o'clock. I make sure all the M&S packaging is crammed down to the bottom of the kitchen bin, cover it with a piece of kitchen roll and then check myself over in the mirror to ensure I don't look like a complete bag lady.

That done, I open the door to see Harry leaning against the frame as if he's on the poster of a terrible romcom.

'Fancy seeing you here,' he says.

I look him up and down. 'Jeans and a jacket again? Don't you own anything else?'

He laughs as he comes in, pecking me on one cheek. It happens so quickly that I don't have time to decide whether or not it's fine. He crosses to the kitchen and puts two large carrier bags down on the counter, then crouches and turns towards Billy.

'So you're the cute little thing I've heard so much about.'

Billy raises his head and opens his eyes wider, then pulls himself up and out of his bed. He crosses a few steps to Harry and sniffs his hand. Harry rubs behind his ears, but Billy's seen enough. He turns his tail and shuffles back to his bed.

Harry stands. 'Does this mean he doesn't like me?'

'I think it means he's indifferent to you.'

The two eye each other and then Harry spins back and opens up the bag on the counter. He doesn't appear to have a problem with my meagre flat. 'I didn't know what you liked to drink,' he says. 'I got a bottle of red, one of white; miniatures of vodka, whisky, gin and rum; plus a four-pack of ale.'

I look at his unveiled haul and then at him. 'Are you trying to get me drunk?'

He mock slams a fist on the counter. 'Damn! You've figured me out.' He straightens himself and then adds: 'I figured we can have whatever you want and then there'll be plenty left for next time…'

There's a twinkle in his eye, but I don't take the bait. The grin is fixed anyway as he carefully removes two small ceramic pots covered with foil.

'These are the volcano cakes,' he says. 'My gran's recipe. They only need to be warmed in the oven.'

'Everyone wants to be a *Bake-Off* contestant nowadays.'

He laughs: 'Better than an *X Factor* wannabe.'

Before we can get any further, the cooker starts to beep, so I shoo Harry out of the kitchen area and unload everything from the oven. There aren't many places to sit in the flat, largely because there's so little room, but I do have a fold-down dining table courtesy of the previous tenant. With a clean tablecloth and cutlery, it almost looks as if I don't live in a one-room dive.

It's not long before I've served everything up, using the only two plates I own, with my only pair of knives and forks. Harry doesn't need to know that.

I usually eat on the sofa and Billy would be pacing, looking for scraps or hand-outs. Perhaps it's the table that's confusing him, but he remains in his bed, half-asleep. Not even an early-evening firework outside does anything other than make him raise an ear.

We start to eat and Harry only needs one bite to tell me my cooking is fabulous. I offer him a sideways raised eyebrow to let him know I'm not *that* easily complimented. Besides, it's not as if I did much myself.

'Nice place you have here,' he adds next.

'You don't have to say that,' I reply. 'What's yours like?'

He brushes it off with a shrug. 'It's an apartment. It is what it is.'

The flat is small enough that the cabinet by the television is within reaching distance. Harry stretches across and picks up one of the photos.

'Is this you?' he asks, pointing to a grinning little girl sandwiched between two proud parents.

'It was after a school play one year,' I reply. 'It's one of my earliest memories. I think I was about six.'

He nods and returns the photo and I can sense him looking around the room for others. Possibly for ones of Ben. I talked about him so much before that it would be no wonder if Harry thinks I'm still somewhat obsessed. Not that I have loads, but everything from the past few years is on my phone anyway.

We continue eating, but it's suddenly awkward. I try to think of the things I might chat to Karen about, but everything is natural with us. These silences don't exist. Harry must feel it too, because he glances up from the plate and smiles weakly.

'The food really is good,' he reiterates.

'Thank you.'

There's more silence and then Harry breaks it in the worst way. I guess things are flatlining to such a degree that there's nowhere else to go. 'What's your favourite movie?' he asks.

I have a momentary panic in which I can't think of any movies other than *Face/Off* – not because I love it, more that it was on television the weekend before last. I've not been to the cinema in years.

'You first,' I reply.

'*Die Hard*,' he says in a flash.

'That's a good choice,' I say, playing for time.

'What's yours?'

'Probably *The Jungle Book*.' The cartoon version is the first film I can remember seeing as a child.

I wonder if Harry will follow it up, but he nods along. At least I didn't claim it was *Citizen Kane* or something like that.

'Favourite song?' he asks.

This one is easy, but there's a stumble as I find myself glancing towards the door. '"Rocket Man",' I say. 'By Elton John.'

'That's an interesting choice.' For a moment, I think he'll tell me his but instead he asks: 'Why?'

I suddenly feel on the spot and vulnerable. As if revealing this information is too personal, like he's asked for my PIN. 'I used to listen to it a lot when I was a kid,' I say. 'I don't know where I first heard it, but it was probably Mum. I used to dream of being an astronaut: saying goodbye to everyone and flying off to the moon, or Mars, or wherever.'

Harry has paused with a forkful of fish halfway to his mouth. 'Do you still dream of that?'

'I guess not.'

He puts the food in his mouth and starts to chew. I find myself wondering when I stopped thinking big. Whether it's something to do with me, or something that all children outgrow. He tells me his favourite song is Sinatra's 'My Way' and it's hard not to pull a face. I've always hated it, probably because I associate it with terrible singers shrieking out karaoke versions.

We go back and forth, talking about books, television shows, comedians, sport and other things. It does make conversation, but the one thing of which I'm certain at the end is that we have almost nothing in common.

As Harry sorts out his desserts, I leave a plate of leftovers for Billy. He barely raises his head but does sit up enough to slowly start to eat. I sit on the floor next to his bed and gently rub the area behind his ears. It is still three days until Bonfire Night but that doesn't stop a steady stream of fireworks fizzing into the air outside. Each bang pricks Billy's ears, but he doesn't hide behind my legs in the way he has before.

Harry soon brings over his volcano cakes, looking over them proudly as if he's just given birth to twins. He talks me through the ingredients and how he makes them every Christmas. 'Or for special occasions,' he adds.

We might have little in common, but there's no question that Harry's Gran knew what she was doing when she came up with the recipe. The chocolate is so gooey that my tongue sticks to the top of my mouth and I'm left gasping for a drink.

When we're done, Harry insists on doing the washing-up, while I dry and put things away. We talk on the sofa for a while, but it's hard to remember what about, even as the conversation is happening.

'What are you doing on Bonfire Night?' he asks.

'I've got to look after Billy,' I reply.

Billy watches us, apparently aware his name is being used. He's finished the scraps of food and licked the plate clean.

'It must be hard at this time of year when you have a dog,' Harry says.

'It used to be one of my favourite times of the year,' I reply. 'Perhaps my overall favourite, even above Christmas. I loved it all as a kid. That was before trick or treating was really a thing – but we'd go to different firework displays. I used to score them out of ten and keep everything in a notebook so I'd remember.' I laugh slightly at my own nerdiness. It feels like a lifetime ago.

'Don't you like it as much now…?'

'No.'

'Because of Billy?'

'It's when Ben died.'

There's not a lot to say after that. It's hard not to hear the bangs overhead and remember the policeman coming along the path to confirm what had happened. Perhaps I'm too honest for my own good, or maybe it's a get-out because it doesn't feel as if Harry and I have connected. There was a definite spark with Ben. Sometimes, when Billy dashes to meet me at the door, his tail wagging, his tongue lolling, I wonder if that's how I used to be with Ben. There was an excitement at having waited a whole day to see him and I was a tail-wagging puppy.

Harry nods along as if he understands and I wonder if he feels the lack of connection, too. Sometimes, things are what they are.

We talk a little more, but there's no substance. Before long, we're on about the weather forecast and how it would be nice to have a white Christmas this year.

Eventually, Harry says he has to go. 'Gotta be up early,' he adds.

I give him back his crockery and insist he doesn't leave all the alcohol, then I lead him the few steps to the front door. As soon as I open it, we both stop. The melodic piano opening of Elton John's 'Rocket Man' has just started from the door across the hallway.

Harry turns between me and the opposing flat. I don't know what to say but, seemingly, neither does he. The hairs on my arm have stood up.

'Shall we do this again?' he asks, not mentioning the coincidence of the music.

It would be brutally easy to say 'no', but I fudge it instead. The lack of chemistry could be because we're at my flat, with no space and no atmosphere. It was almost certainly a mistake to invite him here. 'We'll figure something out,' I reply.

Harry nods and I grab my phone, then we head downstairs to the front door. He says goodnight and leans in as I go to turn. He almost ends up slamming his forehead into the bridge of my nose and then we eye each other, curious as to the other's intentions. In the end, he gives me a peck on the cheek and then heads out.

The door opens and closes, allowing a blast of cold and sulphur into the hall. It's only a moment, but enough for me, so I hurry back up the stairs. As I reach my apartment, Elton is still singing from the one opposite. He's up to the second or third chorus and I hover between the two flats, unsure what to do. The sheer coincidence of it leaves me gnawing my fingernails. I step towards my own door and then briskly change my mind, spinning on my heels and knocking lightly on Jade's old flat.

I wait for a moment, holding my breath, and then knock a second time. Louder this time. 'Hello,' I call.

No answer.

'Could you turn the music down?'

I wait, unsure what to do next, when my phone starts to buzz. It's Unknown once more and I'm lost staring at the screen until the caller rings off.

Back inside my flat, Billy has picked himself up from his bed and is ambling around the apartment sniffing the furniture. I crouch and ruffle his ears.

Perhaps it wasn't only me who felt no connection.

The number 24 bus is packed when I get on. It's busier than it was on Friday when the money ended up in my bag. People are getting off, but it's like a clown car because the amount on board doesn't seem to be decreasing.

As I finally get in front of the driver, I reach into my purse, but my pass isn't there. My stomach sinks once more as I thumb through the other compartments searching for it. It's then that I look up and realise the driver has disappeared. Confused, I turn to see where he's gone, but there are only empty rows of unused seats. I try to breathe, but the air is stuck and, when I look down, I realise my feet are bare. I've forgotten my shoes. Not only that, I'm wearing nothing at all. I cover myself with my arms and it's then that everything begins to buzz. My entire body is shaking involuntarily as the entire world rumbles.

My eyes open suddenly into the gloom of my room. My phone is vibrating across the desk, the light flashing on and off. Through the confusion of sleep, I see the number being displayed on the front and press the screen to answer.

It's a woman's voice: 'Hello? Is that Lucy Denman?'

'Who is this?' I croak.

'My name's Alison and I'm a nurse at the casualty unit,' the voice says. 'We've had a patient admitted and he's given us your name and number.'

TWENTY-ONE

WEDNESDAY

It's hard not to wince as I peer closer at the gash across the back of the patient's head. The medical staff have done a great job to clean and stitch it, but underneath the bandages, it is still a horror story. They've had to cut away some of the hair and the slash stretches from one ear across the back of the cranium almost to the other.

'The police think it was a pole or bat,' Harry says, with an unerring cheerfulness.

He leans forward again and pulls the hair apart to give me an even better look. The darkened reddy-black of the blood has blended with the purply-yellow of the welt to create something that looks like it should have an eighteen certificate attached.

'What does it look like?' he asks.

'What do you *think* it looks like?'

He presses the dressing back onto his head and leans onto the pillows that are propping him up.

'I think it's going to give me a rugged handsomeness.'

'It's on the back of your head.'

He manages a laugh and then pouts a lip as he draws a circle in the air, indicating his face. 'I've already got it going on here, now I've got it going on back there, too.'

I laugh as well, though it's hard to see the humour. I'm chilled simply by looking at it. There are more grazes on the side of his face from where he presumably hit the pavement.

'What happened?' I ask.

'I was walking home and there were these six burly blokes,' Harry says. 'They said, "Give me your volcano cake recipe," and I said, "No, I'm taking it to the grave." Then they said—'

'Can you not joke about this…?'

The smile slips from his face and I wonder if I should have let him continue. Humour might be his way of dealing with it.

'Sorry,' I add.

He shakes his head a fraction but then winces. 'I shouldn't have asked the nurse to call you,' he says. 'I couldn't think of who else to call. My family live nowhere near and, if I'm honest, I don't have a lot of friends in town. I didn't realise how late it was. Everything was a blur.'

I take his hand and squeeze. 'I'm glad you called,' I say.

He bites his bottom lip and glances past me before taking a breath. 'I don't know what happened,' he says more quietly. 'I was most of the way home and the next thing I know, I'm in an ambulance. I've got a massive headache and the paramedic says it looks like someone attacked me.'

I shiver at the thought and he definitely sees it: 'What?' he asks, eyes widening.

There's a moment in which I almost tell him the truth about the similarity of it all. How many coincidences can stack together until it's clear there's no chance involved?

'Nothing,' I say. 'It's just hard to imagine someone doing this…'

I wonder if he'll see through the explanation, but he moves on. 'The police think it's random,' he says. 'They asked if I'd made any enemies and all that, but there wasn't a lot I could tell them. They said something about it being a CCTV blind spot where I was, though they're going to go door to door to see if anyone heard or saw something.'

'Were you robbed?' I ask.

He shakes his head and flinches once more. 'No. My phone and wallet were still in my pocket.'

We sit quietly for a moment and I'm not sure what to say.

A glimmer of a smile flickers across Harry's face, but it's not matched by his eyes. 'You've not got any crazy ex-boyfriends, have you?'

I blink. 'No.'

Because we haven't had enough, there's another awkward moment. It feels like there's a valley between us.

'Sorry,' he says. 'I think the painkillers must be wearing off. It was probably kids having a laugh, something like that.'

Everything's always blamed on kids, as if the young people are inexplicably more feral than they were when we were that age. One generation always blames the next because it's easier to punch down.

I sit at Harry's side for a while as the nurse comes around and checks his bandage and the stitching. She takes his temperature, pulse and blood pressure and then, unexpectedly, says he can be discharged if he wants. Harry seems a little surprised, but I get the sense the hospital needs the bed. He agrees, probably because he doesn't want to spend any more time here than absolutely necessary.

She tells him he has to take it easy. No alcohol, nothing strenuous or stressful. If he's feeling dizzy, he has to stop whatever he's doing and, if it doesn't clear, he has to call either NHS Direct, or 999. It strikes me that if a person is disorientated, using a phone might be a problem – but I guess other people know best.

Harry asks if he's allowed to sleep and she takes the question with a smile, saying it's a myth that patients with concussion or head injuries have to be kept awake.

There are forms to fill at the front counter, a prescription to take – and then we're on the kerb outside, shivering in the early morning darkness. I wave across to one of the taxi drivers and then help Harry into the back.

'Blimey, mate – what happened to you?' the driver asks.

Harry gives a brief rundown – stranger with a bat or pole from behind – and then tells the driver his address. We sit silently in the back together, listening to the sound of early morning talk radio. It's worse than I could have imagined, with every mad opinion amplified by the lunacy of the callers who are awake at this hour.

The driver stops on the corner of Livingstone Street after Harry tells him it's close enough. It's a strangely unique thing to taxi journeys in that passengers say anywhere in the vague region of the destination is 'close enough'. Boats don't just dock anywhere in the general vicinity of a port and pilots don't set down planes at any old airport because it's sort of there.

Either way, I take Harry's arm and help him onto the kerb. He leans into me and I almost overbalance until I press back onto the adjacent wall to support both our weights.

'Which one's yours?' I ask.

He points to an apartment block at the end of the street and we set off hobbling towards it, as if we're in a three-legged race. Harry groans under his breath every few steps, but, when I ask if he's in pain, he insists he's fine. He is a man, after all. I can imagine someone like him in a war zone having their leg shot off, only to turn around to his comrade and say that there's no need to get a doctor involved.

When we reach his building, we stop next to the doors at the front and he nods towards the dimly lit lobby within. 'This is me,' he says. 'I'd invite you in for a brew but I'm probably going to get some sleep.'

'Will you text me when you wake up?' I ask. 'Let me know you're okay…?'

'Of course.'

We stand for a moment and then, stupidly, and for a reason I can't quite fathom, I kiss him. Before I know it, he has a hand on my lower back and the other cradling my neck. He pushes back into me and presses his lips to mine.

It's me who pulls away first and we stare at one another in the gloom. I don't know what to say, so he speaks instead.

'That was nice,' he says.

'It was.' I'm not sure I mean it but I have to say something. It wasn't bad.

He nods and then turns on his heels. 'I do need to sleep, though.'

'You should.'

'I'm going to let myself in via the back. There's a second lift that opens up next to my flat.'

Harry gives a little wave and then disappears around the side of the building. I watch him head between a pair of bushes and continue on around to the corner of the block. He's barely out of sight before I have my phone in my hand and I'm googling 'Alex Peterson'.

Nothing is forgotten in the twenty-first century. If it happened, then it's on the internet forever. The browser blinks and then the headline is there in front of me.

MAN GUILTY OF ASSAULT

I click the link, though the details of the story are worryingly familiar. The guilty man is my former boyfriend's younger brother.

Ben's *dead* younger brother.

The specifics are as precise as I remember: Alex Peterson once went to prison for hitting a man in the back of the head with a bat.

TWENTY-TWO

I read the story through once and then return to the search page before reading a couple more with similar details. In essence, it's relatively straightforward: Alex broke up with his girlfriend. She started seeing someone new and then, after dark, Alex smashed the man in the back of the head with a baseball bat. It happened around half a mile away. He ran off, but there was a witness who identified him. It seems like charges were downgraded from attempted murder to actual bodily harm and, somehow, he got away with a three-month sentence.

There's an emptiness inside me after reading and re-reading the details. Should I tell Harry? Or the police? On its own, it's nothing but, bundled with everything else, it is one more coincidence on a growing stack.

Alex Peterson is dead, after all. I've been going to memorials in which his name is read out for five years now.

It's only as I'm trying to look for more information about other attacks that I realise I can no longer feel my fingers. I could call another taxi, but it's hard to justify more money for that – and it's too early for buses – so I walk instead.

There's another thing that has stuck with me: Harry asking about a 'crazy ex-boyfriend'. It didn't sound like he meant it as a joke, even though he laughed it off. The timing is extraordinary, with it being the anniversary of the crash. First the money, then the police turning up, all the times I've run into Melanie, and now

Harry being attacked. There are little things, too. The phone calls from Unknown, Karen's money.

As for Harry, I shouldn't have kissed him – I know that for certain now. When our lips touched, there was no spark; no weak-at-the-knee moment – if that's even a real thing. The little voice that won't go away tells me I can't be so picky at thirty; that Harry seems nice enough. It's surely better than being alone…?

The streets are largely empty as I walk across town with my hands in my pockets, but it isn't long before light starts to seep around the buildings as the sun creeps above the horizon. In seemingly a blink, the main road is full of queuing traffic, so I cut in a few streets to avoid the fumes. Kids in school uniform are booting a ball along the middle of the road, while one of them commentates on what's going on.

The yawns begin as I round the corner to take me onto the street on which Hamilton House sits. My bed is calling and I can almost feel the softness of the pillows as Billy snuffles at my feet.

I'm at the pelican crossing waiting to get onto the other side of the road when I realise there's somebody standing outside our building. The green light flashes as the beep to cross echoes along the street, but I stand transfixed by the man who's watching Hamilton House.

It's the person who Elaine pointed out was standing close to the hedges near the pub after the memorial service. The gatecrasher. He's wearing the same green fleece as the previous day but has added a backpack this time around. As I watch, he angles his phone up towards the building and takes what I assume to be a photo. It's with a chill that I follow his gaze upwards, realising it might well be *my* apartment he's trying to picture.

I move away from the crossing, tucking myself in next to a hedge and not losing the irony of how our roles are now reversed. The man scratches at his ridiculous sideburns and it's hard to know where the hair begins and ends. I watch for five minutes, but he does little other than check his phone, scratch his backside and watch the building. Figuring he isn't going anywhere soon, I continue along the opposite side of the street behind him and then cross at the far end. There's a lane that runs along the rear of the building and I follow it until I'm at the back door. In the four years I've lived in Hamilton House, I've only used this entrance once. That was after a fire alarm that, predictably, left everyone shivering in the cold all because someone downstairs had burnt their toast.

It takes me a moment to remember which key is the right one, but I eventually bluster my way into a freezing corridor next to the laundry room. I hurry up the stairs and let myself into my apartment. The room is a mess, with the unmade bed down from the wall, taking up enough space that it would give any feng shui expert a coronary.

Billy is in his own bed but clambers to his feet as I enter the flat. His routine has been blown to pieces in the past few days and he must be struggling to know what's going on. I take his lead from the back of the front door, which would usually instigate a mini Staffie-shaped bull rush. Not on this occasion. He mooches over to me with his head down.

I crouch and rub his back. 'Oh, Bill… have you caught something nasty off Judge?'

He nuzzles into my palm but lowers his head enough for me to attach his lead.

'I need you to be big and fearsome,' I tell him.

Fearsome is not Billy on his best of days – he's more likely to lick a person to death, or sleep on their feet to stop them moving. If Judge is ill, then Billy seems to have it, too. I'll have to ask Nick if he took Judge to the vet and, if so, what was said.

Billy traipses down the stairs at my side and we leave via the front door. I head directly towards the man, hoping the presence of Billy will give me something of an edge. It's immediately obvious that the man recognises me. I glance to him and his eyes are wide with recognition, even though I have no idea who he is. His hair is redder up close, especially the beard, and he looks younger – perhaps late twenties, as opposed to the early forties I'd guessed from distance. His green jacket is covered with sew-on badges, though it's hard to make out any specific words or images from a brief look.

I'm not quite sure what I'm doing. There's a part of me that wants to stop and ask him who he is; but another entirely that wants to hide. I sense the man's eyes on me as I walk past with Billy, trying to keep my pace even and my hand steady on the lead, as if I haven't noticed him. If there is any danger, then Billy doesn't seem to realise. I was hoping there might be another person or two on the street, but living in a quiet area has its disadvantages. Either way, I've got my closer look.

As I continue along the street, I try to block out the distant hum of traffic and focus on whether there are footsteps behind me. Would this man really be following openly in something close to daylight?

Billy pulls gently on his lead to head off to a bush where he sniffs and raises his leg. I wait for him, not daring to look behind… not yet. When Billy has finished, I lead him away from the hedge towards a zebra crossing. There's a moment in which I think the BMW is going to plough on through without stopping, but, at the last moment, the driver notices me and stomps on his brake. He scowls through the windscreen at the inconvenience of not being allowed to rattle along residential roads at twice the speed limit.

It's as I step onto the road that I risk the merest of glimpses to the side – to where the man from outside my flat is following at a distance. He's clutching his phone in front of him and possibly filming.

On the other side of the crossing, there is an entrance to a park. The gates are open and a group of children in school uniform are surrounding one of the benches.

I stop a fraction inside the gates and listen for the revs of the BMW's engine. It's humming gently, waiting at the crossing and then, as soon as the car pulls away, I step out from behind the gate and turn to face the man in the green jacket.

He's so stunned that he jumps backwards, almost stumbling off the pavement into the road. I half want Billy to snarl or growl protectively, but he seems uninterested in anything but sniffing the base of the gate.

'Why are you following me?' I ask, trying to sound firm and confident.

The man glances quickly both ways and then notices the group of children. His eyes widen again, the unease apparent. I've seen dramas with seasoned experts at following people. This guy is not a pro.

'You were at the service yesterday,' I add. 'Then at the pub afterwards. Now you're here. Who are you?'

He opens his mouth but no words come out. I wonder if I've misread things because, instead of being overbearing or intimidating, this man is tongue-tied and timid. I don't recognise any of the symbols on his sew-on badges but one has a slogan, 'Believe in Reality'. I have no idea what that's supposed to mean but it seems like the type of supposedly deep nonsense someone would post on Facebook.

I reach for my phone to take a photo, but Billy chooses that moment to pull against his lead and yank me into the park. By the time I've spun around to tell him 'no', the man is rushing away along the pavement at something close to a jog. I could probably catch him, but the young people have noticed something going on. One of them shouts across to ask if I'm all right and I end up flustered, trying to say I am while, at the same time, giving off every indication that I'm not. A couple of the boys in uniform start walking towards me.

'Are you sure you're all right?' one of them asks.

Billy has somehow got his lead wedged between my feet and in an effort to disentangle myself, I stumble into the gatepost before righting myself. When I look up, the man is almost at the corner of the hedge that surrounds the park.

'My dog tangling me up,' I reply.

The lads continue over to me anyway. One of them pokes his head around the corner and looks both ways along the street; then they both crouch to make a fuss of Billy. He's still not quite his exuberant self, but he sniffs both of the lads' hands and lets them pet his head.

'Thanks for checking on me,' I say.

It's not the first time that I've been upstaged by Billy. The lads call him a good boy and smooth his head and back until they realise their friends have started to walk off without them.

The lads stand and take one last look towards me before heading after their friends. When it's just us, I rub the back of Billy's head myself. 'You could've chased after that man,' I tell him. He looks at me as if to say, *I would've done if you weren't busy falling over my lead*. He has a point.

We head back over the zebra crossing and amble towards home. It wasn't that long ago I was ready to return to bed, but the weirdness of being followed has woken me up. I have the sense that the man in the green jacket wanted to talk to me, as opposed to specifically follow.

I'm lost in those thoughts as the shadow of Hamilton House falls across the street. I almost miss it and it's only because Billy pulls towards the lamp post that I don't. Taped to the lamp post is the thing I've been dreading since Friday. There's one big word at the top of the poster: LOST.

TWENTY-THREE

I can't stop staring at the poster: it is simple but effective, with black ink on white paper. It must have been taped sometime since last night. I was so focused on the footsteps behind me that I missed it on my first pass.

> *LOST!*
> *I misplaced something important on the No. 24 bus on Friday 29 October. If you have any information please email me*

There's an email address at the bottom and that's it. It feels incomplete, and yet whoever wrote this could hardly have put, 'I lost £3,640 on the bus'. If he or she had left a phone number, they could have been bombarded with any number of crank calls. I guess it had to be something of this nature.

I could ignore it, pretend it's not there or that I never saw it, but this represents more than that. This is a test of who I am as a person. When I first realised what was inside the envelope, I told myself I would hand it in. Then, when I spent a bit of the money, I told myself I would replace it. Gradually, over the past few days, all of that has eroded to the point that I've blown through a thousand pounds. Am I *that* person, or am I someone who'll email this person and say I found the envelope?

Money does strange things to people.

I take a photo of the poster and, after entering the hall, I let Billy off his lead and we head up to the apartment. He lags behind, tired from the morning walk. I end up waiting for him at the top of the stairs as he nudges past me, head drooped to the ground. After I unlock the door, he pokes his way in and immediately heads for his bed.

It's as I'm about to close the door that I notice a sliver of light arcing across the landing floor. The source is quickly obvious: the door of Jade's old apartment is open a crack. I stare at it for a second, wondering if it means someone's about to pop out or in. When nobody does, I head into my own flat, leaving my door open a small amount in case I hear any movement from the corridor.

I swill out Billy's water bowl and put down a fresh lot, then spoon some of his food into a separate dish. Billy would normally already be getting under my feet, ready to pounce the moment the bowl touches the ground, but when I look over to him, he's on top of the blankets that line his bed, his ears down, eyes closed. I pick up the bowls and cross the room to hunch next to him, before ruffling his ears. His breathing is steady but even and he opens his eyes to acknowledge me.

'Hungry?' I ask him.

Billy rolls his head to the side and I tickle his chin. He laps the water and sniffs the food, though makes no attempt to eat anything. I spend a couple of minutes at his side, but it seems as if all he wants to do is rest – which is something I can understand.

I return to the hall where the apartment door opposite is still ajar. I take my key and pull my own door closed and then check both ways along the empty corridor before stepping across to the other side. I knock on the frame itself and call 'hello…?' through the slit.

Nothing.

I knock once more, check both ways again and then gently give the door a nudge. It creaks open ominously, like something from a horror movie before the bad guy surprises the plucky hero.

'Hello…?'

There's no reply and I take a single step into the apartment. When Jade lived here, I would occasionally catch a glimpse of the room within, but I've never been inside before.

'Hi…?'

I wait on the precipice; one foot in, one out. Nobody comes to interrupt me. If anybody is inside the flat, then they're hiding. The decision is made, so I step fully inside and turn to take in the apartment. For the most part, it's a mirror image of mine. There's one big room, with part of it separated into a kitchenette. The biggest difference is that it's significantly cleaner and emptier. There's a sofa and a small wooden table – but that's it. The floor is covered with the same kind of vinyl that's on mine – but it's brighter and newer. The walls are bare: no photographs or other decoration.

After another check that the corridor is clear, I push the door until it's almost closed behind me and return inside. There is a bed built into the wall, but when I ease it down, it is only a bare mattress. It doesn't look as if anyone has slept here recently.

I push the bed back into the wall and then spot an Ethernet cable plugged into the wall near the window. The lead has been coiled neatly and left on the bare floor and there's no sign of whatever it might have been attached to.

The kitchen cupboards and drawers are empty and there are no products in the shower room. I've done a full lap of the apartment and arrive back at the door, wondering where the music I've heard comes from. All I can think is that it could be somebody's phone hooked up to a Bluetooth speaker. If it is, then there's no sign of a speaker here.

I'm about to leave when I remember the one place I've missed. If our flats truly are mirrors of one another, then there should be a wardrobe built into the wall close to the shower room. The handle is hidden within a foldaway panel, which wrenches outwards with a low, groaning squeak. The inside is dark and the rack is empty except for a single item which beams bright through the gloom.

It's so surprising, so striking, that it's as if I am momentarily paralysed. I stare for a minute, maybe more, until my limbs finally start to work and I reach to remove the coat hanger. On it is dangling a slightly crumpled red anorak.

Melanie's anorak.

It was the first thing I saw when she was on the park bench the morning after the money dropped into my life. It was there again after I'd been fired and walked out of Crosstown Supermarket in disgrace. It's been following me around since Saturday morning and, now, here it is in the apparently empty apartment across the hall from where I live.

I remove the coat from the rack and push the wardrobe door closed. It snaps into place but the creaking continues – which is when I realise the front door is opening behind me.

TWENTY-FOUR

'What are you doing in here?'

'The door was open,' I say.

Karen nods and steps into the apartment. She is by herself and stares around the empty space before focusing back on me. 'Empty, isn't it?' she says. 'I told you it was some bloke with a fancy woman. Nobody's living here. What would they do all day? There's not even a television.'

I step confidently away from the wardrobe as if it's totally normal that I'm here.

'That's what I thought,' I say.

Karen does a lap of the sofa and stops to check the Ethernet cable before deciding it's nothing important. She turns back to me. 'Mark my words,' she says, 'sooner or later, one of us is going to run into him and we'll find out it's some rich city banker who's bringing his women here. Either that, or it'll be a politician. Probably a Tory. You know what they're like. They're all at it. Try and get a photo – the *Sun*'ll give you a few quid.'

She glances towards the red jacket in my hand but says nothing. She either assumes it's mine or doesn't care that I've pilfered it.

I edge across to the door, ready to leave. Karen's seemingly going nowhere, though. She sits on the sofa and squidges herself around to get comfortable.

'Did you hear about Jade?' she asks.

At first I think she's talking about what the police told us, but her accompanying sigh doesn't bode well.

'What?' I ask.

'She was found in a shallow grave out at Dale Park Woods. I found out from one of the girls on the school gates. Her husband's best friend's cousin's half-sister's husband works as a paramedic and she's friendly with someone at the police. They reckon it's a full-blown murder enquiry. They've been covering it up, but it's all going to go public soon.'

Karen's at her gossipy best but stops for a moment, shocked by her own revelations. 'Horrible, isn't it?' she adds.

I nod, not sure how to reply. 'Horrible' feels like a massive understatement.

'Poor girl,' I say.

'I know.'

'Why would they cover it up?' I ask.

There's a pause and then Karen shrugs. 'Dunno. That's what I heard.'

Dale Park Woods is around thirty miles away and encompasses a large country park as well as, obviously, a big wooded area. It's popular in the summer for hikers, dog walkers and children. At this time of year, it's grim.

'Probably some stalker boyfriend,' Karen adds. 'Something like that.'

It occurs to me that, if this is remotely true, the man outside could have been a reporter. Perhaps he'd heard similar rumours and had come to ask residents what they'd heard? And I ended up chasing him away.

We sit for a while and I try to remember the last time I saw Jade. The way she looked and those times she stopped to say hello to Billy. She didn't deserve whatever happened to her.

'Do you think we should be in here?' I ask, suddenly aware of our surroundings.

The answer is largely self-evident, but Karen doesn't seem fazed by it all. She pushes herself up from the sofa and takes another look around before we step into the corridor.

'Should we close the door?' she asks. 'It probably stuck when whoever was leaving, like yours does.'

I make the decision instinctively, clicking the door closed, though continuing to clutch Melanie's jacket under my arm. There's no returning it now.

Karen steps away towards her own flat. 'Gotta get ready for work,' she says. 'I'll let you know if I hear anything else about Jade. There might be more when I get back to the school gates later.'

She's about to go when I stop her. The secrets are building up and mashing together in my mind. Melanie's coat is almost the final thing. I'm not sure how much more I can remain on top of.

'Can I ask you something?' I say.

'Sure.'

'When I was at yours the other day, I found an envelope in one of the kitchen drawers—'

Karen's features shift in an instant. It's not surprise, more embarrassment. She covers her mouth and nose with both hands and half turns away. I end up interrupting myself.

'I wasn't snooping,' I say. 'I was looking for teabags.'

'I know…' She huffs out a long breath and stares past me towards the end of the corridor.

I check over my shoulder, but there's nobody there.

'Come on,' she says, beckoning me towards her place.

'It's none of my business,' I add hastily, but she's already unlocking the door and ushering me inside. She rattles it closed behind us and then rushes to the kitchen drawer and pulls out the envelope I found the other day. Without another word, she upends it, sending the sprawl of notes cascading onto the counter. More bounce onto the floor and she chases them around the kitchen until everything is in hand. There are a mix of twenties and tens, but they're not neatly packed in the way mine were.

Karen shuffles them all together into raggedy piles of mixed amounts; something that hurts my eyes simply to look at.

'There's almost nine-hundred quid here,' she says.

'Wow.'

She unties her hair and runs her fingers through it, pulling out a knot and then stopping to stare at the money. I'm doing the same. It's what I've spent large part of my time doing since Friday.

'Where did it come from?' I ask.

Karen breathes in deeply and stuffs the money back into the envelope. There's no neatness or finesse. It's all rammed in together. She returns the envelope to the drawer and then starts going through her cupboards until she's found a bottle of vodka. She unscrews the cap and then offers it to me.

'No, thanks,' I say.

She eyes the liquid and there's a moment in which I think she's going to wrap her lips around the bottle and neck it. She doesn't. She slowly re-screws the cap and returns it to the cupboard.

'I should've told you before,' she says.

I say nothing, waiting for her to continue.

'When you've been babysitting on the Sundays, it's because I've been earning this.' She nods to the drawer and there's silence as I wait. 'The agency sent a few of us out for a cleaning job a couple of months ago,' she says. 'It was at this big old house in the country. I think they get us in three or four times a year to go bottom to top. There are ten or twelve bedrooms, plus two dining rooms, this other one that's full of art – proper *Downton Abbey* stuff. It takes us a whole week.'

She's out of breath and fills a glass with water from the tap, before swigging it.

'I got talking to the housekeeper and he said there might be a bit of extra work for me if I gave him my number. He told me not to tell the agency. I figured he meant cleaning but, when I phoned him at the end of the week, well… it wasn't that.'

Karen has another glass of water and I realise she's stopped to stare at the drawer in which the money is kept. I know that feeling of being indebted to an idea.

'What was it?' I ask, not completely sure if I want to know the answer.

'There are parties there every Saturday and Sunday night,' she says. She bites her lip and then lowers her voice. '*Sex* parties.'

At first, I think I've misheard her, but then I'm not sure if I should laugh or if this is serious.

'You go to sex parties?' I reply.

'No!' she fires back, before lowering her voice again. 'Well… yes – but not like that.' Her brow wrinkles and she squeezes the top of her nose. 'They were looking for a couple of people to work as greeters on the door. You have to hand out glasses of champagne and these wristband things that people have to keep on. Everyone's supposed to have an invite, so you have to check that, too. Then there's this giant rack where everyone leaves their phones and you have to hand out tokens. That's it. I don't get involved with *any of that*.'

This time I do laugh.

'Stop it!' she scolds – but that only makes me laugh harder. 'I don't understand what's funny,' she says.

'It's the way you said it. "Any of that" – like you're a granny repulsed by the idea of s-e-x.'

A grin creeps onto Karen's face and then she's laughing too.

'It's cash in hand,' she says eventually. 'All I have to do is put on a black dress and be on time. Nobody cares what anybody else looks like. It's every body type you can imagine.'

'So, every time I've been looking after your kids, you've been sexing it up with strangers?'

I burst out laughing before she can answer and she stands with her arms folded.

'You don't mind, do you?' she says.

'Course not. It sounds hilarious.'

The edges of Karen's lips twitch. 'It kind of is.'

'Where do they keep the tokens?' I ask.

'What tokens?'

'People check in their phones and you give them a token for it – but when they're doing all the sex party stuff, where do they keep the token?'

She looks at me and then dissolves into giggles. 'I'm not going to be able to get that out of my head now.'

It's a good ten minutes before we stop sniggering. As soon as I think it's over, the laughing starts once more.

Eventually, Karen says: 'I'm using that money to pay for my birthday party.' She pauses and then adds: 'Can I tell you something?'

'It's your fiftieth?'

'Oi! It's my thirty-sixth.' Her smile fades and she adds quietly: 'What I was going to say was that I've never had a birthday party before…'

The silliness seems to evaporate.

'I went to other kids' but never had one of my own,' she says. 'I wanted to do something for me for once.'

I touch her on the arm and then wrap an arm around her back until my head is resting on her shoulder. It was only a few days ago that the idea of going seemed like such a chore. I've spent days thinking of myself, how seemingly small things mean different things to different people – that lad with his 'only two quid' – but this is the same thing.

'How many are going?' I ask.

'I don't know,' Karen replies. 'People are being flaky. Lots are saying they'll see what they can do, that sort of thing. Maybe fifty, if I'm lucky. There are a few I know from work and others from the building. It'll clash with Bonfire Night, obviously, but there's not a lot I can do about that. I can hardly go back in time and tell Mum to stop pushing for a few hours.'

I feel her body relaxing and, when I let her go, Karen lets out a little grin.

'I've never liked fireworks,' she says.

'I used to.'

'They always stole my thunder,' she says. 'No one seemed bothered about my birthday because they all had fireworks displays to go to.'

'Shall we both agree that Bonfire Night and fireworks in general are rubbish?'

'Definitely.'

I take a step backwards and it feels as if things have changed. There was an innocent reason for all this suspicion – so perhaps that's true of everything else?

The sense of well-being lasts for about a minute until I remember I'm holding onto Melanie's jacket.

'What about you?' Karen says.

'What about me?'

'It feels like there's something on your mind. If you want to share…?'

She's read me better than I thought. There definitely has been something on my mind – more than one thing. I could unload everything on her now and see what she thinks. Tell her about the money and the music from across the hall. About Melanie stumbling back into my life and her jacket. About being fired and the man outside our building, who also happened to be at the memorial service. About Harry and how he was attacked in the same way that Ben's brother went to prison for.

Then I remember the poster from the lamp post – and the fact that somebody wants their money back.

It's all or nothing and I choose nothing.

Or almost nothing.

'I left my job,' I say. 'I didn't want to do it any more.'

Karen stares at me for a second and then leans in, wrapping her arms around my back. 'Oh, you poor thing,' she says.

I suppose I can add lying to the whole fired-for-stealing outcome.

'Can I do anything to help?' she asks.

I pat her back gently, wanting to be released. 'I don't think so,' I say. 'I think I'm going to have to sort it out by myself.'

TWENTY-FIVE

Karen keeps me chatting for a few minutes more, but we quickly run out of steam. I tease her a little more about being a 'sex-person' and then return to my own flat. I put Melanie's red jacket on my counter and am hoping Billy will greet me something like his old self. His food bowl is full and he seems to be asleep. I cross and sit next to him, but, when I touch his ears, he still doesn't open his eyes. His back is rising slowly, but that's the only sign of movement.

'Come on, Bill,' I say.

He doesn't acknowledge his name. His ears don't even twitch. 'Bill?'

I rub his ears and his eyelids give the merest flicker, though barely enough for him to see through.

That feeling of my stomach bottoming out is back again. It's like I'm falling, that everything is zooming past me at such a speed that I cannot focus on anything.

I've not had to take Billy to the vet for two years – and, back then, it was one of the most stressful periods of my life. Not only did I spend weeks nursing him back to health with the medicines, but there was a constant worry every time I left the flat without him. If he was a person, I could have at least called him during the day to see how he was doing. As it was, I'd find myself pulling out small tufts of hair in the ladies' bathroom, or biting my nails down even further than usual. I would pinch the webbing in between my thumb and forefinger for a reason I wasn't sure of then and definitely am not now.

It took me four months to pay off the vet bills and that was with denying myself anything but noodles to eat six days a week. My treat on the other day was an out-of-date pack of Quorn sausages that had got stuck down the back of the fridges at work. Jonathan told me to take them and not tell anyone.

Not this time.

I grab the envelope from the drawer, stuff it into my bag and then go to knock on Karen's door. Her hair is half tied back and she's busy pinning a row of clips.

'Are you all right?' she asks.

'Do you still have that child's buggy?'

She tilts her head, asking without words if I've gone mad.

'Billy's not well,' I say. 'I need to get him to the vet but he can't walk.'

At this, Karen springs into action. She hurries inside and returns a moment later with a pushchair that she folds out. 'I'd help but I have to get to work,' she says. 'Will he fit in there?'

'He'll have to.'

I take the buggy back to the flat and it takes all my strength to lift Billy into it. He opens his eyes a fraction but otherwise doesn't fight. I have to fix him into a semi-sitting position and then fasten the straps across his front. His head lolls to the side, his eyes still closed.

I've done all that without figuring out how I'm going to get him down the stairs. Karen chooses that moment to emerge from her flat. She heads towards me, initially muttering that she's late, and then going quiet when she sees Billy.

'The poor thing,' she coos as she takes the back and I take the front of the pushchair.

Between us, Karen and I get him to the bottom of the stairs – and then we head off in opposite directions to catch different buses. Through all of this, Billy barely moves. His head flops from side to side and he can hardly open his eyes.

I crouch at the side of the buggy and stroke his soft fur. I gently squeeze his paw to see if he might have some reaction, but he does nothing other than open his eyes a fraction.

'Oh, Bill…'

The bus seems to be taking an age to arrive. People pass and glance sideways, expecting to see a child in the buggy. Each time they let off a little 'ooh' when they see a sleeping Staffie strapped into the chair. Nobody actually says anything.

It's a similar reaction when the bus finally does pull in. I get on and show my pass. The driver says 'It's a pound for the little 'un' – but, when I step to the side to show off Billy in the pushchair, the driver makes the same 'ooh' sound.

I wheel him into the pram spaces at the front and sit next to him, gently rubbing his ears. It's hard to ignore the sideways glances from everyone either already on the bus or the people who get on. Everyone does a double take and there are at least five people who take photographs on their phones when they think I don't realise.

If circumstances were different, I suppose it would be funny, but it's like his sickness has spread to me. My throat is dry, my gaze unfocused. It's hard to concentrate on anything other than the softness of his fur. The desperation and desolation is overwhelming. I'd take every note in the envelope and dump it on the vet's counter if it meant them being able to make Billy right again.

The height of the step makes it an effort to get Billy back off the bus – but a man who's getting on helps after giving the obligatory 'ooh'. I'm in such a muddled panic that I start wheeling Billy the wrong way, as if I'm heading to work, before remembering where I am.

By the time I reach the vet's itself, I am a frazzled mess. I can barely get the words out to explain what's going on – but the woman behind the counter understands anyway. She quickly comes around to help Billy out of the pushchair, though all he wants to do is sleep on the floor.

She takes a few details and tells me a general appointment will be £40 – though there might be additional costs. I tell her to 'do whatever'.

After that, Billy is helped into the waiting area… where we do precisely that.

The receptionist is apologetic, saying that someone is already in with the vet, but that she'll try to rush me in next. I understand – but it's little comfort when it feels as if Billy is slipping away at my feet. I sit with him on the floor, running my hand against the length of his back, desperately wanting him to open his eyes. All he does is breathe and, at times, it barely feels as if he's doing that.

Time passes. I'm not sure how long. It's probably minutes, but it feels like an age. A couple come out of the main vet room holding one another and there's no sign of a pet. It's hard not to think the worst as they stand solemnly at the counter, signing various bits of paperwork before disappearing out of the door. They didn't stop holding each other for reassurance the entire time.

Another minute passes, perhaps two, and then the receptionist comes across with a fixed, flat expression, saying I can take Billy in to see the vet.

It's some solace that he walks himself, although it's as if it's in slow motion. His feet don't seem to leave the ground as he shuffles into the office.

The veterinarian is a young man, but I hardly notice him as my eyes stay on Billy. He asks questions about symptoms, usual behaviour, current behaviour, what Billy eats and more. I tell him about the doggy cake – but say it was from the pet store. He is concerned enough to phone them and ask for the ingredients, which they presumably give him, because he says it's fine.

That done, the vet looks Billy over and then shaves a small patch of his fur away, before syringing out a blood sample. The worst moment is when the needle goes in and Billy doesn't react. The vet must notice the horror on my face because he assures me there's nothing unusual for now, although I'm pretty sure not reacting to having a needle jabbed into flesh is – by definition – unusual.

It's time to wait some more. I'm ushered into a second, smaller area while the vet sees another pet. There is nobody else in the room, only a pair of chairs and walls full of posters about pet health. Billy lies on the floor at my feet and I have no idea what to do. There is only emptiness. Everything else that has happened in the past few days suddenly feels irrelevant.

By the time the knock comes on the door, I can barely say 'come in' fast enough.

The vet comes and sits on the seat next to me and reaches to gently stroke Billy's back. The silence is excruciating.

'It's not bad news,' he says, before quickly destroying everything. 'But it's not good news, either.'

'What does that mean?'

'There's nothing specific on the blood test. We can send it off for further examination but it's costly and, if I'm honest, I'm not sure it will be of benefit at the moment.'

'I still don't understand what that means.'

He smiles kindly. 'I think he's probably eaten something that's not quite right,' the vet says. 'Sometimes on a walk, dogs can ingest something they shouldn't. If it was something serious, something to worry about, there would be indications on the blood work.'

It suddenly feels like I can breathe again. 'He's got food poisoning?'

The vet nods. 'Something like that. I don't want to get too far ahead, but I'll give you some medicine that should help settle Billy's tummy. We'll give him some here and you can help him with a second dose later. He'll likely need to sleep it off and you can see how he is tomorrow. If you need to come back, we can look again.'

'He's going to be okay?'

Another nod. 'Give it a few days and he should be back to his old self.'

TWENTY-SIX

After Billy's first injection, the vet says he should be feeling a little sprightlier soon. I pay the receptionist with yet more of the cash from the envelope and then Billy and I sit in the waiting room for a few minutes, waiting to see if he perks up.

With little else to do, I type Jade's name into my phone and search for anything new. Karen's sources might have been dodgily third- or fourth-hand, but they seem to be accurate. Although there's nothing that names Jade specifically, there are now a couple of news stories saying a body was discovered by a couple of hikers at Dale Park Woods. There are few other details, but it is definitely not good. The poor girl.

It's hard not to flash back to the times when I saw her and wonder if I could have done more. Perhaps she was in trouble – and all I did was ask dull questions about how her course was going, or throw out inane lines about it being a bit chilly out, and the like. I remember Lauren, the building manager, calling to ask if I'd seen her – and how I didn't question that Jade had upped and left without paying rent. Karen and I both shrugged it off, while, all the time, something far worse had either happened or was happening.

I'm brought back into the room by Billy rubbing his nose on my ankle. His eyelids are still droopy, but he looks up to me and there's recognition. It's like the sun has emerged after a long winter and I'm filled with such relief that I have to blink away tears.

This time, Billy clambers into the buggy himself. I'm going to have to carry it back to Hamilton House anyway, so he might as well use it. Rather than flopping to the side, he wriggles himself into a sitting position and then waits for me to strap him in. He licks his tongue across his teeth and looks to me as if to say, *Well, what are we waiting for?*

I thank the receptionist again and have an odd moment of déjà vu. I was standing in the same spot what feels like hours ago. I was panicking that Billy might be dying… and now everything feels as if it's going to be okay.

It's a few minutes back to the bus stop and it's while we're waiting there that I get a tap on the shoulder. I turn to see Daff, staring at me curiously. It occurs to me that we've never actually seen one another away from Crosstown Supermarket. For all her offers of nights out and the like, I've never once taken her up. Our entire relationship has been within the four walls of work – and it's like I'm looking at an alternate version of her. She's in skinny jeans and a Pink Floyd vest, with a denim jacket over the top.

'Well, look who it is,' she says with a grin, before turning towards the buggy. 'I didn't know you had a—' Her features dissolve into a curious mix of amusement and confusion. 'I was going to say child,' she adds.

'I had to take him to the vet,' I reply.

Daff takes a moment to go gooey over Billy, showering him with affection that he reluctantly reciprocates by sniffing her hands.

When she's done, Daff turns back and slaps me playfully on the shoulder: 'You abandoned me!' she says. 'Jonathan said you'd left. One minute you were there, then you'd gone. What happened?'

I fight away a smile. I'd been worried about running into anyone from the supermarket in case they all knew the real reason why I'd been fired. But Jonathan kept it to himself. I don't deserve it.

'I was having a few issues,' I say. 'I talked with Jonathan and decided it was best if I left the job.'

It's politician speak. Off to seek new ventures, and all that. Spending some time with the family. Saying nothing in as many words as possible.

Daff isn't stupid. She waits for me to follow up, but, when it's clear that's all there is, she shrugs it away.

'I'm gonna miss our chats,' she says.

'Me, too.'

'Good luck, I guess. You'll have to come out with us one night…'

I smile weakly: 'Maybe.'

She laughs at that and there's a tug from within me, saying that I wasn't as isolated as I thought. It's true that I kept saying no to these offers of friendship – but they kept coming nonetheless. That had to mean something.

'I'll see ya around,' Daff says. She ruffles Billy's ears, gives me a small wave and then bounds off along the street.

There are more sideways glances and illicit photos on the bus. I'll be an Instagram star without even knowing it. Or, more to the point, Billy will. #BuggyDog #BuggyDogOnABus #BusDog

By the time the bus pulls up close to Hamilton House, Billy is straining against the straps, so I let him out to walk on the pavement alongside me. He's still slower than usual and there's none of the curiosity he would usually have for lamp posts, walls and bushes – but the fact he's walking is such an improvement.

After reading the news stories about Jade, I half expect there to be reporters or police hanging around outside the building – but there's no one. I can't help but notice the poster on the lamp post about the item lost on the bus. There's another taped to a pillar on the opposite side of the road, almost as if they're breeding.

Upstairs and Billy finishes his water in one go. I refill the bowl for him, but he's already stomping circles in his bed, trying to get comfortable. The vet bills were a little over £100 and, even if it was my own money, I'd have found a way to pay it.

I sit with him on the floor for a little while, but he shrugs me away, wanting to be left to himself. This is the Billy I know and love. Friendliness is one thing – but affection and sleep do not mix. Or friendliness and *his* sleep. He's fine injecting himself into my rest times.

Leaving him be, I park myself on the sofa and open the laptop. My *new* laptop, bought with someone else's money. I open my email, type in the address from the poster and sit staring at the blank space. This is the test of who I am and I want to be a good person. My fingers tremble as I hover over the keys.

Hi. I found your money. Do you want it back?

There's a moment in which I almost hit send, but then I read back the line and instantly delete it. My next attempt isn't much better:

Hi. I found what you lost. Do you want it back?

I run through half-a-dozen terrible variations until settling on something far simpler.

Hi. I take the same bus as you. What is it you lost?

I read this new version over and then send it from my second email account. It's the one I use to sign up for things online so that all the spam ends up in one place, while emails that actually matter arrive elsewhere. More importantly, the alternate address does not have my real name attached to it.

That done, I send a quick text to Harry, asking how he is. I've barely finished doing that when Annie's name flashes onto the screen as an incoming call. The last time we saw each other, I had essentially dumped her in a graveyard to talk to Gloria instead.

I'm nervous as I press to answer, expecting some sort of unease that doesn't come. Instead, Annie offers a chipper: 'Hey, hun!'

We go back and forth and she asks how things are going. I tell her about Billy being ill and she offers the expected sympathy before breezily moving onto the real reason for calling.

'Do you mind if I ask what you talked to Gloria about?' she says.

Far from being awkward, it feels like a relief that she's asked. 'Not much,' I say. 'It was all a bit strange. She asked if I'd made any money after the crash. When I said that Ben and I weren't married and that I hadn't, she went quiet and dashed away.'

'Hmm…' Annie takes a moment and then adds: 'She just called me with the same thing.'

'What? Why?'

'Something to do with a TV documentary that she's trying to pull together.'

Annie waits, as if expecting me to chime in – but I have no idea how to respond. It is far from what I might have expected.

'I think there's a production company involved,' Annie adds. 'They're trying to get her to sweeten us all up so that they have some idea of who might want to work with them.'

'Why didn't she tell me that?' I ask. 'All she did was run off.'

Annie lets out a dismissive *pfft*. 'Apparently Gloria's been talking to everyone – but only as individuals. You know what she's like: A complete nutter.'

I don't say that I'm not sure what Gloria is like. I don't think I've ever spoken to her properly before the memorial.

Annie continues: 'One of the others reckons there's a budget from the production company. She's trying to figure out how much she'll have to offer people to appear. If someone got a bit insurance pay-out, they might do it for less – that sort of thing. If she can get a load of people on board for lower fees, she'll get more herself. She's been banking on none of us talking to each other.'

'Has anyone signed up?'

'I don't know. Not that I've heard. I do have a second reason for calling you, though.'

She sounds reluctant in saying that.

'What?'

'Someone needs to tip off Alex and Ben's mum. I know you've got issues with Melanie, so I can call if you want, or—'

'I'll do it.'

I'm not completely sure why I say it. I glance across to the kitchen counter, on which her jacket is still resting. I suppose I was going to have to confront Melanie sooner or later.

'Are you sure?' Annie asks.

I don't need to think about the answer. 'Yes.'

TWENTY-SEVEN

I sit with Billy on the floor and he chomps down his food with no hesitation. He rubs his head against my hand and then puts it back down, closing his eyes for another sleep. It's a wrench to leave him but I figure I can get out and back in two hours at the absolute most. He's probably going to rest for most of that time anyway. The vet said he'd need to sleep it off.

Melanie lives in the same house she always has. It's on the furthest side of town from me, tucked on the back end of a post-war housing estate. These are the types of properties built when people knew what they were doing – with large back gardens, patches of green at the front and so much space there could be two or three new-builds rammed into the same area.

The first thing I notice about Melanie's house as I approach is that the curtains are closed upstairs and down. There are no lights in the hallway and no sign that anybody is in. There's no doorbell and a sign that tells doorstop sellers not to bother. The facia boards are brown with muck and the outside of the house is coated with a dusty murk, making it look as if it hasn't been cleaned in a long time.

I knock on the glass of the front door and wait. After thirty seconds, I try again, a little harder this time. I give it another minute and am about to turn to go when a shape appears in the distance through the rippled glass. It's a stand-off as I watch the silhouette slowly make its way towards the door. It's probably a good two minutes since I knocked the door that a timid-sounding 'hello' comes from the other side.

'It's Lucy,' I say.

At first, nothing happens; then there's the sound of five or six bolts unlocking before the door is wrenched inwards. Melanie stands there in tracksuit bottoms and a pyjama vest. She's either not been up long or has been in her nightwear all day. Her overriding feature remains, however – the malice in her stare. Her eyes boggle as if she can't quite believe what she's seeing. Hell has frozen over.

'What do you want?' she says, sternly.

'Can I come in?' I ask.

Melanie has turned into a statue. She's rigid until she bangs the front door open wider into the wall.

I was half expecting her to tell me to do one, but it's as much as an invite as I'm going to get.

There's always an awkward moment in entering someone else's house. They hold open the door, which means the person going in has to gamble at where to go. I bustle along the hallway into a kitchen I've not seen in seven or eight years. The blinds are down, leaving the room shrouded in a gloomy murk. There is mould in the corners of the ceiling and spider's webs in the window frame. The fridge is humming like a jumbo jet coming into land and there's a large tear across the centre of the linoleum flooring.

Melanie stands blocking the kitchen door. 'What do you want?'

I figure there's no point in niceties, so get right to it: 'There's a woman named Gloria who's going around talking to relatives of people from the crash. It's something to do with a TV documentary, but she's asking about money. I—'

'I don't want anyone's money.'

'Me either. I'm here to let you know, in case nobody else has mentioned it. Someone said Gloria has been offered money by a production company and that she's trying to keep as much of it for herself as she can.'

Melanie clucks her tongue and then half turns back towards the hallway. 'Is that it? I guess you can get off then. You've already killed my son.'

I should let it go. I've *been* letting it go for years. It takes some twisting of the truth for her to believe I killed both her sons but I've ignored it because I can't imagine how much she must be hurting from losing both her sons at the same time. Perhaps it's the time I've had with Billy, but something inside of me tugs. My skin tingles and it's like I'm about to erupt. I unzip my bag and pull out the red coat, holding it up triumphantly.

'I knew it!' Melanie shouts, reaching for it.

I pull the jacket away. '*You* knew it?' I shout back.

'You nicked it, didn't you?'

She makes another grab for it, but I pull it away once more; like a low-rent matador on a Channel 5 gameshow.

'What is your problem?' Melanie says.

'*My* problem? What was this doing in my building?'

Melanie stops trying to lunge for it and steps away until she's in front of the fridge. 'Don't play that game with me,' she snarls. 'This was nicked off my line and now you're here, literally red-handed.'

I can't deny that it's a good line. When she snatches for the anorak a third time, I let her pull it away. She glares volcanic fury at me and my anger of moments before has suddenly gone.

'It was stolen off your line?' I say, softer this time.

'Aye – and now I know who did it.'

'Why would I steal your coat?'

Melanie lets out a breath of such force that it's like a llama spitting at a selfie-taker. If I'd been closer, I'd have got a face full. 'You're the one who's been stalking me,' she shouts.

It's now my turn to splutter. I can barely get the words out. 'What are you on about?' I say.

'I'm in the park – and there you are,' she says. 'I'm having a quiet moment on a bench – and there you are. This week of all weeks. Can't you leave me alone? Don't you think you've done enough?'

We stare at one another. She's so convincing that I wonder if, somehow, I *am* the stalker.

'Don't you have anything to say?' she adds.

'I thought you were stalking *me*,' I reply.

'Oh, I get it. *I'm* the crazy one.'

'That's not what I meant.'

We stand on opposite sides of the kitchen and the buzzing fridge makes it seem as if the entire room is vibrating.

'Get out,' Melanie says, nodding towards the front door.

She's right – I should go – so I step past her into the hallway, although I stop almost immediately. There's a photo on the wall of Ben that's so haunting, it feels as if I can't move past it. He's precisely how I remember him – in a vest with the long tattoo along his arm that he'd only had completed a month or so before the crash. He's tanned, which makes the scar under his Adam's apple more apparent, and he has an arm around someone who looks like a younger version of him. It's Alex, of course, his brother. And, yet, in the few times I met Alex I never remembered them looking so similar. There were five years between them. Alex lacks the tattoo and the scar, but from this angle, in this light, they are strikingly similar.

'Look alike, don't they?' Melanie says.

She's uncomfortably close, yet I'd somehow not noticed. There's a smirk in the corner of her mouth as she enjoys my discomfort.

'When was this taken?' I ask.

Melanie shrugs and then, seemingly without thinking, her gaze glances towards the ceiling. I follow her line of sight, but there's nothing there.

'Why was Alex on the train?'

My question takes Melanie by surprise. She steps backwards into the kitchen: 'What?'

'When Ben left in the morning, he never said he was getting on the train with his brother. There's no reason for him to have kept it to himself – so why was Alex on the train?'

Melanie bites her lip. 'I want you to leave.'

I think about it and even take half a step closer to the door before turning back. 'He tried it on with me.'

'Who did?'

'Alex.'

It's as if the back door has been opened. A chill bristles along the hallway from the kitchen. Melanie is lost in the gloom.

'At a barbecue,' I add. 'It was the weekend before the train. He groped my bum and said he could see what his brother did.'

'You're lying.' Her words say one thing but the tone says something else. She knows it's not beyond the realms of something that could have happened.

'He asked if I wanted to pop upstairs.'

'You're a filthy liar.'

'I'm not. Why would I lie? He'd only been out of prison for a few weeks after whacking that bloke with a bat.'

It's true. All of it.

Melanie doesn't move, but her voice is a slithering snake's: 'He was provoked.'

'Because smashing someone with a bat *from behind* is always the way to deal with a problem…'

We stand apart, in more ways than one. I've never told her this before, never told anyone about Alex trying it on with me. Ben had an important week with work and I didn't want to interrupt that with tales about his brother groping me. I was also worried that he might not believe it.

After the crash, when it was revealed that Alex was among the dead, there seemed no reason to mention it, plus who was I going to tell? Things feel different now. I've never had that much animosity towards Melanie before, but I can't escape the sense that

I've missed something. Her jacket was in the flat opposite mine. The one from which music has been taunting me. I don't believe her that it was stolen.

'Go,' Melanie says. Her voice is a low growl. 'Go, or I'll call the police.'

I move towards the front door but turn back to where Melanie hasn't moved from the dimness of the kitchen. This is what I've been waiting five years to say.

'You can't keep blaming me for what happened,' I say, 'I wanted to marry Ben. I wanted the house and all that – but I had a job, too. I thought we both wanted the same thing. I never forced him to go on trips and, even if I had, I didn't know he was spending our savings to fund it all. He stole everything I had. He lied to me and he lied to you. We both have that in common.'

I can barely see Melanie among the shadow, but her outline slumps to the side as she rests on the counter behind. She says nothing. I know she'll never concede this point, even though she knows it is true. She tells herself I killed Ben because I pushed him to buy me nice things. She told me I killed Alex because Ben roped him into whatever get-rich-quick scheme they had going on.

'Just go,' she says.

'If you didn't leave your coat in my building, then who did?'

I'm not expecting an answer and Melanie sighs wearily. 'Go.'

So I do.

It's only as I'm out the door, down the path, and halfway back to the bus stop that I remember what she said in the kitchen. *You already killed my son.*

In the days and weeks after the crash, she would rage at me regularly at how I was responsible for killing her boys.

Boys. Plural. Suddenly, now, only 'son'.

TWENTY-EIGHT

Billy's ears prick as a firework booms into the night sky. There are still two days until Bonfire Night but nobody seems to care. Bluey-green sprinkles of light seep through my blinds, even though they're closed. It truly is the time of year when all the knobheads come out. All sorts of weapons are rightfully banned in the UK – but tubes filled with gunpowder? Go for it, mate.

The fact Billy is reacting to the fireworks is something, though. He's alert, awake and wanting assurance. He's eaten a little more food and didn't mind his second dose of medicine. He was awake when I got home from Melanie's and the turnaround is incredible.

I'm comforting him as much as he's comforting me. There was something about the photo of Ben and Alex that stuck with me in a way I cannot explain. The completeness of Ben's arm tattoo means it would have had to be taken close to the crash – and the brothers looked so similar. Perhaps they always had and I'd somehow missed it? It's hard to know.

For some reason, I picture the wolf that Tyler pointed out when we were trick or treating. There was a moment, in the murk, when the costumed head was down, in which I saw Ben. It was the light, I'm sure, and yet Alex was five years younger than his brother. Five years have passed.

And then poor Harry was bashed in the back of the head by someone in the exact kind of attack for which Alex went to prison.

You've already killed my son.

Singular.

I blink away the thoughts and keep Billy close as I fill in yet more information for the job agency. While I'm doing that, I refresh my email over and over, waiting to see if the person who put up the posters has contacted me. There's nothing but marketing. There never is. Dare to buy something small from a company once and they email three times a week for the rest of eternity.

The agency's questionnaire asks about, essentially, everything I've ever done since being conceived. I'm busy trying to remember what job I was doing eleven years ago when a new email alert pings.

Can we meet?

That's all it says. I reload the page in case it hasn't loaded properly but there are only three words. I think about leaving it there. Whoever this is doesn't know me and he or she had a chance to reply properly. Instead, this is what was sent.

I close the page and return to the questionnaire – except that I cannot concentrate. It still feels as if this is a test of who I am. Honest or not? Someone who takes responsibility for their actions, or a person who runs from them?

It takes me a few attempts to figure out how to reply.

What did you lose?

The response fires back after barely a minute:

I think you know. Can we meet?

It feels as if someone has breathed into my ear. My entire body shivers. If I was in any doubt that this person is talking about the money, then that's now gone. *I think you know*. It reads like a threat.

I only noticed the posters after finding the guy in the green jacket covered in sew-on badges outside the building. It could have been him who put them up. I wonder if whoever it is can now trace me via the IP address on my email. I've heard of doxing and that sort of thing. Perhaps the posters were a trap and I fell into it…?

Despite that, I still can't escape the sense that this isn't who I want to be. I was an honest person. I *am* an honest person.

I can't leave my flat tonight. What did you lose?

I read the email back before sending and then realise my mistake.

I can't leave home tonight. What did you lose? If you don't tell me, I will not reply.

The new version feels a bit punchier. I do hold the cards, after all. Or, to be more precise, I hold the money. No point in letting him or her know that I live in a flat, either.

The previous reply came after a minute, but nothing fires back this time. I refresh over and over until fifteen minutes have passed. After that, I manage to finish the agency questionnaire and then, for the first time in what feels like weeks, I go to the Open University website. With Billy at my side, things feel clearer and I finally get a little work done. No sooner am I on a roll, however, than my phone starts to ring. It's an 07 mobile number that I don't recognise. It's dark outside, close to nine o'clock. It's rare that anyone calls me at all, let alone at this time.

'Hello…?'

A tentative-sounding man's voice replies. 'Uh… we spoke the other day,' he says.

'Sorry, who is this?'

'I'm from the bus company. You called about CCTV footage…?'

In everything that's happened, I'd forgotten about my moment of madness where I pretended I was some love-struck woman searching for a mystery man on the bus.

He continues talking. 'Sorry for the delay, but I've, um, got them.'

'Got what?'

'The stills from your bus. There are about fifty. I didn't know who you were or what I was looking for. There were loads of people standing, so I grabbed the lot. You can have them all and figure out who you're after.'

He speaks quickly, one word blending into the next in a wave of nervous spluttering. I'm not sure if I picked up on it the other day but he sounds young. He has one of those voices that has definitely broken but still lurches an octave or two on the odd word.

'Can you email them to me?' I ask, partly because my email is open in front of me.

'I've already printed them,' he says. 'It's cash only.'

He stumbles over 'cash' and there's a part of me that feels sorry for him. I can imagine some kid straight out of school hovering around a printer while checking over his shoulder in case a supervisor comes by.

'Hundred quid,' he says.

'Um…'

'Okay, seventy,' he adds quickly, already talking his own price down. He's got the negotiating skills and business brain of someone whose last name is Trump.

'When do you want to meet?' I ask.

'Now?'

I almost say yes – but am reluctant to be out in the dark. 'It's a bit late.'

'I've got work in the morning.'

He sounds so pathetic that I almost laugh. I glance across to Billy, who raises his head as if anticipating what's about to happen.

'I'll have to bring my dog,' I say.

There's a sigh from the other end: 'Fine.'

TWENTY-NINE

'I'm so sorry, Bill.'

Billy is decked out in his winter coat and booties that protect his paws from the salt they put on the pavements when the frost comes. He's walking slowly and stopping every time another firework goes off. I figured being with him outside with the fireworks was better than leaving him inside by himself. After the scare at the vet's, I'm not sure I want to leave him anyway.

The guy from the bus company must live close because he suggested the park that's nearest to where I live. I walk to the gates where I confronted the man with the green jacket covered in sew-on badges. It seems like days ago, but it was only this morning. So much has happened. It's only when I get there that I realise the gates might be shut. There's a sign about the park closing at sunset each day – but, though the gates are closed, there's no lock. They open with a loud creak and I hurry inside, pulling them behind me.

This park is part of Billy's regular walking route and he seems to recognise it, tugging on his lead to go in one direction as I head in the other.

'Come on, Bill,' I hiss and he does as he's told, following at my side.

I agreed to meet here without really thinking about it. It was close, so I thought it would be simple – but I now realise how vulnerable I am. It's dark and there are no street lamps. The only permanent light comes from the moon attempting to glimmer through the low cloud. There's temporary illumination too. Sulphur hangs in the air and another rocket whizzes up over the trees on the far side of the park. There's a bang and pink sparks fly in all directions. Poor Billy stops walking and I have to crouch at his side to persuade him to continue.

The 'bench near the fountain' that my mystery man mentioned is a quarter way around the path that loops the park. There's no one around when I get there, although Billy does pull ahead to lap the water at the bottom of the fountain. I let him at first – and then remember what the vet said about him possibly ingesting something harmful, so pull him away.

Another firework fizzes and bangs from the same direction as the previous one. There's a second or two in which the entire park is illuminated and then, as quickly as the light came, it's gone. As far as I can tell, there's nobody here but me.

I do a lap of the fountain and then arrive back at the bench. The shadows feel darker and deeper than they did moments before. I'm not sure what else to do, so I sit. Billy takes this as a cue and plops himself on my feet. The cold wood of the bench is like needles through my jeans.

'Sorry, Bill,' I whisper. It's cold enough that I can see my own breath.

I check my watch. The person on the phone said ten but it's already five past.

I almost jump off the bench when my phone buzzes with a text. It's Harry, telling me he's slept most of the day. He's attached a selfie of him with the bandage stretched diagonally across his head. 'What do you think of my war wound?' he asks, along with a smiley face and thumbs-up emoji. I think about replying but do nothing for the time being. I've already led him on with the kiss and don't want to make it worse.

Another firework bursts from the beyond the trees and then, as if from nowhere, someone in a hoody is barely steps away. The person's head is down, hands in pockets. Billy hasn't moved and I yelp in alarm. This stops the hoody on the spot. I have to wriggle my feet out from underneath Billy's body so I can stand.

'Have you got the money?' the hoody asks. If anything, he sounds even younger in person. His voice trembles as his breath spirals into the air.

'Have you got the photos?'

He reaches into his top and pulls out an envelope. 'Money first,' he says – and I'm as sure as I can be that he's seen this in a film at some point.

I take three twenties and a ten from my pocket – more of the money that isn't mine – and hold it towards him. He stretches for the cash with one hand while slowly offering the envelope with his other. It's laughable, really. As if it's a cartoon Cold War and we're completing some sort of illicit handover. I suppose we are in a park after dark.

He takes the money and I end up with the envelope – but, when that's done, neither of us quite knows what to do next. It's more shy than spy.

The hoody bobs on the spot and puts his hands in his pockets. 'Right, see ya then,' he says. The stuttering nerves have gone now he has the money and he's talking as if we're mates who'll catch up again in a few hours.

'Bye,' I reply, and then he turns and dashes off towards the gates.

I unstick the envelope and pull out a stack of paper, though it's too dark to make out anything more than vague shapes on the pages. I tell Billy it's time to go and then we follow after the hoody. By the time we're through the gates and onto the pavement, the road is clear. It's a short walk back to Hamilton House and then, when we get into the flat, Billy saunters off to his bed, while I sit on the sofa.

The contents of the envelope are seemingly as promised. Images from a bus security camera have been printed on regular paper. They're grainy and monochrome and, initially, I'm sure they're from the wrong bus. I can't find myself in any of the first dozen pictures – but then I realise it's because I'm hidden by Mr Stinky. Once I identify him with his raised arm and phone in the other hand, I see myself slotted in behind. It's like a Where's Wally? puzzle.

The bus is even more packed than I'd realised at the time. The me from the past is looking down in every image, a complete irrelevance. When I was in the middle of it, the crowd felt hostile and overbearing. From the images, there's more of a friendliness. Many people are talking and smiling. Of everyone featured, it feels like it's only me who is disengaged.

Each image is time-stamped in roughly thirty-second intervals. I can see the moment after the bus had stopped and everyone moved around. The woman who was bleating about foreigners appears and, in the next shot, Mr Stinky has his arm down.

There's a claustrophobia that's hard to avoid even by looking at the pictures. One after another, there are limbs wrapped around limbs. People packed far too tightly for it to ever be safe.

I keep working through the stack until I reach the one in which I'm moving towards the front, trying to get off. I'm there in one; gone in the next. By that point, the envelope of money was already in my bag.

Unsure of what I'm looking for, I go back to the beginning. It's like a badly made flickbook of jumping images. People's heads jerk wildly, limbs flap uncontrollably… and then I see it. A face I recognise belonging to a person standing directly behind me. A face that, surely, shouldn't be there.

I'm looking at the floor, oblivious to who and what is around me – while, at the same time, there is a person so close I could've touched him.

Harry.

THIRTY

THURSDAY

One of the most common pieces of advice people give, or get, is to 'sleep on it'. It's often followed up with something like, 'It'll seem different in the morning', or 'It'll feel better in daylight'. None of that makes it clear what to do if sleep proves near impossible because of the situation, or if things seem exactly the same by sunrise.

I sleep in short bursts but constantly jump awake, thinking Harry is standing at the side of the bed. It's as if his presence edges across me and then I'm alert.

At the time the CCTV still was taken, we had been messaging back and forth on the dating app for a couple of weeks. We had swapped photos but didn't meet for real until we were in The Garden Café a little more than twenty-four hours later. I can't quite get my head around the images. Harry is in seven consecutive photos, but I can't work out if he's already on the bus and works his way forward through the mass, or if he gets on at one of the stops. There are only two pictures in which it's clearly him. One with a sideways profile; the other where he's glancing up towards the camera and it's a full front-on image. In the other five, he's either looking down or turning away. There's an umbrella in his hand, but he's wearing jeans and jacket, like the other times I've seen him. In all of the seven images, I don't look up once. I'm paying no attention to anyone around me.

When Harry and I first saw one another at The Garden Café, I remember seeing something in his eyes that I thought was a hint of recognition. I didn't know him, but I considered if he knew me.

I wonder if, perhaps, Harry takes the same bus as me regularly and, for whatever reason, I've never noticed him. It could be possible.

I scan through the faces of everyone else in the images and recognise perhaps one person – even though I took the same bus at the same time every day I was at work. That could be it, of course. I had a routine that was easy to follow if somebody wanted.

But why?

What reason would Harry – or anyone else – have for leaving the envelope of money in my bag? Could he be some sort of secret millionaire-type who's playing a strange game? It does seem like the type of thing Channel 4 would show.

I fold my bed away and check on Billy. He's awake but lethargic and I hide the next dose of his medicine in his food. He eats it without too much complaint and then I take him outside for a short walk.

Back upstairs and there's an email waiting for me. Whoever put up the posters replied a little after three in the morning. I'd said I wasn't going to contact him or her any more if the person didn't tell me what was misplaced on the bus. I half expected to receive nothing, but the message is straightforward enough:

I lost an envelope. I think you know that. Can we meet?

It's hard not to wonder now whether this is Harry playing games. If it is, then what is the trick? He is asking to meet. Is he gambling that I won't show up? Or is this going to be the big reveal that it was a joke, or an experiment, all along? I can't work out what I think is real, so decide to be assertive.

I can meet today. 11 a.m. at Chappie's café.

It puts the onus back on the sender – whether or not it's Harry: *Meet me or don't meet me.* It takes less than a minute for the reply to come.

See you at 11.

There's something unerringly uneasy about the confidence of the reply. I thought the time of day might put the person off – or the public location – but it is seemingly fine. He or she is unfazed by daylight and isn't at work. I could not turn up, of course, but there's a big part of me that wants to figure out the mystery. I also realise that, in all our communication, I've given this person no way of knowing who I am. I won't recognise him or her either, and so, unless the café is empty, there's still some anonymity.

I check Harry's last text – the one in which he sent a selfie while wearing the bandage. 'What do you think of my war wound?' it says underneath. It's a little flirty. I didn't reply last night and don't now.

As has been happening so often, I find myself counting the cash in the envelope. After everything else, plus the vet bill and bribe for the bus company employee, there is a little under £2,400 left. I've spent more than £1,200 in less than a week. I pack the cash into the same envelope in which it arrived and slip it into my bag, then I say goodbye to Billy.

Chappie's is one of the trendy new breed of café-bars that open before I get up for work and close long past my bedtime. The days of greasy spoons and the smell of chip fat in the morning is largely a goner. Now, it is all inoffensive background lift music and lattes made with any kind of milk, as long as it comes from a nut. By the evening it is imported beer from Portugal or Croatia

– nowhere too obvious – plus craft ales from up and down the country that are called things like 'Bloated Emperor Penguin' or 'Flighty Orange Fox'.

I order the cheapest coffee on the menu and it still comes to more than two pounds. I sit cradling it on one of the tables towards the back, far away from the windows. It gives me a good view of anyone entering the café.

The reason for choosing this place is that, despite the prices, it is comfortably the most popular café in the area. There are people all around. *Witnesses* all around. Admittedly, many are either hammering away on their MacBooks or sitting cross-kneed in suits and talking about things like 'this month's portfolio' and how Veena from accounting 'can't operate the photocopier, let alone an entire payroll'. It still seems like the worst thing that can happen here is that someone's poached egg is a little overcooked.

It's ten minutes to eleven as I sit and wait, listening into other people's conversations and meticulously watching the door for even a hint of movement. A waitress shuffles by and asks if everything's all right. It's hard to get a coffee wrong, so I tell her it's fine and she moves on.

Five minutes later and the only people who've entered are a pair of mums whose infants immediately begin crying. One child seemingly eggs the other on and, before anyone knows, everyone else in the café is shooting sideways death stares towards the women. The men in suits have seen enough. One leaves a twenty-pound note on the table and then they disappear. Meanwhile, the mothers have ordered a pair of pumpkin-spiced sugar-filled monstrosities that masquerade as drinks. Yet more pumpkinisation of the country. I wonder where it'll all end. Pumpkin Coca-Cola? Pumpkin tap water? Pumpkin Steak Bakes at Gregg's? There'll be riots.

Eleven o'clock comes and goes and, if someone is coming to confront me about the money, then he or she is not here. Or, they were here before me – and they're looking out for me in the way I'm looking out for them.

I eye the other singles around the café – and there's a bloke in shorts. There's always one. I'd bet that whenever there's an Arctic expedition, some fella rolls up in shorts and then shrugs something about not feeling the cold. He's busy beating a MacBook to death so is perhaps writing a novel or something. Either that, or cranking out one of those massive Facebook posts that only maniacs come up with and are definitely not a cry for attention.

There's a woman reading a paperback – but, if she is the person wanting to find out where her missing money has gone, she's doing a fantastic job of never looking up.

Other than that, it's all couples and groups.

I check emails on my phone, but there's no reply since the ominous sounding, 'See you at 11'. It's gone 11 and I'm not seeing anyone.

At five-past, a man in double denim walks in. He has a blow-dried mullet and looks a bit like Kevin Bacon in *Footloose* – if the Hollywood actor had been run over by a bus and then spent the following three or four years doing nothing except eating.

There's a fleeting second in which he glances towards the back of the café, settling on me. I figure this is it – he's going to come and ask what I've done with his money – but then he slinks over to an armchair next to a bookcase and waves across to the waitress. Two minutes later and his wife or girlfriend strides in and takes a seat across from him.

By ten-past, the waitress comes over and asks if I want another coffee. It will be two more pounds that I don't want to spend. I tell her I'm all right for now and she slips a bill onto the table while clearing everything else away. There are still no more emails. Quarter-past comes and the only newcomers are a pensioner couple.

My phone rings, but it's the job agency. The same enthusiastic woman from the other day asks if I can get to an interview on

Saturday. I try not to sound surprised, but the 'oh' is already out before I can stop it. I ask her where and it's an office close to Crosstown Supermarket. I've walked past it day after day for years and barely paid any attention. She tells me it's mainly answering phones, along with a bit of secretarial work. I'll have Sundays and Mondays off and work eight til four every other day. It sounds perfect. The money's not great, but it's no worse than Crosstown. It'll mean the same number 24 bus… my life won't change that much.

'Do I need to take anything?' I ask.

'Just yourself. They have your CV and questionnaire. They're looking forward to seeing you.'

That last bit does sound suspiciously made up, but it gives me a swell of anticipation. Perhaps they are looking forward to seeing me?

I almost forget to ask the time, but the woman at the agency is on the ball anyway. She also tells me that I should be there fifteen minutes before to fill in 'some form or another'. There are always more forms…

By the time I've finished talking to her, the waitress has done three separate passes of the table to see if I've left any money. She gives a small 'in your own time' wave that really means, 'I'm calling the police to evict you in ten minutes' – and so I check my emails one final time. It is 11:23 and I've not had anything since the last message.

I still can't get my head around the CCTV images of Harry from the bus. I wasn't sure if I expected him to be here, but, either way, I've been stood up.

After leaving some coins on the table – *my* money, not what came from the envelope – I get up and leave. The mothers are focusing on their kids; deformed Kevin Bacon is chatting to his other half and the waitress is clearing my table. None of them are paying me any attention – but, as I step out of the door, it's hard to escape the tingling sense of unease that, somewhere near, someone has been watching me this entire time.

THIRTY-ONE

When I get home, I go full internet nutjob by googling 'Harry Smith'. It's way too common a name, of course. There are news anchors, wrestlers, bakers and many, many others all called the same thing. Back when we were chatting via the dating app, I'd looked up Harry when he first told me his name and encountered the same problem. This should probably be the first lesson with online dating: never, ever choose someone with a normal name. Dave Brown? Do one, mate. Salamander Higglebottom The Third? Here's my number.

Next, I try searching for Harry's name alongside 'internet security', which is the field in which he told me he works. Results are still muddled, but I stumble across a LinkedIn page for a British Harry Smith who lists himself as a 'White Hat Hacker', working for 'Bright White Enterprises'.

The name makes it all sounds a bit supremacist, but it doesn't take much to discover that it's actually an industry in which 'good' hackers find flaws in the website or security systems of companies. They are either hired directly by companies to find holes or they do it off their own back in order to claim bounties. Some bloke made millions by finding an iPhone exploit and telling Apple about it. As well as making money, these types of people help protect the public from having their details stolen. It makes sense, but is the first I've known of this kind of job. I've always heard 'computer hacking' and thought it was a bad thing.

I can't find out for certain whether the LinkedIn Harry Smith is the same as my Harry Smith. The only real clue is that Bright White Enterprises has an office based on an industrial estate a few miles away. Either there are two Harry Smiths who both work locally in internet security, or it's the same person.

I take a few minutes to check on Billy and he's almost back to his old self. He has finished one bowl of water, so I lay him down another. When he paws at the door, I take him down to the green at the back of the building and wait until he's done his business. All the while, a thought is beginning to seed that's so clear it's hard to dismiss: could Harry have hacked into my computer?

He sent the first contact via our dating app – but part of the appeal was that we seemingly had so much in common. But what if he was able to make it appear that way because he had access to my emails, my social media and everything else? He *knew* what I liked and so turned himself into the ideal person for me?

There are a few issues around this. Not least an inflated sense of my own ego. *Why?* I live in a flat with one room. Two, if the shower is counted separately. I have no savings and barely anything to my name. I offer little except myself – and do I really believe I'm so dazzling a companion that a stranger would go to such lengths?

Secondly, if it was Harry who dropped the money into my bag on the bus, what does he get from it?

I finally reply to Harry's previous text, the one with a selfie in which he asked what I thought of his war wound?

How are the injuries now?

I've barely sent it when a single-word reply pings back:

Recovering!

I take a moment or two to think about a response and then go for:

Do you fancy lunch?

He texts back almost immediately:

Can't. Got things to do. Catch up soon.

There's a sad face and then a smiley face. I'm not sure what to think. I could ask something far simpler – whether he gets the same bus as me; whether he knew me before we met at The Garden Café – but they don't feel like the type of questions I can fire off in a text message.

Before I know it, I've taken Billy back upstairs and am hurrying back out of Hamilton House alone in the direction of Harry's apartment building. It's one o'clock, but the day seems to be getting colder. Clouds have started to close ranks, bringing a stinging breeze that fizzes between buildings and whips fallen leaves into a swirling frenzy. I was in such a rush that I forgot to pick up a proper jacket.

It takes an hour until I eventually reach the spot where the taxi dropped off Harry and me the morning after he'd been attacked. It felt different in the dark; emptier and quieter. In the middle of the day, it's brighter and more vibrant. There is an express supermarket on the corner that I'd missed when I was last here. People are streaming in and out, carrying sandwiches, pastries, bottles of water and coffees.

I follow the road to his apartment block and then realise I have no idea which specific flat might be his. There's a screen built into the wall outside, with a list of numbers and names of who lives within and the buzzer number. It is presumably to help couriers get hold of people they're delivering to – and far more advanced than anything in Hamilton House. There, the postman leaves everything in our hallway.

I scroll through the list but there's no 'Harry Smith' or 'H Smith'. There's nothing that's close – although there are a handful of empty spaces in the list of occupants for the thirty flats.

As I'm looking through the names, a woman comes out of the building with a little dog on a lead. It's one of those animals that's a cross between a rat and a canine. The sparkly pink collar is more or less the only giveaway. The dog tugs its way over to me, probably smelling Billy on my clothes.

'Sorry,' the woman says. She's wearing sunglasses for a reason that's probably best not to ask about. She's either a celebrity, a cataract sufferer or a lunatic.

'Do you live here?' I ask.

She glances back to the apartment block and then me. 'Yes…'

'Do you know someone named Harry who lives here?'

I can't see her eyes, but her forehead wrinkles. 'Should I?'

'I guess not…'

She gives a dismissive shrug and then hurries away with her dog. It's only when she's gone that I remember Harry telling me that his building doesn't allow pets. It's an eerie moment as I walk back to the road and turn in a circle, wondering if I've somehow come to the wrong place.

I haven't – it was definitely here that Harry stood outside and told me that he was going to get some sleep… He then walked around the *back* of the building. I never actually saw him go in. I head back to the main doors and then follow the path around to the side in the way he did. There's a garden at the back with a grubby sandpit nearby. There is a door through which people *could* enter – but it's hard to see why they would. I stand and watch the stream of cars on the far side of the road, wondering if Harry said goodbye to me, rounded the building and then disappeared off to wherever he *actually* lives.

I eventually do a full lap of the building and end up back where I started. As I reach the main doors, a man is exiting with a football under his arm. He holds the door open for me with a smile and, without thinking, I take the offer and head inside, giving a quick 'thank you' as if this is all perfectly normal.

The lobby to the building has a large unoccupied desk off to one side, two lifts opposite the main doors and a bank of mailboxes on the other wall. A slim tab accompanies each box, with a name of a person for each flat. I scan through them all twice, but there's no 'Smith'. If Harry is living with someone, then he never mentioned it. Otherwise, why wouldn't his name be on either the directory? Or the mailboxes?

I hang around the lobby for a minute or so, not sure what to do. There's nothing conclusive, not yet… but it's disturbing. I search for him on my phone again and re-find the LinkedIn profile. There are no pictures, no significant details about past education or the like – only the name and 'Bright White Enterprises'.

There's a local phone number attached to the company listing, so I call it. The three rings take an age, but then a man's voice sounds a chirpy: 'Bright White.'

'Could you put me through to Harry, please?'

'Who?'

I feel certain the man on the other end can hear my heart pounding. 'Harry Smith? I think he works there.'

'Don't think so. Are you sure you've got the right company?'

'Is that Bright White Enterprises? You're in internet security?'

'That's us. Still no Harrys, though…'

I stumble over something that I hope is a thank you and then hang up.

As far as I can tell, Harry Smith – if that is his real name – has lied about knowing me, about where he lives and where he works. On top of that, for a reason of which I'm not sure, he might have given me £3,640.

THIRTY-TWO

I realise as I'm walking home that not everything has to be quite as it seems. The LinkedIn Harry Smith could have added any company to his bio. He could've claimed to work at the BBC, or as Prime Minister. It's not as if anyone would be going around to check. Someone else could have set it up in his name. Other than asking Harry outright, I'm not sure how else I can check what's true and what isn't.

When I arrive back at Hamilton House, there is a small gathering outside. Karen is there with two strangers and, when she notices me, she says, 'Here she is,' with a sigh of relief. As I get closer, she adds specifically to me: 'These are Jade's parents.'

Away from their view, she raises her eyebrows a fraction in a clear apology for dropping me into whatever it is I've been dropped into.

The pair introduce themselves as Doug and Faith. They're younger than I would have thought and I doubt either of them are touching fifty. They are both wearing thick waterproof jackets and trousers, as if they've hiked across a moor to get here. Faith looks astonishingly like her daughter, so much so that I have to stop myself from staring at her. They have the same narrow face, with striking green eyes. I wonder if that's how Jade got her name. If so, it would be apt.

'I suppose you've heard,' Faith says. She's on the brink of tears already, not that I blame her. I assume she's talking about the discovery of Jade's body.

'I'm so sorry,' I say.

Both parents nod, although Doug is struggling. He's staring at the ground, biting his bottom lip.

'Did you know her well?' Faith asks.

'A bit,' I reply. 'She lived across the hall. We said hello a lot. She liked my dog and would sometimes buy him a pack of doggy biscuits.' I tail off, not entirely sure what to say because I *didn't* know their daughter. Not really.

There's an uncomfortable moment in which nobody knows what to say. I end up breaking this by asking them if they want to come up. It's with the eagerness of their thank you's that I realise this is what they were hoping for.

The four of us head up the stairs. Karen is at the front and halts outside my apartment. Faith and Doug understand the significance by stopping and turning to face the door of the flat in which Jade lived.

'Is this it?' Doug asks. He's gruff and his accent is far stronger than his wife's.

'Yes,' I say.

They stand solemnly staring at the door. In the meanwhile, Karen leans in close to me and whispers, 'I need a word.'

'You okay?' I mouth.

She shrugs, whispers, 'When you're done.' and then clears her throat. 'I've got to get back.' She shakes hands with both of Jade's parents and wishes them a safe journey.

'Do you want to come in?' I ask, nodding at my own apartment.

'That'd be nice,' Faith replies, and so I unlock the door and head in. If I had any doubts about Billy's recovery, then they disappear immediately as he trots across to Jade's parents and gives them a good sniff. His tail wags enthusiastically and I wonder if he can smell a link from these newcomers to the woman who used to give him treats. Faith crouches and makes a fuss of him as her husband watches on.

'Have you ever been here before?' I ask.

'No,' Faith replies. 'We live up near Dunblane and it's so far to come. Whenever we suggested something, Jade said not to. She came up for the holidays anyway.' She pauses for a moment and then adds: 'Does someone else live there now?'

'I think so,' I say. 'I've not seen whoever it is, but there's music sometimes. The building manager thought Jade had taken off without paying rent…' I tail off. 'Sorry,' I add, not sure why I blurted out the last bit.

Faith stands and waves it away. 'The police already told us that,' she says. 'When we reported her missing, they spoke to someone…' She swirls a hand around and then says: 'Lauren, I think. We had a bit of a row with the police because they were saying there wasn't much they could do.'

She sighs loudly and then we stand around for a second before I offer them the sofa. I ask if they want tea and then get to work in the kitchen. Billy comes over to check on me before mooching around the living room area, looking for attention.

As I make the tea, Jade's parents mutter quietly to one another. I can't make out a word, but there is urgent annoyance in Doug's tone. When Faith catches my eye, she presses her lips together and glances back to her husband. The whispering stops straight away.

When their teas are ready, I put the mugs on the table in front of them and then drag across one of the dining chairs. The room suddenly feels even smaller than usual.

'Was her flat like this?' Doug asks. I get the sense he doesn't necessarily mean to sound abrupt, but there's something rough around the edges with his tone. He'd tell someone he loves them and it would come out like a headbutt.

'They were mirrors,' I reply. 'Mine overlooks the road, while hers had a view of the community centre.'

He turns to look towards the window but doesn't say anything. I can almost hear his thoughts as he wonders if a one-room apartment is what their daughter's life had come to.

I have no idea what to say – but then I barely knew their daughter. Sometimes politeness leads to any number of inexplicable decisions. I'm sitting with a pair of strangers in my flat because I wasn't sure what else to do.

'Why did Jade choose to come here?' I ask.

Doug and Faith exchange a sideways glance and I can tell this is a point of contention. Neither of them speak for a moment and then, before the silence can become too uncomfortable, Faith lets out a small cough.

'She was looking to explore new places,' Faith says. I get the sense she's chosen these words carefully. 'She could have done her course in a lot of places. We tried to encourage her to go to Stirling, but it was too close. After that, we talked about Edinburgh, but she seemed determined to come to England.'

Doug snorts but seems oblivious to how we've both turned to look at him. He clearly did not approve.

'It's not a crime,' Faith says firmly.

It takes a second for her husband to realise she's talking to him. 'What's not a crime?' he replies.

'To be young and independent,' Faith says. 'If she wanted to put a bit of distance between herself and us, that's more an issue for us than it is for her.'

'*Was* for her,' Doug hisses. 'Not *is.*'

'She didn't die because she left home.'

Faith speaks with a sharp hiss. They stare at one another and then Doug thrusts himself to his feet. He mutters something like, 'See you in the car,' and then he's across the room and through the door. His footsteps echo away to nothingness.

Faith picks up her tea and sips. Doug's is untouched.

'Sorry about that,' she says after a while. 'It's hit him hard.' She has another sip and then puts her mug down. I have no idea what to say.

'Do you have kids?' Faith asks.

'No.'

She glances around the room, probably without meaning to. Even without speaking, she has a point. Where would they go?

'There were no real problems between Jade and us,' Faith says. 'She was home last Christmas and then over the summer. She liked her space, that's all. There's not a lot to do where we live and I think she wanted to be around people of her own age on her own terms. I don't think she even looked at courses in Scotland.'

Billy, dear Billy, picks his moment; trotting across the floor and settling next to Faith. He looks over to me with his endless dark eyes, as if he wants permission, and then he turns back to Faith. She rubs his head and he lets out a low, appreciative moan before lying on her feet.

'She was living somewhere else around here at first,' Faith says. 'I'm not sure where. It was too expensive for her, though – so she was happy when she found this place.' She gulps and then adds: 'Do you think she was happy here?'

It feels as if there's a spotlight on me. The truth is that I have no idea. Not really. What I do know is that, sometimes, telling a white lie is the right thing to do.

'I think so,' I say. 'She always stopped to say hello to me – and she loved Billy.'

That last bit is true and Faith bites her lip and glances away to the corner of the room as she rubs Billy's back.

'Have the police been around?'

'Yes,' I reply.

'Did they ask you about whether Jade was ever in trouble? Or if she was in a bad relationship? Anything like that?'

I nod. 'There wasn't much I could tell them. I'm not sure I ever saw Jade with anyone here. If she had a boyfriend, she never told me. If she was in trouble, I never saw it. She got in late a few times – but that's something we've all done. She was really quiet. The perfect neighbour, really.'

Faith nods again and gulps. It takes her a good minute to reply.

'I just wish we had a reason. I don't understand any of it. She'd call us once or twice a week – and would probably text most days. Sometimes it was just to say she had a lot of work on. We contacted the police after we'd not heard from her in over a weekend. They didn't do much at first. Our force said they'd contact the officers down here, but I don't know if that happened. By the time we finally got to speak to someone who understood, six more days had gone. It all got really dragged out. They were saying she was an adult, then I'd say, "Adults can still go missing." We talked to that Lauren, but she seemed more concerned that Jade had taken off without paying rent. We'd have come down, but the police talked us out of it. I don't know why we listened…' She tails off. It sounds like someone made a mistake somewhere, but it's all a bit late now.

Faith downs the rest of her tea in one.

'This has been very kind of you,' she says. 'I've imposed enough, though – and Doug will be wanting to get back.'

She stands and so do I. Billy follows us to the door and then, in the corridor, Faith stops to press a hand to the door opposite. I watch but say nothing. She stands with her hand on the wood for thirty seconds or so and, when she turns, there are tears streaming over her cheeks.

'I've gotta go,' she says quickly. Before I can reply, she hurries for the stairs and then I hear her running all the way down until the main door clangs open and closed.

THIRTY-THREE

Karen opens her door before I can knock. She winces dramatically as she holds it open.

'Sorry,' she says. 'I was on my way in and they were outside. We got talking and, before I knew it, I was blabbing about how I live on the same floor as Jade; that you live opposite and all that. After that, I could hardly wave them goodbye and nick off. Then you appeared and, er…'

'You dumped them on me…'

'Yes.'

'It's fine,' I say. 'I think Jade's mum needed someone to talk to.'

'I couldn't face it. When they were talking about Jade, I was thinking about Ty and Quinn. Sorry to pull the mother card.' She frowns slightly and then adds: 'Are you all right? You're white.'

I press a hand to my forehead but can't feel anything untoward. 'I think I might have a cold coming on,' I say. 'Billy was a bit poorly and Nick said Judge wasn't feeling well, either. Perhaps there's something going around and the dogs caught it first?'

Karen shrugs as if to say she doesn't have a clue.

'What did you want a word about?' I ask.

Her eyes widen as if she'd completely forgotten. 'It's a weird one,' she replies. 'I found some random chunks of meat in the hall.'

'What do you mean?'

She waves me across to the kitchenette and opens the cupboard under the sink before pulling out the bin. I suppose this is what friendship really is – showing each other the contents of your bin. If strangers did such a thing, there'd be police involved.

Sitting on the top are four chunks of what looks like beef or lamb. They've been cooked until they're a grey-brown colour.

'Where did you find these?' I ask.

'I'll show you.'

Karen takes me back out into the hallway, to the corner, where the light was out the other day.

'Lauren never got back to me,' Karen says, holding up the flashlight on her phone as if to emphasise the point. 'I texted her to say the light was out.'

I remember how odd it looked against the background of the other dim orange bulbs that line the hallway. I should have contacted Lauren myself. She's never that great at getting onto things if only one person calls or messages. It takes a degree of coordinated harassment to get anything done.

'Where was the meat?' I ask.

Karen takes a step towards the shadows and points at the ground. 'Down there. I'm not even sure why I saw it. It was in the dark, but I guess it caught my eye, or something.'

I step into the shadows, but there's nothing to see except the floorboards. There's no particular smell; nothing odd at all… until I look up. We'd assumed the light was out because the bulb had blown. It's not uncommon in the hallways – except that's not what's occurred here.

'What's wrong?' Karen asks.

'Someone's taken away the bulb,' I reply, pointing upwards.

Karen gets closer to me and, together, we both stare at the hanging light fitting. The lack of a bulb is something that, ironically, is hidden by the darkness.

'You found the meat here?' I ask, pointing to the floor.

'Right there,' Karen replies, indicating the spot on which we're standing.

She lives in the final flat at the end of our floor. There's nobody else who has any legitimate reason to be at this end other than her.

'I thought you should know,' she adds, 'in case Billy eats it. I know he wanders around the corridors. Wouldn't want him to eat anything that's gone off.'

She seems oblivious to what she's said. As if someone has accidentally left a bit of their dinner in the hallway. My thoughts are racing.

'I've got to get back,' she says quickly. 'I have things to do. Are you still coming tomorrow night?'

It takes me a few seconds to remember she means her birthday party. 'Of course,' I reply. 'Wouldn't miss it for anything.'

Karen heads back into her apartment, but I feel lost. The vet said Billy might have eaten something that poisoned his stomach. Judge was similarly poorly, too – and the pair of them have been allowed to roam the hall. That's what happens when dogs are kept in small spaces like this: there's nowhere else for them to walk.

Did someone poison Billy? On *purpose*?

I head along the corridor until I'm outside Nick's door. I assume he'll be at work, but it's hard to know in this building – everyone seems to keep different hours. Until recently I'd have been out during the day.

Nick answers not long after I knock. He's barefooted and wearing shorts plus a sweatshirt with a Marvel character on the front. His hair is unusually askew and it doesn't look like he's left the sofa – or bed – all day. Judge pokes his head around the door and the creeps onto the landing, looking both ways as if to ask where Billy is.

'Was I being noisy?' he asks.

It's only now that I notice that music is seeping out through his open door. I don't recognise the song, but it's some auto-tuned nonsense. That's all there ever is nowadays.

'No,' I say, angling towards the darkened corner. 'Karen found some chunks of meat left on the floor over there. I didn't know if you'd noticed anything?'

He stares past me and narrows his eyes. 'Meat?'

'Beef or lamb – something like that. She picked it up. I had to take Billy to the vet because he wasn't feeling well. The vet said he probably ate something that gave him a bad tummy. I didn't know if that's what happened to Judge…?'

Nick turns to look at Judge, who is ambling along the corridor in the vague direction of the corner. Nick calls him back and the dog turns and comes back to him with reluctance.

'How is Judge?' I ask.

'He was ill for a day or so – but seemed to get over it. If he'd been down for any longer, I'd have gone to the vet.'

We both turn to look towards the darkened corner of the corridor.

'That bloody Mark,' Nick says out of nowhere.

'*Mark?*'

'From downstairs. I told you about him aiming a kick at Judge. He's always had a thing about dogs.'

'Oh…'

For whatever reason, Mark's name hadn't occurred to me. 'He shouted at me, too,' I say.

'Did he?'

'He was playing loud music last week and keeping up Vicky from downstairs. She's got a young baby, so I went and knocked on his door to ask him to turn it down. He didn't seem too happy about it.'

'Give me a minute.'

At that, Nick disappears back into his apartment and pushes the door closed. I wait in the corridor, not sure what to do. A minute or so later, Nick reappears, wearing jeans, a shirt and shoes. There's something about his focused, determined stare that makes me uneasy. He re-closes his door before Judge can leave and then he marches downstairs, with me tucked in a little behind.

When we get to the ground floor, Nick turns and strides towards Mark's door before pounding on it with the palm of his hand. He waits three or four seconds before blasting the door a second time.

When the door opens, Mark is wearing loose basketball shorts and nothing else. His chest is like a Gruffalo's plughole that's not been cleared in a few years. The smell of tobacco and marijuana drifts into the hallway as a sloppy grin falls onto his face. When he spies Nick, Mark starts giggling to himself.

'What did you do to our dogs?' Nick demands. The sternness of his tone is somewhat offset by the way Mark is sniggering like an overexcited toddler who's been snorting milkshake powder all morning.

'You what, mate?'

The way he spits the word 'mate' makes it sound like a swear word.

'Did you poison our dogs?' Nick says.

'What are you on about?'

Nick huffs out in annoyance and jabs his finger towards Mark, who slaps it away. Nick steps forward, chest puffed out, but Mark is a good six inches taller and it is clearly the wrong move. Mark shoves Nick hard in the shoulder and, possibly because Nick is off balance – but likely because of the difference in size – Nick stumbles backwards, clipping his heels together and faltering into the wall. I reach for his arm to help him up, but his pride's been hurt more than his body and he shrugs me away.

Mark laughs. 'Whatever you've got your thong in a twist for is nothing to do with me,' he says.

Nick pulls himself up and straightens his top. His fists are balled.

'Don't,' I say.

'Yeah, *don't*,' Mark taunts.

I put myself in the middle of the two men and, though Nick only has eyes for Mark, he takes a small step backwards.

'Listen to your little girlfriend,' Mark adds, still laughing.

'We don't know it was him,' I say quietly to Nick. He glances to me, but there's something dangerous in his eyes. He's always been the quiet bloke down the hall and I've never seen this side of him.

'Run along,' Mark says, shooing us away with his hand.

There's a moment in which I think Nick is going to jump around me. His arms are tensed and there's a vein in his neck that's bulging.

'Can we go?' I say quietly.

It feels like an age, but slowly, almost imperceptibly, Nick's shoulders drop. He steps backwards towards the stairs, which only makes Mark laugh more.

'Is that it?' he sneers.

Nick mercifully continues to move away, but it's only when we're a floor up that the sound of Mark's door slamming echoes through the hall and I breathe a little more easily. When we get back to Nick's apartment, the embarrassment has started to set in. He mumbles something about keeping an eye on Judge and then heads inside and closes the door.

I'm in the hallway by myself, not quite sure what to do. Perhaps it was Mark who left the meat down for the dogs? Perhaps the meat isn't poisonous at all and there's a misunderstanding? I don't know any longer. Mark did tell me to 'watch yourself' after I asked him to turn the music down. He's not a fan of dogs, plus, generally speaking, he's a bit of an arsehole. There is a difference between being an arsehole and deliberately setting out to harm another creature, though.

I move back towards my own door, but as soon as I start to push it open, Elton John starts singing 'Rocket Man' from Jade's old apartment. I stop and turn. It can't be a coincidence. Not this time.

It's only a step across the corridor and then I knock loudly on the door. I'm not certain, but it feels as if the music is turned up a little after I knock. I try to peer through the eyehole, but get no more luck than I did the last time. Pressing my ear to the door gives no clues as to who's inside, so I knock again; harder this time.

Nothing.

'Melanie?'

The volume nudges up a little more.

'Harry?'

I wait, but there's no reply. There's nothing else to do, so I stomp into my apartment and slam the door. Poor Billy scuttles off to the corner and watches me sideways in case I start throwing things. I fumble with my phone, almost dropping it twice, before finding Lauren's name. She answers on the second ring with a cheery, 'Hi!'

I tell her who I am and then add: 'I need you to tell me about our new neighbour.'

There's a gap of a second or two and I wonder if the call has dropped. Lauren is one of those people who is constantly softly-spoken, even when telling a person to get stuffed.

'Is there a problem?' she asks.

'It's their music.'

'They're playing loud music?'

'Yes. Well, no. Sort of…'

'Hang on.'

The line goes muffled for a moment and there's a distant sound of Lauren chatting to someone else. When she returns, it sounds as if she's been laughing.

'I'm not sure what you're asking me to do,' she says.

'Can you tell me who lives there? Is it a man? A woman? Just a name.'

I'm sounding desperate and weird; something at which I'm apparently good.

There's another silence and, when Lauren replies, there's pity in her voice. 'There are privacy issues, Lucy. I can't go around telling tenants the details of other tenants. If there's a problem, I can deal with that…'

I could make something up – but I've already done too much of that in recent days. If I were to claim the music was loud, one of the first things Lauren would do is ask other tenants if they've heard anything. Regardless of their response, it wouldn't get me the name of who's on the other side of the hall. It all feels rather hopeless.

'It's okay,' I say. 'Sorry for bothering you.'

Lauren offers a brisk 'no worries' and then she's gone.

I open my door a crack and listen as 'Rocket Man' loops back to the beginning. Aside from bashing down the door, I'm not sure what else I can do.

THIRTY-FOUR

I lock my door and then wedge one of the dining chairs in front of it. Everything is a swirling mess of suspicion. There's Harry, with whom I've had two dates. Is he some strange internet hacker and stalker? There's the bloke with badges on his jacket who was hanging around outside the building and the memorial. Melanie's coat was in the opposite apartment – and whoever's in there keeps playing what was – at one point – my favourite song. Someone poisoned Billy – but was it Mark? Melanie? Harry? And then, beyond all that, someone left me more than three and a half thousand pounds for seemingly no reason.

I apologise to Billy, but he doesn't seem quite ready to accept it. It's not often I go around slamming doors and shouting at people. He remains in his corner and closes a single eye, watching me with the other in case I haven't got the tantrum out of my system.

There are no emails from the person who put up posters about losing the envelope. The last one I received read a simple 'See you at 11' – except I waited at Chappie's and nobody appeared. I send a new message:

Where were you?

I wait for a minute or two, but there's no instant reply. After that, I go back through the CCTV photos from the bus again; looking through all the images, not only the ones with Harry. There are other people who are impossible to identify. Some are wearing caps or beanies; others are angled away from the camera and never turn to look at it. There is one image in which someone in a cap is between Harry and myself, but they are gone in the next shot. It's hard to know what to think.

My phone rings with a number I don't recognise, which reminds me I've not been bothered by 'Unknown' for a little while.

When I answer, it's a woman's voice: 'Is that Lucy?'

'Who's calling?' I ask.

'It's Gloria, love. We spoke at the pub after the memorial.'

She's right in as much as we definitely spoke – but that's only half of what happened.

'What do you want?' I ask.

'Sorry about the other day. I think we might have got our wires crossed somewhere along the line.'

'Do you mean when you ran away after the memorial?'

'Well, er… yes… I'm sorry about that. Things were a bit emotional after the service and…'

She's presumably waiting for me to say it's fine, but I stay quiet and she's forced to fill her own silence.

'I should've told you the other day, but I'm working on a documentary,' Gloria says. 'It's all a bit hush-hush, so I'm sure you understand, but—'

'I'm not interested.'

Gloria has barely stopped for breath but hesitates and then ends up almost talking over herself: 'Sorry, did you say you *weren't* interested?'

She sounds stunned at this development.

'I don't want to do it,' I reiterate.

'Ah, but you've not heard what I have to say. There's a fee involved. Probably a few hundred. I thought—'

'I'm still not interested.'

Silence.

When her reply eventually comes, Gloria's forced sweetness of moments before is a thing of the past. 'You know, Lucy, you could at least show a little gratitude. I've gone out a limb for you. I know your financial situation isn't great, so I'm trying to help you out. The least you could do is—'

I hang up. Even on the best of days, I don't have time for this sort of thing. It feels like such a long time ago that she phoned and wanted to talk about money. It seems so naïve now that I thought she might have somehow been responsible for the envelope.

Gloria rings me straight back but I ignore the call.

Seconds later, a text arrives:

Did we get cut off? Can you call me back? X

I have no idea why she attached a kiss. I delete the text and then block her number. It's not even about the documentary. I probably wouldn't have been interested anyway – but if she'd asked in the right way, by explaining what it was about, I might have said yes. If it had the right tone, I'd have done it for free. I've never wanted to profit from the crash or what happened to Ben and I've had enough deception in my life. Approaching the relatives of people who've died to see who might tell their story for the least amount of money is hardly the right way to do things.

I return to my laptop, but there's still no reply to my email from whoever put up the posters. I'm not sure what to do next. Confronting Harry doesn't feel like a good idea – largely because doing that with Melanie gave me more questions than answers.

Billy is still a little wary of me and I find myself by the window, staring out to the road below. Groups of kids in school uniform are scuffing their way home and the light is starting to go. I always hate it when the clocks go back. It feels as if the final vestiges of summer have given up and there's only cold, dark and grimness ahead. For as long as I live, I'll never understand people who like winter. Summer is sun and light; it's optimism and hope. Winter is everything summer isn't.

Condensation is starting to cling to the glass and I feel my mood being pulled down to align with the murk outside. It's as the gloom is settling, in more ways than one, that I spot a familiar figure standing on the opposite side of the road. I duck instinctively, only risking the merest of peeps over the ledge in case I've been seen. I crouch and almost crawl away from the window until I'm out of sight from the road. Billy eyes me suspiciously and I don't blame him.

I unwedge the chair from the door and, when I get onto the landing, the music from across the hall has gone silent. No time for that now. I rush down the stairs and head for the back door but am moving so single-mindedly that I almost bump into Vicky in the hall. She steps out of the way with an 'oh' and almost falls into her door.

'Sorry,' I say, still edging towards the door at the back.

Vicky reaches out a hand to stop me. There's more clarity than when I last saw her in the laundry room. The tiredness has lifted.

'Did you, um…' She looks both ways and then leans closer. 'Someone put money under my door. You're the only person I told about being short on rent. I kept meaning to knock on your door and ask if it was you, but…' The sentence meanders away into a nervous smile.

'I won a bit of money on a scratch card,' I say.

She glances over her shoulder to make sure nobody's there and then turns back. 'I'll pay you back.'

'You don't have to.'

'I've got a job now. It all happened really suddenly. One of my friends saw a sign in a café and I went over there. Got chatting to the owner and started the next day. I think it might work out.' She digs into her back pocket and comes out with a crumpled twenty-pound note, which she offers. 'Here,' she says.

'I don't want your money.'

'Please take it. I don't want charity.'

She strains forward a little further and it feels as if I have no choice. I take the money and push it into my own pocket.

'Can we call the rest a gift?' I say. 'Not charity. I had a bit of luck and I wanted to share that luck with you.'

Vicky presses her lips together and takes a small step backwards. 'Okay,' she says. Somehow, in that one word, there's a crack in her voice.

'I have to go,' I say.

She nods and whispers 'thank you', before stepping to the side.

Some of my momentum has been lost, but the fresh air of being outside reinvigorates my thoughts. I hurry along the back of Hamilton House and then loop around until I'm halfway along the road.

The man with the jacket that's covered in sew-on badges is standing next to a postbox, partly in the shadows. His face is lit by the light from his phone, which at least means he's not quite paying attention.

I move as quietly as I can along the street until I'm within a few metres of him. He hasn't looked up from his phone and is busy typing out a message, when I grab his upper arm. He spins and reels back at the sight of me.

'Don't run,' I say. 'I'll scream if you do, say that you attacked me.'

The street isn't busy, but there are a handful of people going about their day. His gaze fizzes sideways as he weighs his options.

'What do you want?' I say. I'm trying to sound assured and in control, even though I feel anything but. I'm hoping the panic isn't burned onto my face.

The man seems cornered. He glances across the street and there's a moment I think he's going to run. Instead, he pockets his phone and takes a breath.

'I've got vital information,' he says.

I can't pick his accent, but it isn't local.

'Information about what?' I reply.

'About your husband?'

I stare at him and can see the realisation that he knows he's made a mistake. 'Not your husband,' he says. 'Ben Peterson.'

There's something about hearing the name that always takes me by surprise. Like hearing the name of someone who was once at school a long time ago. Someone forgotten that never quite goes away.

'You have vital information about Ben?' I say, although the words don't make sense.

The man nods. 'His brother, too.' There's a falter and then: 'Alex Peterson.'

'What about them?' I ask.

'I think the government killed them.'

THIRTY-FIVE

I'm not sure if there's a correct response to this sort of statement. The best I manage is 'Er… what?'

'The government,' he repeats, as if this explains everything.

There's a low wall near the postbox and I suddenly need to sit. It's been a long few days and this goes far beyond anything in my comfort zone. I rub the bridge of my nose.

'I think you should probably go home,' I say.

The man is pacing on the pavement in front of me but then stops to sit on the wall at my side. 'Don't you want to hear what I have to say?'

'You've been hanging around outside my flat for two days now. You were at the memorial service and then the pub afterwards. That's stalking. You should tell the police what you have to say.'

'I have!'

I turn to look at him, focusing in on the 'believe in reality' badge that's sewn onto his jacket. It's hard to guess his age. There are acne pockmarks around his cheeks but much is covered by his gingery beard. It's the lack of wrinkles around his eyes that give away his youth.

'You spoke to the police?' I say, disbelievingly.

'More than once. They don't want to know.'

There's a huge part of me that also doesn't want to know, but it feels like I'm too far into the hole to turn back.

'What's your name?' I ask.

'Steven.'

'What do you want to say?'

'The train crash was faked,' he replies.

I struggle not to sigh at this. From the moment he mentioned the government, I feared this was what was coming.

'How do you fake a train crash?' I reply. 'I saw the wreckage. Everyone did – it was all over the news. There was a helicopter beaming live footage. There were photographers on the ground.'

'The crash was real,' Steven replies, 'it was the reasons that were faked.'

'What reasons?'

'They said it was an issue with the signalling; then the lights and the brakes – but our research shows there was a Russian spy on board. It was an undercover job to kill the spy and make everything else *look* like an accident. Everyone who died was collateral damage.'

I turn to stare at him, but he gazes back at me with such earnest certainty that I have to look away again.

'It was an undercover job to make it *look* like an accident,' he adds.

'You believe the moon landings were faked, don't you?' I reply.

'They were!'

'And that 9/11 was staged. That the London bombings in 2005 were an MI6 plot.'

'MI5,' he corrects.

It's hard not to sigh again. I rub my forehead, but Steven seems oblivious to my scepticism.

'Why are you telling me this?' I ask. 'Twenty-five people died in the crash and I only knew two of them.'

Steven shrugs. 'Alphabetical order. A for Alex, B for Ben. The police weren't listening and nobody was visiting my website. What else was I supposed to do?'

'Leave it?' I reply.

'That's what they want people to do.'

'Of course they do.'

Steven doesn't pick up on the sarcasm or exasperation.

'How did you know where I live?' I ask.

'Google and the electoral roll. I'm going to talk to everyone eventually.'

He holds up his phone to illustrate the point and I resolve that, as soon as I'm done here, I'll put my first post on the secret Facebook page to warn people. I didn't realise people's addresses could be found so easily simply because they'd registered to vote. That's assuming he's telling the truth.

I figure I might as well get the full story from him in order to pass it on.

'You're saying "they" deliberately staged a train crash in order to assassinate a Russian agent?' I ask.

'Exactly! They say the driver died in the crash, but our sources have him living in Venezuela. He was in on the whole thing.'

'Who's "they"?' I ask.

'The government, the MSM, the NWO. All of them.'

'And why is the driver in Venezuela?'

'We've not been able to get proof of that yet.'

I don't ask about the 'we' to whom he's referring, nor what MSM or NWO stand for. I could probably check the internet – but I'm guessing that's where many of Steven's theories have come from. I should probably leave. The number of cars and people passing has slowed to a minimum and we're in the shadows. It's not that I feel unsafe, more uneasy. I wish Billy was here, if only as comfort.

All of a sudden, Steven's shoulders slump. 'You don't believe me, do you?' he says wearily.

'No, I don't.'

He wags his phone towards me, but it's more comical than threatening. 'Tell me this,' he says. 'Say the crash was perfectly normal. It was an "accident"' – he makes bunny ears with his fingers – 'where did you bury Ben Peterson's body?'

'You already know the answer, so why ask?'

He claps his hands together as if he's caught me out. 'Exactly,' he says. 'You didn't bury him. And, why?'

I wait, not particularly wanting to engage but somehow needing to hear it.

'Because that fire,' he adds, 'if there was one – burned so hot that all they found was ash.'

'They found more than ash,' I say.

'Well, yes… bags and jewellery, that sort of thing—'

'And there was definitely a fire,' I say. 'There are photos of it.'

'Photos can be doctored.'

'There are video images *from a helicopter*. There are scorch marks on the ground. Parts of the rails melted. Someone was live-streaming it from their bedroom with their phone.'

'Well, okay, there probably was a fire but—'

'There was *definitely* a fire.'

'Right, but that's not important. What's important is that you never buried a body. Hardly anybody did. Most of the coffins were empty.'

This is one thing on which we can agree. Most of the coffins *were* empty. Not that it means very much. There was a fire after the crash and, in one carriage in particular, there was very little left. There was a public inquiry that discovered serious safety lapses on the maintenance.

'How can a train burn that much?' Steven asks.

'I don't know. I'm not an expert – but there was an expert at the inquiry and she said—'

'She was a plant. An actress. We found stills of her starring in a Ukrainian soap opera. Where did the extra fuel come from?'

'I don't know what you're talking about.'

'Exactly!'

He thrusts his phone forward again, like this is a huge a-ha moment. That he's caught me out. The 'believe in reality' badge on his lapel reads increasingly like the rantings of a nutjob. I *do* believe in reality; I think it's Steven who doesn't.

'There's more,' he says.

'I think I've heard enough.'

Steven throws his hands up and jumps off the wall. It's such a shock that I almost tumble backwards in an attempt to escape one of his flailing arms.

'Fine!' he shouts. 'Don't believe me. Maybe you're in on it too? I didn't realise it went this far. You're one of them.'

'One of who?'

'The illuminati.'

I sigh and rub my forehead once more, pushing myself up until I'm standing. The lights from Hamilton House seem so appealing. The central heating will have kicked in by now and, despite what I think of it, my flat can be deliciously cosy on these types of evening.

'Is this the lizard thing?' I say. 'Because, if it is, I'm definitely not a lizard.'

'Of course it's not the lizard thing,' he replies – as if *I'm* the one spouting conspiracy theories. He digs into an inside pocket and pulls out a card that he thrusts towards me. I take it, largely through politeness. 'Contact me if you want to talk like a rational human being,' he says. 'My phone and email is on there – but don't use those. They can watch that. Use Signal.'

I start to ask what Signal is and then stop myself, not wanting to know. I definitely won't be contacting him.

'My website's on there, too,' he says. 'If your mind isn't completely closed, have a look.'

'I will,' I say, not meaning it.

It seems to take him by surprise because he stops flapping and straightens his jacket instead.

'Oh,' he says.

'Is that it?' I ask.

'Check the website,' he replies. 'There's so much more.'

THIRTY-SIX

Curiosity got the better of me. If there was one thing about which Steven was correct, it is that there is definitely 'so much more' on his website. It's a wacky mess of bright colours and flashing slogans. It's hard not to wonder if I'm going to end up on some government watch list simply for browsing it. There are theories about everything from the existence of the Loch Ness Monster (an alien) to why *Coronation Street* is on so often (brainwashing through subliminal messages).

The section on the train crash is largely what Steven told me. Something to do with a Russian spy, MI5, Venezuela… and plenty more. There are grainy freeze-frames of overseas news broadcasts that are thrown up as 'proof', even though it's impossible to make out what anything is. I scan for my name but, thankfully, there's no sign. None of the victims are named and it's hard to tell why Steven thinks now is the best time to bring everything up. I can only imagine it's because of the anniversary.

There are articles about the 'big ones' – the moon landings, 9/11, JFK, and so on. The general conclusion seems to be that it was all faked by the government illuminati. I was aware of this corner of the internet – but had never done much exploring. I wish I'd maintained that record.

I'm distracted by a knock at the door. It's Nick with Judge at his side. He offers a knowing smile.

'Sorry about earlier,' he says. 'I don't know what came over me. I think it was the thought of someone wanting to hurt Judge.'

The dog has scampered past me and is egging on Billy to get up to no good. There doesn't seem to be a lot wrong with either of them now as they twist in circles, sniffing one another's backsides.

'Do you want to sit in together?' he adds, nodding towards the window. 'I think it's going to be a noisy one tonight.'

It seems like a far more appealing thing to do than continue to browse conspiracy theories, so it's an easy choice. The hall is silent as I follow Nick back to his apartment; the two dogs in pursuit. His flat is the same size as mine but filled with an array of throws, quilts and carpets. It's like a market stall of Marrakesh – or at least the photos. I've never seen the curtains open and the entire space seems to live in permanent murk. Not that the dogs mind. As soon as Nick opens the door, they shoot past us and start playing with the squeaky toys in the corner. Content and occupied, neither seems to notice the booming firework that explodes into the evening sky outside. Bonfire Night is still twenty-four hours away – but the fizzes and bangs tonight won't be far off tomorrow's total.

Nick offers me a drink, either flavoured water, kombucha or some sort of fruity wine. I go for the wine and then, after I've shifted a dozen cushions, we settle on the sofa.

'I still think it was Mark who tried to poison the dogs,' Nick says.

'There's not a lot anyone can do without proof.'

'Who else would it be? I don't have any other enemies in the building. Do you?'

I say that I don't and fail to bring up the new occupant of the flat opposite mine – whoever that may be.

Nick wants to gossip about Jade – and so that's what we do. I'm not sure if he knew her any better than me, but he does bring up a night the pair of them went drinking together. 'She was completely ratted,' he says – but there's not a lot more information than that. Nobody seems to have a bad word to say about her. That's always the way, I suppose. Whenever something unexpected happens in a community, it's either, 'We never guessed it could have been him' or 'Yeah, we all knew he was a lunatic'. There's never a middle ground.

The dogs start begging to be let into the hallway and it's clear they're a bad influence on one another. Nick is staring at his phone but glances up to tell Judge there will be no more excursions around the corridors and it doesn't seem as if we have any other choice. Someone in the building left meat that was probably poisoned and there's nothing to stop whoever it was doing the same again.

Nick asks about Karen's party and seems far more excited than I am. Neither of us are sure if it's fancy dress, but he says he's going as a sexy zombie anyway. I don't ask what that entails.

We chat and laugh as Nick gets gradually tipsier. The dogs need regular assurance that the bangs outside aren't going to get them and it's not long before I have Judge and Billy resting themselves across me on the sofa.

We've been chatting for a while when Nick's phone rings. He's been checking it intermittently and his features darken when he says 'I've got to take this', before nipping into the corridor. I suddenly get the sense he's been expecting whoever this is to call through the evening. Part of the reason he's invited me over is for moral support after whatever happens.

The dogs are both asleep and I'm somewhat trapped, so take out my phone. It's as I'm reading Harry's texts that I realise I'm a little tipsy, too. Rather than being a concern, it suddenly feels hilarious that he might be stalking me.

I have a strange sense of self-awareness in that I know it's a bad idea to contact him and yet the booze on an empty stomach makes me wonder if it is, in fact, a terrific idea. They say there's a fine line between genius and lunacy and I feel like walking it.

My first message is as direct as can be:

Can we meet?

Harry's reply doesn't take long:

Sure! When were you thinking?

The excessive exclamation points are really becoming quite the plague. It's a bit like herpes: a person should remain single until they've got rid of it.

I type out 'later?' and then delete it, before going for:

Tomorrow?

Even in my tipsy state, I realise that this evening would be a bad idea. I'm going to need to plan what to say and to be a good eighty per cent less giggly than I currently am.

I down what's left in my glass and refill it with Nick's wine. It isn't even that good – but that isn't the point. I find myself wondering if Harry is currently sitting in the apartment opposite mine, playing Elton John. Perhaps he already knew about Ben – and then stole Melanie's coat to throw me off the scent?

The madder my thoughts, the funnier I find it all – and then I'm texting again, before he's had time to reply:

How are you?

I picture him in the hospital, his head dented from when he was hit.

His reply comes almost immediately:

The painkillers help! Self-medicating with Jack Daniel's! Looking fwd to seeing you! What time?! Where?!

Give! It! A! Rest!

It's the alcohol, I know, but I wonder if he was really attacked. If this was all some massive ruse to woo me. Give me money to get me off guard, convince me he likes everything I do and, if things aren't going perfectly, concoct some sort of attack to make me feel sorry for him. When Harry was in hospital, it was *me* he called. Not family or friends – a woman he'd only met twice.

It doesn't add up.

At Chappie's Café? 11 a.m.? Do the police have any leads about who attacked you?

I'm not sure what I expect back, but the reply is straightforward enough:

11 is good. Haven't heard from the police. CU2moz!

The biggest problem I have with all this is why would anybody bother with it all? If Harry is trying to con me into a relationship, am I that desirable? Do I offer something that another person couldn't? Or is he after something else?

I leave the text messages there and it's only a few seconds later that Nick returns. He seems shattered and pours himself the rest of the wine, downing half a glass in one.

'It's Ravi,' he says. 'He wants to break up.'

I let Nick talk and offer the odd consoling word. Alcohol gets me giddy, but it's all tears for Nick as he tells me everything that's been going on in his relationship for, seemingly, the past two years. He opens a second bottle, but I wave it away, worried I'll have a thick head in the morning.

It's possibly because he's been talking for so long, but I almost miss Nick's throwaway line. I have to stop him with, 'Sorry, what did you say?'

He pauses mid-sentence and then repeats what I thought he had. 'I said perhaps I should cry on the shoulder of the guy across the hall from you.'

'You've seen the person who lives opposite me?' I reply, suddenly feeling sober.

Nick shrugs as if this is a perfectly normal thing. 'He was on his way out one day. We nodded to each other on the stairs.'

'You *nodded*?'

He breaks into a boozy giggle. 'Is it that hard to believe?'

My thoughts suddenly feel very focused. It's not Melanie who's been across the hall: it's a man. Perhaps it is Harry…?

'What does he look like?' I ask.

Nick purses his lips and holds his arm up. 'Tall and dark. A bit stubbly. My type.'

I dig for my phone and swipe through the pictures until I find one of Harry. 'Like this?' I ask, flipping the screen around.

Nick shakes his head. 'It's not like I was staring – but I'm pretty sure that's not him.' He pauses and then adds: 'Why? Do you think you know him?'

'I don't know.'

We sit for a moment and I'm almost disappointed. There's a huge part of me that wants to be wrong about Harry – but things would've been so much clearer if Nick had said yes.

I keep scrolling through photos, flicking further and further back in time. There are so many of Billy. He's in the park, chasing around with another dog; he's at Parkrun; he's on the beach barking at the ocean; he's pounced on an ice cream that I dropped. The years flash by until it's before Billy came into my life. There's an enormous gap that means only desolation and acceptance. My life changed for the worse and I didn't feel the need to catalogue it. Back further and there he is. It's Ben and me at a festival the summer before the train crash. I'm in a pork pie hat and he's giving the camera a thumbs-up. Memories never die in these modern times.

I'm not sure why I do it, but I zoom in on Ben's face and then turn the phone for Nick to see.

'How about him?' I ask.

I expect a shake of the head, an instant 'no', but that's not what happens.

Nick pouts out his bottom lip and squints.

'Maybe… he was sort of similar, but this guy had longer hair. He was wearing a cap. It's hard to say.'

I have no idea how to reply and Nick follows up with, 'Do you know him?'

'Perhaps…'

Nick reaches for the phone and has a closer look. He leans in and pinches the screen before handing the phone back with a scratch of the head. 'This guy is a bit different. I can't explain what I mean. The same but not the same.'

'Like a brother?'

He clicks his fingers. 'Yeah,' Nick says. 'Like a brother.'

THIRTY-SEVEN

FRIDAY

I have no idea what people with no job fill their time with. After waking up, I decide I'm definitely going to do some university work, but then resolve that I won't be able to concentrate until I've had my showdown with Harry. I try television, but Piers Morgan's face is as appealing as a yeast infection. After that, it's the radio – but there's a phone-in and Steve from Basildon is arguing with a Nobel prize-winning economist about how finance works, so that goes off, too.

I take Billy for a walk that's as long as he can handle and, as best I can tell, he's back to his old self. He dives off into the nooks and alleys, wanting to explore, though I keep a close eye on anything he tries to pick up from the paths. I think about last night and Nick partially recognising Ben… but I wonder if it was because he'd had too much to drink. Not that I'm one to talk.

Back at Hamilton House, the corner near Karen's apartment is clear. If it *was* Mark who left something there, then he hasn't been back. The bulb hasn't been replaced, though.

I can't think of anything else to do through the morning so spend my time pacing the flat going over the conversation with Harry. He'll say such-and-such, so I'll fire back with a killer line and then he'll melt and have to tell me the truth. I waste so much of the morning talking myself in circles that I almost forget I actually have to go and meet him.

It's some relief that I get to Chappie's Café before Harry does, although there is a certain sense of déjà vu. Deformed Kevin Bacon is here, this time by himself; as are the mothers from before and the bloke in shorts – who is *still* wearing shorts and hammering away on a MacBook. The poor keyboard must be on its last legs. I'm even nodded at by the same waitress, who offers a 'sit wherever you want'. I don't think she recognises me.

I order the same as yesterday – the cheapest coffee – and then sit around psyching myself up. Harry arrives at a minute to eleven in jeans and a jacket. He's got an open-necked shirt and seems slightly more tanned than the last time I saw him. He gives me a small wave and a grin and then says something to the waitress before joining me. He takes off his jacket and puts it on the back of his chair, then sits.

'This is a nice place,' he says as he turns to look at the various prints on the wall.

'Have you been in before?'

He shakes his head. 'You?'

I think about saying 'yesterday', but then he might ask why and I'm not sure I could come up with something that sounds plausible.

'How's the head?' I ask.

Harry turns and parts his hair so that I can see the welt on the back of his skull. Whether or not it was set up, there is one hell of a gash in the skin.

'That looks nasty,' I say.

'I've been sleeping about fourteen hours a day. I checked with the doctor, but she reckons it's normal.'

The waitress arrives with a tray that includes a coffee for me and a coconut milk latte for Harry. We thank her and then each sip our drinks.

'How have you been?' he asks.

I hide behind my mug, summoning the courage to say something. All those phantom conversations are proving to be precisely that.

'Who are you?' I ask, still using the mug to cover my mouth.

Probably unsurprisingly, it takes a second or two to get a response. Harry's eyebrows arc downwards.

'Pardon?' he says.

'Who are you?'

'What do you mean?'

'You hacked my computer.'

I say it as if it's a fact. Something that's on record and indisputable. I'm looking for a response, but all I get is a frown.

'I did what?'

I'm not sure why I thought he'd fold and confess all. As if my deductions were of such genius that he'd be able to do nothing but collapse and ask for forgiveness. It all feels rather silly, but it's a bit late to back off now.

'You're a computer hacker,' I say.

'Oh… kay…' A pause and then: 'I told you I worked in internet security.'

'You didn't say hacker, though.'

He holds both hands palms-up. 'Because we don't call it hacking. I'm not sure what you're saying.'

'That you hacked into my computer to find out what I liked so that, when we connected on the app, you could make it seem like we had a lot in common.'

Harry stares at me as if I'm a new creature he's never encountered before.

'You poisoned my dog,' I add.

It's at this point that I realise I'm raving. Somehow, when I was thinking this through, it all sounded logical. In between the thoughts and the words, it has become apparent that I'm utterly mad. The problem is that there's no turning back now.

'What are you talking about?' Harry says. He pushes himself up from the table until he's standing over me. It feels like he's going to turn and storm away – but I still have my trump card.

'You were on my bus,' I say.

His eyes widen and slowly, very slowly, he returns to his seat. This time, I know it's the truth.

'The number 24,' I add. 'That's why you recognised me at The Garden Café.'

Harry picks up the small biscotti that came with his drink and bites it in half. He's staring at me, looking for some sort of reasoning. It's a good fifteen seconds before he says anything. When he does speak, it's in a tone I've not heard before. The playfulness has gone, replaced by something harder.

'I was disappointed,' he says. 'When we met at The Garden Café.'

'By what?'

'That you didn't recognise me. I get on that bus a couple of times a week and I see you all the time. When we swapped pictures on the app, I thought it was you but didn't want to say anything in case it wasn't. Then, when we met properly, I realised it *was* you. I recognised you straight away but you had no idea who I was.'

'Oh…'

It feels like I'm a balloon that's deflating. This is not how things went in my head. Even from the photos it's obvious that all I do on the bus is avoid eye contact. I wouldn't recognise anyone except, perhaps, the driver.

'Do you have a problem with me?' he asks.

I have no idea what to do. My argument now seems flimsy and not well thought through, like something one of my old school reports might say.

'I went to your apartment block,' I say.

'I know – I was there.'

'No… I went again afterwards. You went around the side when we were together. When I went back on my own, nobody knew who you were. Your name isn't on the directory or any of the mailboxes.'

Harry's frown now slips into a full-on scowl. 'You went to my home?'

'I, um…'

'Do you know everyone in *your* building? How many people did you ask at mine? Did you talk to either of my next-door neighbours? Or Stacy across the corridor? Or Caitlin down the hall?'

'Er…'

'I'm not on the directory because it isn't working properly.'

He cradles his head in his hands and, as I glance around, I realise people are starting to watch. There's a trio of mothers this morning and they're offering sideways glances from the front window while pretending to keep an eye on their kids. Deformed Kevin Bacon isn't bothering to hide it – his mouth is open as he watches us openly. The waitress is leaning on the counter, pad in hand, and quickly glances away when I look to her. I don't blame them. It's better morning entertainment than guessing which of Piers Morgan's five chins he'll dribble on first.

'You said pets weren't allowed in the building,' I say.

'They're not.'

'But I saw someone coming out with a dog.'

If it's a triumph, then it doesn't feel like it. The smoking gun is more like a soppy water pistol.

'Was it a little rat thing?' he asks.

I feel tiny. 'Yes…'

'That's Veronica. She's lived there for fifteen years or so. When the building council changed the rules to ban pets, she already had the dog. They could hardly stop her having it, so it was a ban from then on. There are no *new* pets.'

'Oh…'

My evidence is suddenly thinner than the plot of a *Fast And The Furious* movie.

'What about your job?' I say.

'What about it?'

'I called Bright White Enterprises and nobody knew you?'

The silence is worse than the incredulity. I can hear a spoon clinking on a mug across the room and there's a vague rattling coming from the kitchen. Other than that, everyone is quiet.

'You called my office?' Harry says after an excruciating pause.

'Yes. The guy said there's no Harry Smith working there.'

'That's because nobody there calls me Harry. It's "Haitch" or "Aitch". That's what people called me at school and it's continued. Everyone calls me that – but I didn't want to say that to you because it sounds a bit silly.'

Harry pushes himself up and takes the jacket from the back of his chair. He puts it on and does the keys, wallet, phone check. He takes a step away from the table and then moves back, leaning in close so that nobody can overhear.

'I don't want to be mean,' he says, 'but I can't think of a nicer way to say this. You've got problems, Lucy. Serious, psychological problems. This is not normal. I hope you know that.' He stands straighter, thinks about it and then crouches once more. 'Also, I don't think we should see each other again.'

With that, he stands, drops a ten-pound note on the table, nods to the waitress and then strides out of the café and out of my life.

THIRTY-EIGHT

Billy senses my mood when I get home. He follows me around the apartment and then snuggles into me on the sofa. He doesn't even beg for food.

'Well, Bill,' I tell him. 'I'm an idiot.'

He looks up to me and doesn't disagree. It takes an incredible degree of obliviousness to think someone else is a stalker – and then pay for CCTV photos that end up proving the person with a problem is me.

I flick through the pictures once more and, in frame after frame, I'm ignoring the world around me. The truth is that anyone could have dropped that envelope into my bag; the music across the corridor *could* be a coincidence and Mark *might* have poisoned Billy and Judge.

That leaves one thing that's harder to resolve – why Melanie's jacket was in Jade's old apartment. Was the door left open by accident, or was I meant to find it? I suppose it could be a coat *like* Melanie's – and hers was stolen from the line at the same time. It would be taking flukes to a new level, but I suppose crazier things have happened.

I spend a few hours doing little other than not really watching television, while cringing every time I think about the way I embarrassed myself. It's only as the clock ticks around to six that I remember it's Karen's big night.

I'm not in the partying mood – but that's something I could have said on almost every day of my life. It's only my specific birthdays up to the age of about eleven or twelve on which I might have felt differently. After that, it's been a consistent lifetime of not being in the mood for revelling.

That said, I do have enough self-awareness to realise that tonight is not about me. Karen's never had a birthday party, so the least I can do as her friend is actually go to this one.

Even with the money I've spent, I've done very little to expand my wardrobe, so there's not a lot of choice when it comes to what to wear. Karen never mentioned fancy dress to me, even though Nick says he's going as a sexy zombie. If he's the only one, there's going to be quite the clash of style… although if an attack of the undead does ever happen, they could launch it at Halloween and it would only be the morning after that anyone would notice a problem. Either way, I go for jeans and a warm blankety top. It's November after all.

The Rec Centre is a council-run building that's used for everything from Sunday-morning yoga classes, to drop-in citizens' advice sessions, to a polling station every time the government decides to call an election or referendum. That seems to happen with alarming regularity at the moment. It's the type of council resource that will be cut sooner or later – and then disappear for good. Considering the building is literally on our doorstep, it's probably to my shame that I never use it for anything. When it *is* cut, it will be because of people like me.

Billy and I head down to the party at almost eight o'clock. The posters say seven – but only nutters will show up that early. Half-past is still dicing with trouble at being one of the first to arrive. It's an awkward time in that there might be a high strangers-to-friends ratio, which means talking to somebody unknown is a real possibility. Not only that, but it's hard to know if going to the buffet that early is acceptable. Nobody wants to be the first. Waiting an hour seems the most sensible option.

The party is being held in the room at the back of the centre. There are handwritten signs with 'party' over the top of an arrow stuck to the glass doors at the front. I follow the building around until I'm at the back where there's a large expanse of grass and a children's play park. Sulphur hangs in the air and there's a cloud of smoke clinging to the trees at the furthest end. There is the faintest orangey haze beyond the hedge line, so there's either a bonfire, or something's ablaze at the back of the industrial park. Tonight must be a pyromaniac's dream.

Intermittent whizzes and bangs from overhead have Billy on edge and he keeps close to my legs, to such a degree that I almost fall over him twice on the way to the doors at the back of the Rec Centre.

There are floor-to-ceiling windows attached to the hall, with patio doors that are wide open. A song I vaguely recognise is seeping through, while spinning coloured lights are flickering back and forth.

When we get inside, Billy seemingly forgets the trauma of the fireworks outside – largely because there are almost as many dogs present as people. The floor is the same type of varnished wood that was in the gym when I was at school and Billy tugs at his lead, scratching and sliding his way across it until he's in a clutch of wagging tails with all the other pets. I let him off his lead and he darts in small circles, as happy as I've seen him. He sniffs around Judge – and then moves onto the others. Someone's Yorkshire terrier is dressed as a pumpkin, while a French bulldog is wearing a ninja turtle outfit. I wonder if the other dogs feel underdressed.

Karen spots us straight away. She's in a sparkly black dress and, from the speed at which she's talking, already tipsy.

'You're here!' she says excitedly before gripping me in a hug that's borderline assault. I gasp for breath until she releases me. 'I'm so glad you came.'

'Of course I was going to be here.'

She crouches and strokes Billy's back – although he's unaware because he's busy flirting with the ninja turtle. He always was more sociable than me.

'Good showing, isn't it?' she says.

I turn and take in the room. There are birthday banners across the doors and three disco balls hanging from the ceiling – but, more importantly, a good forty to fifty people mingling.

'There's a pound off at the bar for people who live at Hamilton,' Karen says. 'Just tell them your flat number. Jamie's on top of it all.'

Karen waves across towards the bar, which is set up in one of the corners. There are two smartly dressed barmen in waistcoats and the taller of the two waves back at her.

Karen nods across to a speaker on the edge of the stage: 'The DJ wanted £200, so I set up a playlist on my phone,' she adds. 'It's all eighties, nineties and two-thousands stuff. None of the new rubbish. If you want a request, I can add it to the playlist if I've got it on my phone.'

'I think I'll leave the music to you,' I say.

'There's a lot of Kylie on this playlist.' She laughs to herself and then points across to the buffet. 'There's a special doggy treat section. I had to put a load of signs around it in case people accidentally ate the biscuits themselves.' The grin has barely left her face as she waves across to someone I don't recognise. She turns back to me and says: 'Have you seen the state of Nick?'

He's in the corner chatting to three women. From what I can tell, he is the only person in fancy dress. He's gone all-in, too – it's not some cheap mask with scraggy jeans. He's either way more talented than I realised, or he has a friend who's a make-up artist. His face is covered with drawn-on flesh wounds, while the rest of his skin has a greyish tone. There are some sort of entrails hanging from underneath his ripped top.

'I think he thought it was fancy dress,' I say.

'I think he wanted to dress up regardless,' Karen replies with a smile.

'Good point.'

Karen waves to someone else and then says she'll catch up with me later. She hugs me one more time and then, as if on schedule, there is momentary pause in between tracks before Kylie's 'Spinning Around' comes on. Karen does the half-walk, half-dance that people do when they're on the way to drunkenness and disappears away to talk to other people.

I watch her, wondering how many people would come to a birthday party of mine. Definitely not this many. From feeling happy for her, I suddenly feel a little sorry for myself. I have Billy and, after that, I'm not too sure. Even when I find someone I like on, of all things, a dating app, it's me who turns out to be the mental one.

I coax Billy over to the buffet and give him a couple of the doggy biscuits. He makes a mess of crumbs, which is more or less a given, and then trots back to socialise with his new friends. Even *he*'d have more attendees at a birthday party.

I follow him back and, before I know it, I'm chatting to the bloke whose French bulldog is dressed as a ninja turtle. I strongly suspect his biggest reason for having the dog is to try to pick up women. He's youngish and hipstery; all beard, hair wax and no chance of ever buying a house. There's a charm to him, though, and we're soon banging on about the things all dog owners do. There's an unspoken checklist – he or she? – age? – breed? – and then it's on to bigger issues. He knows Karen because he used to work with her on a production line. He's gone back to university since, but they are friends on Facebook and blah-di-blah-di-blah. These are the exact kinds of relationship I don't have.

The music continues to scroll through hits mainly from the nineties as more people arrive. There are probably eighty or ninety people milling around now. Few are dancing but most seem to be drinking and chatting. It's a Friday night and this is an alternative to pubs, clubs, or the organised bonfire displays. It seems the dogs are a popular attraction, too. Many people arrive, ditch their coats, and then head straight for the congregation of animals to say hello.

Billy is loving it all and there's no question this is a better place for him than my flat would have been. The fireworks would've made it the worst evening of the year for him, but now, because of Karen, he's having one of his best.

I go on a lap of the hall, trying to make it look as if I have friends and know how to be sociable. It amazes me that this is natural for some people. As I'm on my way around, I spot Vicky standing close to the buffet by herself. She's tugging on the ring through her nose but nods and smiles when she sees me. There's a moment in which it feels as if we're both experiencing the same degree of awkwardness, but I amble over towards her. The music seems to have got louder, so I lean in to talk into her ear.

'No baby tonight?' I ask, although it's largely stating the obvious.

'Mum said she'd take her,' Vicky replies. She pulls away momentarily and then angles in again. 'I want to pay you back the money. I know what you said, but it doesn't feel right.'

She doesn't want to catch my eye, so I don't force it. I touch her on the arm instead, to say I understand. 'Whatever makes you happier,' I reply. 'But you don't have to.'

Vicky is about to say something else when the music stops fleetingly between songs. It's the difference between a DJ and a playlist and means that there's almost always a drop in the volume of conversations, if only for a second. When the music returns, a shiver whispers along my spine. Elton John is singing about a woman packing her bags. It's nine in the morning.

Vicky has been talking, but I've heard none of it.

'Sorry, I'm not feeling well,' I say. Or think I do. Everything is a bit of a blur and the spinning lights above are suddenly disorientating. The hall is as it was. People are chatting, drinking and dancing. The dogs have their own corner, although some are now settling down for a snooze. Zombie Nick is still surrounded by women. Karen is dancing with a man I've never met before. She's swaying tipsily and laughing to herself. Nobody seems to have noticed that anything out of the ordinary has happened.

I drift through the crowd on autopilot until I'm close to the stage. There are two large speakers on either side, but I head towards the one at which Karen pointed. There's a small table, half hidden by a curtain. Her phone is sitting on top, its garish purple case unmistakeable. There is a cable trailing away from the table but, instead of being plugged into Karen's phone, it is now clipped into a small, plasticky MP3 player. It's the type of thing that was once close to the height of technology but now sells for a tenner on a market stall. Karen's phone screen is locked but the MP3 player has a photo of Elton on the front.

It feels as if someone has breathed down my neck, but, when I turn, there is nobody there. That sense of being watched eats away at me once more. It was there as I walked away from Chappie's Café after I was supposed to meet whoever had put up the posters. I've felt it in the hallways of Hamilton House and it was there when I was trick or treating with Karen's boys last weekend.

I pull myself up onto the stage and turn to take in the floor. The attendance is even more impressive from higher up. I never realised Karen knew so many people, though I recognise almost nobody. There's no one identifiably out of place; nothing untoward… except, almost as if it was timed, a firework explodes into the sky beyond the glass doors at the back. A shower of shadow and light splays wide across the lawn and, in that second, there's a flicker of movement, a shadow… probably nothing. It's gone as soon as it was there. But the chill is back.

I clamber off the stage and work my way through the crowd, to the doors and onto the grass beyond. It's colder than it was and I wrap my arms around myself. My breath spirals up and into the night sky. From behind, Elton's tones are muffled and yet, somehow, that makes it more powerful. It feels like a dream; a memory.

The moon is shrouded by cloud, leaving everything doused in dark or dim, vague shadows. It's in my periphery that I see another glimmer of movement. A ghost in the night. I follow it over towards the play park. For a moment, I feel weak at the knees, but then I realise the ground is covered with the springy, spongey material that coats all playgrounds nowadays. It's like walking on a trampoline as I bob across the surface, searching for the shadow that's no longer there. I can barely hear Karen's music any longer.

'Hello…?'

My voice echoes into the night without reply, but my heart leaps as a rocket fizzes high above the houses beyond, exploding into blue and purple droplets. The boom comes a fraction of a second later and then it all dissolves into nothingness, as if it was never there. I've been holding my breath and puff a thick, chilly cloud into the dark.

'Hi.'

The word makes me yelp with alarm. It's so close that I can feel the man's breath on my neck. I spin, but there's nobody there.

Except that there is. He's not directly behind me; he's further back, rocking gently on one of the swings.

I take a few steps towards him and then he speaks again: 'Hi, Luce. It's been a while.'

Never Lucy, always *Luce*.

Closer. The shape of his face is unerringly familiar, even in the night. Another firework explodes into the sky above and, in that second, I can see who it is. He's smiling at me lopsidedly; still the same, even after all these years.

'You're dead,' I tell him.

'Am I?'

'Alex…?'

I move closer still and he stops rocking, sitting still and looking up to me. Perhaps it's fate, or maybe it's an accident of nature – but the moon chooses that moment to emerge from behind a cloud. Gloomy white light seeps across the playground and the scar is suddenly clear underneath his Adam's apple. The old rugby injury.

'Nearly,' Ben says.

THIRTY-NINE

Ben rolls up his sleeve to show me the tattoo he had etched onto his arm a month before the train crash. There are spiky shapes that always looked disjointed to me, but it's darker than I remember; more intricate. I was never sure if I liked it. It all seemed a bit low-rent. The type of thing some bloke might have on show while throwing around chairs outside an all-day breakfast place on the Costa del Sol as he bellows 'English' at the Spanish owner. I never told Ben that, of course. It's one of those unwritten rules: if someone shows off their tattoo, they have to be told it looks great.

Ben shivers and rubs his arm: 'Bit chilly, innit?' he says.

I feel it now, too. There's a wind that sizzles between the trees. Everything feels like a dream. An impossible dream.

Another firework booms overhead and Ben holds up his hands. When the bang has evaporated, a small smile crinkles onto his face. 'Your favourite night of the year,' he says.

I shake my head. 'It used to be.'

He doesn't object as I stretch for his arm and rub the tattoo with my thumb. I half expect it to smudge but it remains intact.

'It's real,' he says. 'I'm real.'

'How?'

Ben tugs his sleeve down and sets himself rocking steadily on the swing. I have to step to the side.

'I've been trying to give you clues,' he says. 'To ease you into it. I didn't want it to be such a shock. I thought you might've figured it out by now.'

'Figured it out? You're dead.'

He shrugs in the way I always hated. It never did suit him. He says nothing in reply and, almost because of the weight of expectation, I sit on the swing next to his, allowing my legs to dangle.

'Have you been living opposite?' I ask.

'Not living. I've spent some time in there. I wanted to be close to you. I've missed you.'

He makes it sound as if this is all normal. 'There was a funeral for you,' I say. 'A *joint* funeral. There have been memorials every year.'

I pinch the webbing in between the thumb and finger on my right hand, half expecting to jump awake and still be at home. I don't. I'm here on the swings.

'I wasn't feeling well,' Ben says. 'Do you remember?'

'"Last night's sushi",' I reply. Of course I remember. Those words, those stupid words, have been burned into my memory.

He laughs a little, though there's no humour there.

'Right. The sushi. It saved my life. My stomach was in knots and the toilets on the train were out of order. I ended up getting off at the final stop before the crash. It was one of those smaller ones that are only used by window-lickers and bumpkins. I was going to sort myself out and then get on the next train an hour later.'

'You weren't on the train...?' I reply, thinking of Steven and his stupid conspiracies. There never was a body.

Ben doesn't reply. I suppose the very fact he's here is a response.

'What about Alex?' I ask.

'Alex...' Ben repeats the name with a sigh and stops rocking on the swing. He presses his feet into the floor and leans forward a little. 'I thought it would look better in front of the investor if there were two of us. We were in matching suits to look united. When I got off the train, I told Alex to stay on and that I'd catch him up. We didn't know where we were going at the other end and I said that if he could figure out where everything was, we wouldn't lose that much time…' He tails off and then whispers: 'I *told* him to stay on…'

Neither of us speak for a while. I pinch the webbing on my hand again but nothing happens. I'm not sure if I even feel the pain. Everything's numb.

'There were no toilets at the station,' Ben says. 'It was basically just a platform. I was in this café over the road when the crash came on the news.'

He leans backwards and the swing bounces back and then forward. It feels as if this is all he's going to say; as if this is an explanation for everything.

I turn and stare sideways at him.

'Why didn't you call?' I ask. 'Or come home? I don't understand.'

He bites his lip and turns to face me. I can see the subtle differences in his appearance now. There are gentle lines around the corners of his eyes and more of a crease to his lips. Age comes to everyone.

'The reason I was seeing the investor in the first place is because I was out of money. I actually *did* call you – but hung up before it connected. I had no idea what to say. It was going to come out sooner or later that we were broke.'

'*We?*'

Ben doesn't react at first, but then it comes: 'I had this weird moment of clarity,' he says. 'That this was my way out. I had a bit of cash hidden at Mum's house – but that was it—'

'Your mum knew?'

He holds up a hand to stop me. 'I met a guy in a bar one time when I was away. He reckoned he was a private investigator. I thought it was a joke but I'd kept his card for some reason and then I saw it all clearly. I didn't want to let you down any more. I waited until Mum was out and then went and got my money. I used that to pay the investigator and he sorted me out with a new driving licence and some other things. As long as I had the money, he didn't bother with many questions. I think he'd done it before.'

I've turned away but, when he pauses, I can sense him wanting me to twist back. I ignore him for a few seconds and then the tug is too much.

He waits until I'm looking at him and then says: 'It's not like I *tried* to fake my own death. It just sort of… *happened*.'

'Are you joking?'

'No.'

'Things like this don't just happen.'

I twist around in the swing so that my back is to him.

'Luce…'

'Don't call me that.'

He says nothing and then I feel the fury boiling. It's like I'm going to be sick. 'Then what?' I spin, rotating back towards him. 'You had what was left of our money.'

He shrugs. That damn shrug.

'I moved,' he says. 'I started again. I'd learned my lessons about day trading. I made money second time around. I took fewer risks and it started to come together. I pooled my money with some people I found online and we made a decent profit.'

'You've been doing fine all this time, while I've been struggling with *your* debts…?'

'It wasn't—'

'I didn't owe any money. You took loans out in my name.'

'If you'd just—'

'If I'd just *what*?'

'That's in the past.'

He clamps his lips together but I feel like I need some sort of answers.

'Where did you move to?' I ask, hoping for something.

He shrugs again. 'Does it matter?'

'YES!' I'm shouting, unable to keep it in. I'm gripping the chain of the swing so tightly that the links are imprinted into my palms. 'All this matters.'

Ben sighs and now it's him that wants to turn away. 'Can we stop talking about the past and think about the future?' he says.

It's so outlandish, so ridiculous, that it takes me a few seconds to take it in. '*Future?*' I say. 'What future? Everyone thinks you're dead. I have a copy of the death certificate. You can't just come back.'

'I don't need to. I have another ID. I'm not Ben Peterson, I'm Peter now.'

I actually laugh at that and it's not fake or forced. It explodes in a guff of air. '*That's* the name you chose? How long did you have to think about it?'

He shrugs.

'Stop shrugging!'

He lowers his shoulders, seemingly chastened. I wonder if everyone has these types of traits that follow a person through their life. Whether there's something I do that annoys everyone else.

'I didn't choose the name,' he says. 'When you get an ID, you get what you're given. The point is that I don't *need* to come back. We can be together as Lucy and Peter. Ben *is* dead.'

He says something else, but it's lost among an exploding firework. The explosion crackles along the sky, finishing with a series of smaller fizzes. When it's over, Ben is no longer speaking.

'Does your mum know?' I ask.

He doesn't reply, but, when I turn to him, he shakes his head. 'I couldn't tell her,' he says. 'I thought about it. I wanted to.'

'You stole her coat from her washing line?'

I watch his eyes narrow, probably wondering how I knew. If it is that, then he doesn't ask.

'I wanted to feel closer to her,' he says, not seeming to realise how creepy it sounds. How creepy all this sounds. 'It's not her I'm back for,' he adds.

'You'll keep letting her think you're dead?'

'Ben *is* dead. I think it's kinder. Don't you?'

'Don't bring me into this.'

I push myself up from the swing and step away. Ben mutters 'don't', but that's not the reason I stop and turn. A horrible suspicion is starting to settle.

'What did you mean "ease me into it"?'

There's a pause and Ben has his lips pressed together.

'Tell me,' I say.

'I couldn't just turn up at your door and say, "Tada! It's me".'

'What else?'

I know him better than I realised. He stares at the floor. 'I enjoyed the chase,' Ben says. 'It was like the old days. I was trying to prove to you that I wanted you. It was fun. Didn't you enjoy it?'

He glances up and I can the sincerity in his thoughts. He really believes the last week has been enjoyable. I close my eyes and can see the CCTV stills from the bus. They're imprinted on my memory. Ben was the man in the cap from the bus. The one who was in only a single picture.

'Why did you give me the money?' I ask.

He starts to shrug and then catches himself. 'I wanted you to enjoy your life again,' he says. 'I hated seeing you live like this.'

'Like what?'

'Poky flat, rubbish job. It's no way to live, is it?'

I want to be furious with him. He doesn't think it's an insult but it is. I'm not happy with my life – but that isn't because of my flat, or the people. It's because everything I earn goes into paying off rent or his debts. It *is* a miserable way to live – but I'm also trying to change it.

'I like a lot about my life,' I say. 'I have friends. I'm studying for my future. I have a job interview tomorrow morning.'

He snorts. 'What? I thought you were working at a supermarket? You can't be happy doing those jobs? Come off it.'

Ben doesn't seem to know I no longer work there. I suppose my downfall at Crosstown was all my own. 'It's a means to an end,' I say.

'You don't need that now. You have me.'

'You *left* me. You stole our savings.'

Ben bites his lip again. 'Bygones…?'

It's my turn to snort now. It's hard not to. Ben barely responds.

'You put up the posters, didn't you?' I say.

He doesn't answer.

'You made me email you.'

'I didn't *make* you do anything.'

'I was trying to be honest! You had me chase around and arrange a meeting and then you didn't turn up.'

'I wanted to see you,' he says. There's something about the pathetic tone to his voice that makes me believe him. 'I didn't know if I could hold off until now,' he adds. 'Being close to you kept making me want to say something. I almost opened the apartment door to you so many times when you were in the corridor. I almost walked into the café. I kept stopping myself because I wanted it to be tonight.'

'Why tonight?'

We lock eyes and there's a moment in which I realise he doesn't understand what the past five years have done to me. There's an obliviousness, a lack of realisation.

'Because it's your favourite time of the year,' he says.

'It's not. It's the time of year when my boyfriend died and I realised he'd taken out loans in my name. It's the time of year when everything fell apart. When I realised I'd been lied to over and over.'

He sucks in his cheeks and stares at the floor.

'I'm happier with Billy,' I say.

The reply is under his breath, so quiet that I barely catch it. 'That mangy thing.' He spits the words and suddenly I know.

'You poisoned him, didn't you?' I say.

Ben shrugs. Again. 'You don't need him now you have me.'

I look back towards the hall, where Billy and the other dogs will still be hanging around in their corner, going about their evening while protected from the bangs overhead. There's such innocence there that I can barely square it with everything out here. It's darkness and light.

'Did you attack Harry?' I ask.

'Is that his name? He's not right for you.'

It's not an answer, but Ben speaks like it is.

'You got the idea from Alex.'

Ben spins, his shoulders tensed, fists balled. 'Don't say his name.'

For the first time since coming outside, a ripple of fear teases its way through me. It's dark and there's nobody else around. I could scream but won't be heard over the music from the hall. I look across towards the party, hoping people will be starting to leave and head along the path. But there's no one. Just us.

I take a step away from the swings, towards the hall. It's only a simple movement – but Ben pulls himself up from the swing and stretches out a hand as if to take mine. I move another pace away.

'I've been planning all this,' he says. 'Well… not all of it. I didn't know about the party until the flyer came under my door. I wanted it to be special. I did all this for you. I messed up five years ago, but I've put it right. I have money – lots of it. It won't be like before.'

'Life isn't all about money.'

'Not *all* about money – but it helps. Look what you've done with it this past week. I wanted to show you that. We can be happy.'

'No—'

'All those things you wanted. The stables, the house—'

'It wasn't me who wanted them. I could've had a small wedding. I didn't need the big house. You wanted those.'

A shrug: 'Right, but we can both have them now…'

We're off the padded matting now, onto the grass. I risk a glance backwards to the hall, but, when I turn back, Ben is another step closer.

'No,' I say.

He stops, frozen half in shadow. I can only see the right side of his face, but there's puzzlement there. 'What do you mean no?'

I try to sound bold and assertive even though I feel the opposite. 'I don't want this. If you're alive, then good for you. Go and enjoy your life as Peter. Tell your mum or don't tell her. I don't want any part of it. I'm my own person and I have a life. You're not in it.'

It's hard not to stumble with my next step backwards. There's a hidden ridge in the grass and I panic that Ben is going to launch himself forward as I try to right myself. He doesn't though. He's still. I take more steps away from him until there's a gap of ten metres or more and I can barely see him among the shadows. He hasn't moved. I almost stop to ask if he's okay.

Almost.

But I don't. I turn and run until I'm at the back of the hall once more. Lights are still spinning; music is playing. It's Kylie again: one of the oldies from her *Neighbours* days. Warmth seeps out from the inside, catching in my lungs. I'm out of breath and my mouth is dry. It's only when I step into the hall that the horrifying, haunting thought hits me.

I turn back to the park, but there's no figure there any longer. No sign that Ben was ever there at all. It's hard not to wonder, though. If he did all this, then what wouldn't he do?

And what happened to Jade?

FORTY

I drift across to the speakers near the stage, where the MP3 player has been unplugged and is sitting on top of the small table. Karen's phone has become dominant once more. Kylie becomes Jason and all our youthful pasts flood back in a blur of dodgy perms and lunchtimes skiving off school to watch *Neighbours*. I check that nobody's paying me any attention and then grab the music player and stuff it into a pocket, almost to prove that this happened.

When I turn around, Billy is there, watching me with his ears pricked, as if waiting to hear what I have to say for myself. I crouch and rub his back, but this is insufficient as he turns and mooches back towards the other dogs in the corner.

I have no idea what to do.

If I called the police, what would I say? That my dead boyfriend is back? He assaulted someone with whom I'd been on a date, poisoned my dog and might have killed the person who lived opposite me? All I know about his life now is that he's called Peter. He could disappear back to wherever he was before with no proof he was ever here. I'd sound like a madwoman.

I head back towards the doors and stare out to the green and the darkened play park. Seeing Ben already feels like something of a dream. A shadowy figure on a shadowy child's swing at a time of year that's known for ghosts and ghouls.

Someone I don't recognise nudges past me with an apology. People are starting to leave the party, which means a series of lengthy goodbyes. There are hugs, handshakes, air-kisses and actual kisses, accompanied by empty platitudes like, 'I'll call', or 'I'll be in touch'. When it comes to any social gathering, nobody can ever just leave. I've had shorter sleeps than some people spend saying goodbye to one another.

I'm still staring out towards the park when a hand touches my shoulder. I jump and spin around, expecting the worst – but it's Karen. She doesn't seem to notice my alarm, largely because she's swaying slightly from side to side.

'What happened with the music?' I ask.

'Someone playing around,' she replies.

'I think I'm going to leave. I've got an interview tomorrow morning and—'

'You have an interview?'

'Didn't I say? It's at an office close to Crosstown? It's only filing and that sort of stuff, but I want to make sure I get a good sleep. It's—'

Karen lunges at me, wrapping both arms around my back and stroking my hair. 'Oh, honey. I'm so happy for you…'

I tap her gently on the back, unsure how to respond. At least in part, it's drunk talk. Karen is slurring her words as she presses hard into the crook of my neck.

'You deserve this,' she says.

It takes me a few seconds to extricate myself and then it's our turn for the lengthy goodbye. I promise to let Karen know how the interview goes and she says I'll have to come over for dinner soon. After that, I put Billy back on his lead and tug him away from his new friends. There are more goodbyes – mainly from me – and then I'm finally outside, on the way home.

It's a short walk, but I spend the whole time peering into the shadows. As if trying to give me a heart attack, a cat jumps from a wall, landing with elegant ease on the pavement in front of us. Billy's ears prick up, but he's too tired to go chasing tonight. The cat stands and watches, almost daring us on. It's nothing to worry about and yet I still walk in the middle of the road for the short distance back. It's where there's more light; where I am furthest from the bleakness of the overgrown bushes and the high walls behind which anyone could be hiding. It's late, but I want to call Lauren to tell her that I know who's living opposite. That she's rented the apartment to a fraud. It's only the fact I'm sober that stops me.

After getting into Hamilton House, I find myself edging up the stairs, expecting a surprise around every corner. There's no one there; nobody in the hall outside my door.

Jade's door is unlocked and slightly open. There's silence as I wait in the corridor and only darkness within. I knock hard on the door frame and then, when there's no reply, push the door open with my foot?

'Hello? Ben?'

There's still no reply, so I poke my head inside and flick on the light, only to see that there's nothing inside, except for the sofa and small table. The ethernet cable has disappeared from the back of the room and the cupboard door in which I found Melanie's coat is open. The apartment feels different than it did when I was last here. It *felt* occupied then, even though there was so little furniture. Now, there's an emptiness to the air and it feels abandoned.

I exit back to the corridor and leave the door as I found it. After getting into my own apartment, I close the door and lock it; then carry a chair across the room and wedge it underneath the handle.

Billy is already in his bed, head down, ready to sleep. It's past his bedtime and he's had a busy day. I don't pull out the bed, instead sitting on the sofa and huddling under a blanket. It doesn't feel as if I'll be able to sleep. Sometimes I might have the television on for background noise – but not this evening. I close my eyes and strain to listen for any sounds from the corridor.

It's hard to explain, but I feel like I've lost something, even though the opposite is true. Perhaps it's that I no longer have the sense of security I once had? Or that there are certain things in life that can be taken for granted? The sky is blue and the night is dark – but I'm not sure what to believe any longer. Absolutes are no longer absolute.

I lay my head on the armrest and open my eyes to watch Billy. He's on his side, head tucked underneath his paw. His ribs are rising and falling in steady rhythm and I wish his innocence was mine. I won't sleep tonight. I know I won't.

FORTY-ONE

SATURDAY

I'm pinned to the sofa, my legs dead and useless. I try to lift up from my hips but there's no strength below my waist. It's a mass of paralysis, with added pins and needles. When I open my eyes, there's a familiar sight.

'C'mon, Bill,' I say. 'Let me up.'

Billy opens a single eye and groans slightly. There's a sliver of slobber around his lips and his eyelids flutter sleepily. He's comfy and the fact he's laid across the entirety of my lower half is seemingly a problem for me, not him. I don't remember falling asleep, something emphasised by the jabbing jolts of pain in my neck. I've slept with my head twisted at an L-angle to the rest of my body. The curtains are open and light floods across the apartment, but it's only when I spot the chair wedged under the front door handle that I remember what happened last night. Now, even more than then, it feels like a figment of my imagination. Could I have somehow imagined it all?

I push myself up, sliding my legs out from underneath Billy's frame. He rolls over and once again shoots me his best betrayed look. The pins and needles start to fade as I knead my fists into my thighs and twitch my toes. My initial few steps are unsteady, a baby duckling waddling onto shore for the first time, but the feeling is almost back as I get to the front door. I remove the chair and then open the door to stare into the corridor. The door to the apartment opposite is still slightly agape, a reminder of what was and what's gone.

This time I do call Lauren, who answers with a brusque, 'Yes?'

'It's Lucy,' I tell her. 'From Hamilton House.'

'Oh. You know it's Saturday…?'

I have to resist answering with sarcasm that, yes, I do understand the concept of a seven-day week.

'It's Jade's old flat,' I say.

'What about it?'

'The door's open. I couldn't help but seeing inside – and it looks like it's been cleared out. I think whoever was there has gone.'

Lauren sighs: 'Are you sure?'

'They might have invisible furniture, I suppose…'

'At least he paid to the end of the year.' Another sigh: 'All right. I'll be over later. Can you close the door?'

I step into the hallway and the floor creaks gently underneath my foot. 'Can you tell me who lived there?' I ask.

'We did talk about this. I can go—'

'Was it someone called Peter?'

There's a pause that's long enough to serve as confirmation.

'I'll be over later,' Lauren says, more firmly this time. 'Is there anything else?'

'I don't think so.'

Lauren says goodbye and then hangs up. It's only as my phone flashes back to the main screen that I realise the time. I have a job interview in exactly an hour.

There's a part of me that can't quite comprehend going to it given everything that's happened in the past twelve hours or so. It feels like such a normal thing in a world that's now abnormal. I'm not sure what the alternative is, though. There might be a link from Lauren to Ben – or Peter as he calls himself. I could tell the police and let them look into it, but, for now, if I miss that interview then I'm not sure where it leaves me. If Ben *has* gone for good, or even if he hasn't, I still have a life to lead.

I blink away thoughts of Jade and what happened to her. It's selfish, I know, but it isn't like I'm forgetting her for good. I pull the door to her old apartment closed and then rush back into my flat for a shower.

Fifteen minutes later and I'm almost ready to go – with one small problem.

I hurry down the hall to Karen's, partly to check that she's still sentient. The last time I saw her, she was swaying from side to side and slurring. She answers moments after I knock and, to great surprise, is wearing yoga leggings, a vest and her running shoes.

'I know!' she says as I goggle at her.

'I was checking you were all right,' I say. 'I didn't expect you to be in anything other than a dressing gown at best.'

'It's a miracle. I drank so much, I thought I'd be hung-over until the kids are back tomorrow night – but I've defied science. I'm a medical marvel. I'm going to Parkrun in a bit.'

'Could you take Billy? I've got my interview and—'

'Of course. Drop him round. He's going to have to run a bit slower with me, though.'

Karen is on her way out but waits in the corridor for a couple of minutes as I collect Billy and check I have everything I need. The fact it's all such a rush is probably a good thing because I've not had time to be nervous about the interview itself. There are bigger things clouding my mind.

Billy doesn't seem to mind and happily trots down the stairs at Karen's side. It's hard to know who's the traitor – me for abandoning him, or him for dutifully ambling along with somebody else.

When we get outside, Karen heads towards the park, or, more to the point, Billy sets off towards the park with Karen in tow. She laughs a cheery 'good luck' and then she's off around the corner of the building. I head the other way to the community centre and the bus stop beyond. The last time I walked this way, I was in the middle of the road in the dark, nervously checking the shadows in case Ben had stayed around. It feels different now. Leaves are billowing along the gutters as a pair of lads in football kit walk along the other side of the road. One has a ball under his arm and both have string bags on their backs. There's nobody else in sight, including at the deserted bus stop.

It's hard to stop my mind wandering as I wait. I want to think about the interview, how I don't have a job and that I need this. Ben's money is upstairs in my flat, but the allure has gone. I'm not sure if I'll be able to spend it. Jade's face keeps eclipsing everything else. As mad as I'll sound, I need to tell the police that I saw Ben and that he's calling himself Peter. They can check with Lauren and, if there's a paper trail, they could find him.

The bus chugs into the stop with a guff of noxious air and the doors fizz open. I flash my pass to the driver, who barely looks at it before nodding and punching a button to close the door behind me. The bus is probably half full, with almost everyone staring at their phones. I move along the aisle, but the driver sets off before I sit and I stumble into an empty pair of seats largely by default. The CCTV dome is a row ahead of me and I can't believe I never noticed it. I stare at it now, thinking of the person on the other side who might have to wade through the footage if a nutter like me phones up.

My thoughts slip to barely a week ago when it all started on this bus. I was standing a couple of metres from where I am now when that envelope of money dropped into my bag and everything changed. Or, to some degree, nothing changed. I'm still paying off somebody else's debts and living pay packet to pay packet. Everything's different except nothing is. I might spend the rest of my life wondering if Ben – or Peter – will return. Or, perhaps the memory of last night will dim and I'll be left questioning whether it happened at all.

The bus pulls in at the next stop and a couple bluster their way along the aisle from behind me to get off. A small queue of people replaces them. Some head past me along the aisle; others risk the disabled seats at the front, hoping nobody with a wheelchair gets on.

I check the address of the office for my interview on my phone and then try to give myself a pep talk. *Be confident, be yourself,* all that. It's all fine as long as they're looking for someone like me.

Another stop and more people get on and off. My palms are starting to sweat now. It's probably fifteen minutes until my stop – and then, forget being myself, I have to somehow pretend to be a competent, sociable human being. That's life, I suppose. Pretend we know what's going on until it becomes apparent to everyone else that we clearly do not. Sometimes that can take a day, other times it is years. Life is a collection of people not really knowing what they're doing.

I check the address again, even though it's etched in my mind. The bus is filling up and there's a shuffling from behind until someone drops in next to me. I glance sideways in the way people do when trying to look at a person without making it too obvious. This time, I stop and stare.

'Hi,' Ben says. He's wearing a cap that's pulled down and covering his eyebrows. The shape of his face is unmistakeable.

'I—'

'Shhhhhhh,' he says so quietly that I barely hear him. He's staring straight ahead, not looking at me, but then his gaze flickers down to his arm. I don't notice it at first, but now I see the glimmer of light catching the tip of the knife that's protruding a few centimetres from his jacket.

'What—'

'Shhhhhhh,' he coos. 'We're going to sit here nice and quietly. Okay?'

FORTY-TWO

I do as I'm told. Ben has withdrawn the blade back into his sleeve, but I can sense its presence at my hip. He is staring at the back of the person's head in front, with a curious, knowing half-smile on his face. I watch him sideways for a while, but it's too disconcerting and I have to turn back to looking at my own lap and then out the window. Ben is sitting a little over the gap that separates the two seats, pressing me towards the window.

A couple are having a mini-domestic in the row behind. She's whispering about how he's always late and he's going on about something that happened in Cardiff last year. She replies that he always brings that up. Back and forth they go in something that's close to domestic bliss compared to what's going on within touching distance of where they're sitting.

The bus pulls into the next stop and Ben gently presses his sleeve into my leg, making it clear I shouldn't move. I can't feel the point of the blade through the material as Ben continues to smile and stare. When the doors hiss open, I consider shouting or screaming – except there's no way I can get past Ben before something terrible happens. He's too close.

'Shhhhhhh,' he whispers, as if reading my mind.

More people shuffle onto the bus and I risk a quick glance backwards to see that the seats are now full.

'Be smart,' he says, and I turn back to the front.

'What are you doing?' I say.

'Wait.'

That's all I can do. I move a little closer to the window to try to give myself some space, but Ben shifts further across the divide, wedging me in even tighter.

'Ben—'

'Patience,' he replies.

The bus starts and stops once more and the same thoughts flicker through me. I should jump up, shout, tell everyone that he has a knife – except it's as if Ben knows this is what's going through my mind. This time, he presses the tip of the knife itself into my thigh, without the shield of his sleeve. It doesn't hurt, not really, it's more the awareness that makes me straighten. When the bus pulls away, Ben withdraws the blade into his jacket.

We've been travelling for another minute or so when Ben presses the button on the pole next to his seat. The bell dings.

'We're getting off,' he whispers.

'I have an interview.'

It sounds so stupid; so completely mad given what's happening, but the words are out before I can stop them.

Ben turns a little, not quite looking at me, though his eye twitches. 'Be smart,' he repeats.

When the bus pulls in at the next stop, Ben clambers out of the seat and takes a step backwards, giving me room to walk in front of him. It's the most space I've had in a while – but Ben is still only an arm's length from me. He doesn't need to say anything, but I do what's requested anyway. As soon as I'm on my feet, he slots in at my back. I try to make eye contact with the other passengers as I'm moving along the aisle, hoping one of them – anyone – will see the panic in my face and realise what's happening. Everyone is staring at their phones or their feet. Nobody pays me any attention.

When I get to the driver, I think about saying something – but what then? Ben stabs me? Stabs the driver? By the time I've weighed up whether I should say something, I'm already off the bus and Ben is at my side.

I realise we are outside the house that Ben said he'd buy for me. It's only now that I see how spooky it is. It's tall and detached, with leafless trees on either side that are swaying in the breeze. The lower half is hard to see because of the overgrown hedges, but there are boards across the windows at the front. Even on a clear day, like today, it feels like the kind of place from which ghostly cries would seep onto the street and terrify young children. I wonder how I've never seen this before. Perhaps it's enhanced because the hedges are so unwieldly.

'It was owned by an old woman,' Ben says. He grips my wrist and pulls me along the pavement towards the gate. 'She died three years ago, but there's a dispute going on between her kids. They're squabbling over who gets what. One of them wants to sell it for the land; another wants to live in it. Everything's a mess.'

'How do you know that?'

'Because I asked.'

Ben leads me past the gate, but, as I think we're going to head around the house, he steps sideways through a gap in the hedge. I'm given no choice but to follow, albeit with a yelp of alarm at moving so quickly.

'Shhhhhhh,' Ben says, out loud this time.

After getting through, I glance back towards the hedge. The branches have grown into one another on the outside, but, from the inside, they've been trimmed short. From the pavement, nobody would know this was a way to get into the garden.

Ben pulls me closer towards him, where he's staring up at the house. Even though there's a creepiness to it, there is undoubted beauty. At one point, this place would have been majestic, with its pretty window ledges and wood-slat decoration. There's a porch, like something from a 1950's American movie.

'What do you think?' he asks.

'What do you mean?'

'I could still buy it.'

I turn to take him in, but Ben is transfixed by the house. His grip on my wrist is loose and I could probably pull clear if I wanted.

'We could live here,' he says.

'You died,' I reply. 'People would see you. They'd know.'

A shrug. An annoying damn shrug. 'I'm not stupid. I know that, but I never stopped thinking about buying it for you. It's what you always wanted.'

I say nothing. There's no reason to point out that there's a difference between what *I* wanted and what *he* did.

Ben lets go of my wrist and takes a few steps towards the side of the house. He turns back and looks at me as if to say, *Are you coming?*

'Will you let me go?' I ask, glancing to the way his sleeve is still dangling across his hand. 'We can go our own ways. I promise I'll never tell anyone about you.'

Ben doesn't acknowledge what I've said. He nods towards the side of the house. 'Come on.'

He takes a step away, but I don't move.

'Luce?'

'Please let me go?'

'Come and look first.'

I want to leave but he raises his sleeve just enough to show me the blade. I wouldn't get far and it doesn't feel like I have much of a choice. He was never violent with me when we were together. There was never anything physical, though I've realised in the years since how I cowered from him. How I avoided confrontation. How I was *scared* of him. That, perhaps, deep down, I always realised he was capable of something awful.

Ben waits for me to get in front of him and I follow the path around towards the back of the house. There are more towering hedges here, dousing the lengthy garden in shadow. There is so much more land than I imagined.

'Where?' I ask.

'Inside.'

I turn back to the house and shiver from the cold. There's a large wooden plank across the back door, but the hook is empty. On the ground next to it sits the broken remains of a thick padlock.

'I'd like to go,' I say.

Ben moves quickly across to me and pushes the tip of the knife into my side. 'Inside,' he repeats, more firmly this time.

'Ben…'

'Inside.'

I do as I'm told once more, pushing open the back door and moving into the house. Dust immediately catches in my nose as the freshness of the air outside is replaced by throat-clogging mustiness. Ben is directly behind me as I move into what turns out to be a kitchen. The windows have been covered with paper and the only light comes through a patch that has been peeled away. It takes a few moments for my eyes to adjust to the murk, in which time Ben has closed the door behind us.

The tiles on the floor are cracked and the fridge door hangs open. There is a bottle of washing-up liquid in the windowsill and crusty old dishes in the sink.

'It needs a bit of work in here,' Ben says. 'New fridge and freezer, obviously. I'd probably rip out the cooker, but there's a lot of room for something more modern. The piping seems solid, though. It's got central heating, which I didn't expect.'

He's perched on the corner of a unit, speaking with his hands as if an estate agent trying to close a deal.

'We could knock this wall through,' he says, pointing to an area behind me. I turn to look where he means. 'There's a pantry through there,' he adds, 'but it could easily be converted into an integrated dining room along with this kitchen.'

Almost through expectation, I poke my head into the room beyond, which is a large cupboard filled with tins of food that are covered with dust. Aside from footprints in the dust, it doesn't feel as if anyone's lived here – *properly* lived here – in a long while.

Ben's clearly spent time here, though. I guess he was only using Jade's flat to keep half an eye on me. It would explain why there was barely anything there.

He's in another of the doorways and beckons me through into a hallway and then a living room. The wooden floorboards creak ominously as I head inside – and this room does seem more lived in. There is a sleeping bag on the floor, next to a large rucksack. The walls are lined with bookcases and there's a rocking chair in the corner.

'Nice, isn't it?' Ben says. 'Probably wouldn't need much work in here, other than a clean.'

I shiver again, it's hard not to. He always seemed to have a life planned for us and now, after everything that's happened, he still has. 'Will you let me go?' I say. 'I promise I won't say anything about you.'

Ben is blocking the door and there's only one way in and out. He says nothing at first, but I can see his frame rising and falling as he breathes. He scratches his wrist and then rests his head on the door frame. I can see his silhouette; his Adam's apple bobbing.

'I did so much for you,' he says. 'It took a bit of luck, admittedly – but it was mainly planning. I wanted to surprise you on Bonfire Night, to make it right. I wanted to start again.'

'I don't want any of that.'

It feels dangerous, but it's the only reply I can give.

'You don't want to be loved, do you?' he says, harshly. 'You want that stupid job. You want a piss-poor job serving groceries to greasy nobodies. You want your stupid friends in that stupid building with their stupid parties.' Ben's voice has been steady and controlled, but he gets gradually louder as he speaks. 'You want to wallow in this mess you've made. You—'

'This isn't *my* mess,' I say. 'They aren't my debts.'

It's the years of frustration that makes the words come out. It's one thing to take responsibilities for things done wrong – but when they are other people's errors, it's a lot to accept.

Ben's frame rises and falls once more.

I'm in too deeply now.

'Did you kill Jade?' I ask. The thought has been creeping up on me.

The words seep into the corners of the house. Buildings like this have a personality of their own. Quirks and creaks; a history that is hard to match. This has to be a new thing for it.

Ben doesn't reply at first. He pushes himself up from the door frame until he's standing straight once more and takes a step into the room, towards me. I shuffle backwards, trying to put the rocking chair between us.

'I told you,' he says. 'I did so much for you.'

I gasp and the sob nearly comes. 'You killed her *for me*?' I manage.

'To be close to you,' Ben replies, his voice not wavering. 'I wanted to show you how much I care. But you didn't appreciate it, did you? You never did. I was away for five years putting things right. I plan this massive surprise and you don't even acknowledge it.'

I wonder if I there was a part of me that knew I was his obsession instead of his girlfriend. Perhaps I knew that and liked it? Everyone wants to be wanted. But then he never really wanted me, not like that. He used me to get the money he wanted. Our dreams for the future were always his. If it hadn't have been for the train, I'd have found out his true nature so much earlier.

I slot in behind the rocking chair, but Ben reaches forward and jolts it to the side. It's only me and him now and there's nowhere for me to go. He slips the knife from his sleeve and I can see the shape fully. It's much longer than I thought; the type from a kitchen that's serrated and viciously sharp.

'Well,' he says with a sigh, 'if you don't appreciate me, what use are you?'

His eyes widen as his arm straightens.

'I *do* appreciate you.'

My voice cracks as I speak, but it's too late anyway. I'm in the corner and Ben takes another step forward.

'No,' he says, 'you don't.'

FORTY-THREE

There's a clarity to my thoughts that's hard to explain. Ben is still silhouetted by the light and, as he breathes in, I lunge forward and thump the side of my hand into his windpipe. I can picture the scar underneath his Adam's apple – the old rugby injury on which he had surgery.

He gasps and creases forward and, in that moment, I'm past him. I race for the door as Ben roars behind me. With a skid, I'm tearing along the hall and into the kitchen. The back door is unlocked and it's only a second until the crisp, clean air of the real world floods forth. I half-run, half-stumble onto the lawn. My legs are like a baby giraffe's and don't seem stable. Ben is right behind me, coughing and rasping. I race for the side of the house but have hesitated for too long. From nowhere, Ben slips in front, so that he's blocking the route away. We're facing one another as he holds his hands wide.

'Where are you gonna go?' he croaks, voice husky.

I step away, but there's only the garden that backs onto the park behind us. The hedge is too tall to climb and there are no overlooking properties. I keep moving backwards and Ben follows. His eyes are wide and wild, the knife clutched tightly in his right hand. I've never seen him like this before.

'Help!' I shout as loud as I can, but there's a steady hum from the road and a general clatter of a cement mixer from somewhere a street or two away.

Ben grins as he moves, knowing I won't be heard – or, if I am, it will be too late for someone to do anything about it.

'I offered you everything,' he says.

'No, you *took* everything,' I reply, still moving backwards. I'm hoping I'll somehow be able to slip around him and dash for the front of the house.

'Ungrateful…' He's keeping a distance, giving me no space to dodge around his arms.

'What are you going to do?' I say. 'Kill me here?'

Ben raises the knife slightly, as if to say it sounds like an idea. 'Who's going to suspect a dead guy?' he asks – and I realise that he's right. There will never be justice for Jade, or me. He'll go to ground and that will be the end. I keep edging away, but the hedge is close to my back now.

'Help!'

Ben grins. 'I want you to know that you did this.'

He takes another step forward and there's nowhere to go this time. I'm trapped between him and the hedge, with only the knife between us. Time feels frozen and then…

There's a ruffle from the hedge behind, a scratching, and, from nowhere, Billy bursts from the bush. I open my mouth to say his name, but he's not the same creature who slept on my feet last night. The kind, loving animal has gone and he's a snarling, spitting creature of fury. He doesn't wait for me, instead launching himself teeth first at Ben's forearm. The knife slips onto the turf as Billy and Ben tumble backwards over one another. I'm frozen to the spot, transfixed with stunned shock as Billy ends up on top, his teeth still sunk into Ben's forearm.

Ben is screeching and flapping around, completely taken by surprise. It's when he uses his free hand to punch Billy in the side that something within me snaps. I race across the grass, snatch the knife from the ground and charge to where they're fighting. Ben continues to thump Billy in the side until I hurl myself onto the grass next to them. There's a flurry of movement between them and they're so close that I can feel the heat from Billy's breath. He's spitting and snorting in a way I've never seen before.

I hold the knife up and Ben's eyes widen.

'Stop,' I say.

His free arm goes limp, but his other is still pushing back against Billy.

'Let him go, Bill,' I say calmly.

The snarling dampens immediately and then, a moment later, Ben's other arm is released. I'm holding the knife a few centimetres from Ben's throat, not breaking eye contact.

'Roll over,' I tell Ben – and he does.

A couple of seconds later, there's a snaffling from the bushes. I glance up – but only for a moment – to see Karen blusters her way through. She's out of breath and red in the face. 'Billy! Bil—'

She stops speaking and I can sense her watching us, even though I'm focused on Ben.

'Lucy?'

'Call the police,' I tell her.

Ben's wriggling, his head tilted towards me. I hold the knife a little further forward, making sure he can see it. Billy is sitting calmly, panting and waiting for any other order.

'You'll never use that,' Ben says.

'Touch my dog one more time and let's see.'

FORTY-FOUR

ONE WEEK LATER

Billy strains on his lead as he pulls along the path towards the park. I call him back but he's eager to get to Parkrun.

'He basically walks himself,' Karen says.

'I thought he'd be slowing down by now,' I say.

'I've hardly seen you in days, what with the police and all. Didn't expect to see you this morning.'

'I fancied getting out. Billy's been cooped up for too long as well.'

Billy stops and waits at the crossing, knowing exactly where he's going. We stand with him and wait for the flashing green man.

'I still can't believe it,' Karen says.

'I don't think the police can either. It was only when they checked his DNA against his mother's that they stopped thinking I was a nutter.'

She breathes out loudly: 'What next?'

'A new 5K PB, I reckon.'

The green man flashes and the box beeps as we start to cross the road. Billy is back to pulling me along again. He leads us over the crossing and around the next corner.

'After that,' Karen says. She knows me too well and sees right through the bluster.

'I've got another job interview on Monday.'

'You know what I mean.'

'That *is* what I mean. Life goes on.'

Karen doesn't reply instantly. I know it's a bit of a fudge but, in essence, it's true.

'Ben died,' I add. 'The Ben I know is still dead. Whoever that was in the garden isn't the same person. He stole everything I had and he broke my heart. The fact he was hiding for five years doesn't mean much. I heard from one of the officers that he'd set up a new life with some woman over in Wales. She kicked him out at the start of the year after an argument and I guess that's when he decided to come back. He's a serial love addict. It's all or nothing. He wants to force people to love him. I think he was always like that. He played with me because he enjoyed the chase and thought his money was more important than the life I had.'

It's grandiose stuff – I know that – but I don't know what else to say. I was rehearsing it in the mirror this morning. Sometimes it does play out that one person will say something expected, so the reply is already practised.

We carry on walking and Karen is silent for a while longer. Some people assume that if a person has no money, then they must be stupid. Being poor is somehow a choice. Karen isn't like that – she knows this isn't the real answer.

'I think he killed Jade,' I say.

'Did you tell the police?'

'Of course – but things take time. I know he hasn't confessed to anything. They're looking into it. I'm sure they'll get him.' A beat passes: 'I *hope* they get him.'

'He tried to kill you…'

'Maybe.'

'And he punched Billy.'

That gets a little laugh. It's not that it's funny, more that a person can commit any amount of heinous crime – but it's only when an animal is harmed that people *really* get annoyed. I know it was him bashing Billy that made the red mist descend.

We keep walking, but Billy slows as we take the turn onto the road on which the now infamous house lies. It used to be owned by a Mrs Cheeseman. Everything Ben said was true – she died three years ago and her children have been arguing about what to do with it ever since.

'How did Ben's mother take it?' Karen asks.

'I don't know. Probably worse than me. She's been grieving for him. I saw her at the police station and she was grey. Haunted.'

'Did she say anything to you?'

'We sat next to each other for almost half an hour and never spoke. That's almost an apology for her. I think she always knew the problem was her son and not me. It's hard to blame someone who was dead, so she put it all on me instead.'

A pause: 'Are you sure she didn't know?'

'It's possible, but I don't think she's a good enough actress to fake it all these years. Ben told the police she didn't know anything.'

We slow even further until we're standing outside the house. One of the police officers told me it's called Tannerman Terrace, which is an oddity considering it stands by itself. Billy stops and sits at my feet as we peer over the gate towards the house beyond. Much of the mystery and spookiness I felt a week ago has gone. It's just a house. The real evil lies within people, not buildings.

'I should've told you about the money before,' I say. 'It was all a bit overwhelming. You have nothing and then it feels like you have everything.'

I stare down at my feet and the shoes bought with Ben's money. I don't want to wear them now I know where the cash came from – but I don't have anything else. It always comes back to money.

'I think I'd have spent it faster than you,' Karen says. 'Do they know where he got his money?'

'I don't know. He said he was a day trader, like he used to be, but I suppose it'll all come out eventually. I'm not sure it matters. A big part of me doesn't want to know.'

We start moving again and it's hard not to feel the pull from the house. The park is around the corner and then it's time to run again. Billy will hopefully get himself a full couple of laps in this time.

'What now?' Karen asks.

'I told you,' I reply. 'A new 5K personal best.'

A LETTER FROM KERRY

For quite a while, I've wanted to write about a character like Lucy. So much media, be it movies, TV, or books, are consumed by a rampant middle-classishness. There's nothing particularly wrong with that. People create things that reflect the world around them, even if it's not necessarily *about* themselves. "Write what you know" doesn't literally have to be a doctor creating something about being a doctor because, if it was, science fiction and fantasy wouldn't exist. There aren't too many sabre-rattling warriors fighting dinosaurs in outer space around who can write stories about sabre-rattling warriors fighting dinosaurs in outer space.

What it does often mean is that, regardless of genre, creators end up writing about *people* like themselves.

I am definitely guilty of this. I would imagine everyone who has ever written something is.

But there was a time when I worked for minimum wage; when I used to work night shifts, or had to trot off to a factory at 5.30 in the morning. There was a time when I had to budget everything religiously in order to make sure rent was covered and that I had enough left to buy food. When I could go a full month and only buy things I specifically *needed*, not wanted, and still have nothing left at the end of it all. It was fine. It's not like I didn't want for things, or hope for better days… but I wasn't unhappy. I wasn't furious with the world because things weren't how I wanted them.

Within all that, I wanted to write something to reflect that. If a person is short of money, there are obviously times in which it's hard to feel anything other than helplessness. But, at the same time, life isn't an endless misery. I really *really* hate the long parade of TV shows specifically that portray being working-class as some sort of non-stop nightmare in which everyone involved hates themselves. I don't believe anyone who writes like that has ever actually lived in such a situation. If it isn't that, then it's a long parade of books *specifically* that act as if nobody exists other than middle-class people in middle-class homes with middle-class lives. There is an enormous group of people completely forgotten by writers.

That isn't me saying I'm above anyone, or that I think this is the greatest work of fiction known to man. It's simply me saying that I've not forgotten how things once were. Admittedly, not everyone has ghosts returning from the past, or a kick-arse dog, but there you go. I hope you enjoyed the read, either way.

As ever, you can find out what's next from me at kerrywilkinson. com. You can also email me from there, or I drivel on about various things on Twitter (@kerrywk) and the like.

Cheers for reading.
Kerry Wilkinson

kerrywilkinson.com

@kerrywk

Printed in Great Britain
by Amazon